Her Sweetest Rogue

The Worthington Legacy
Book Six

Marie Higgins

ARE YOU SIGNED UP FOR DRAGONBLADE'S BLOG?

You'll get the latest news and information on exclusive giveaways, exclusive excerpts, coming releases, sales, free books, cover reveals and more.

Check out our complete list of authors, too!

No spam, no junk. That's a promise!

Sign Up Here

www.dragonbladepublishing.com

Dearest Reader;

Thank you for your support of a small press. At Dragonblade Publishing, we strive to bring you the highest quality Historical Romance from some of the best authors in the business. Without your support, there is no 'us', so we sincerely hope you adore these stories and find some new favorite authors along the way.

Happy Reading!

CEO, Dragonblade Publishing

Additional Dragonblade books by Author Marie Higgins

The Worthington Legacy
Her Perfect Scoundrel (Book 1)
Her Dreamy Deceiver (Book 2)
Her Adorable Cad (Book 3)
Her Irresistible Charmer (Book 4)
Her Captain Enchanter (Book 5)
Her Sweetest Rogue (Book 6)

Love's Addiction Series
A Wallflower to Love (Book 1)
A Governess to Protect (Book 2)
A Maiden to Remember (Book 3)

Lord Trey Worthington has sworn off love, determined to avoid a marriage like his parents'. When his mother brings Miss Judith Faraday into their home to sponsor her into Society, Trey is tasked with preparing her for her debut. As he spends more time with her, he finds his barriers crumbling and feelings he never anticipated. However, Judith seeks a faithful husband, a role Trey fears he can never fulfill, creating a tension that challenges his deepest convictions.

Judith Faraday dreams of marrying her naval officer and having a life full of love. However, she doubts this will happen while living as the ward of the dowager duchess. As she spends more time with the dowager's son, Trey, an unexpected and irresistible attraction begins to blossom. Judith now wonders if God has different plans, as Trey doesn't believe in the sanctity of marriage, something she cannot live without.

Chapter One

England, 1822

SILENCE WAS MOST important. It could mean the difference between freedom and imprisonment.

Judith Faraday lifted on the tiptoes of her riding boots, the worn leather whispering against the polished wood floor, and crept out of her second-story bedroom. Her breath hitched, her ears attuned to the faintest sound as she inched down the corridor. The grand manor was shrouded in predawn stillness, and she strained to catch any rustling from the servants. But this early in the morning, the house was cloaked in silence. Each step was deliberate and cautious, her heart thudding in her chest like a frantic drum. She reached the top of the stairs, where the shadows pooled in the corners, deep and forbidding.

As she descended, her weight pressed onto a loose tread board, the creak slicing through the silence and reverberating off the high walls. With taut muscles, she froze as her breath caught in her throat. The echo seemed to linger, magnifying her presence in the sleeping house. Her pulse pounded louder, drowning out her thoughts.

She held her breath, ears straining to catch any sign of stirring, her senses heightened to the brink of pain. The wild beating of her heart was the only response, a stark reminder of the risk she was taking. She remained still, counting the seconds, until she was certain the silence was unbroken, and then she moved again, stealthy and determined.

Some might think Judith was rebellious, but it wasn't in her nature to stand back and allow everyone to make decisions for her, especially now that she was almost in her twenty-third year. The large inheritance would take care of her for a while, along with her servants. She didn't need anyone to be her guardian, especially someone she hadn't seen since she was a child. Yet if she didn't leave now, she'd become the ward to the Dowager Duchess of Kenbridge. Judith was certain the older woman didn't remember the spitfire Judith had been as a youngster, or the poor woman wouldn't be planning to bring her to Mayfair.

Rubbing her forehead to relieve the pressure of a headache, she tiptoed across the floor toward the back door, each step a careful, measured effort to remain silent. Frustration bubbled up inside her. What had Ma and Pa been thinking, entrusting her to the dowager? They had raised her to be self-reliant, instilling in her the values of independence and strength from a young age. She should be anticipating marriage, not becoming the ward of an elderly woman. The thought gnawed at her, adding to the tension already gripping her mind.

Judith remembered a few things about the Worthington family, but what stood out most was their ill-mannered son. Trey, the youngest, had tormented her endlessly with his cruel pranks. Though years had passed and he was surely a man by now—possibly even married with children—the mere thought of seeing him again sent a shiver down her spine. His mocking laughter and the sting of his tricks were etched in her memory, shadows of a past she wished she could erase.

Unfortunately, she was destined to see him sooner than she had hoped. As she recalled the dowager's condolence letter, her heart sank. The woman had mentioned her own illness and informed Judith that her youngest son, Lord Trey, would be the one to escort her to the Worthington estate. The words had practically leapt off the page, tightening the knot of anxiety in her chest. She could almost hear the disdain dripping in his voice and see the smug look in his eyes. The thought of facing him again, especially under such circumstances, made her stomach churn.

It would happen tomorrow. But she mustn't allow her life to change in such a terrible way.

Finally reaching the stable, she took a glance back at the house. Curtains covered every window. The servants and, more importantly, her unwanted companion—assigned to stay beside her until the dowager took over—were still asleep and wouldn't miss her for another hour. At least, that was her hope.

On the horizon, the waking sun peeked between the trees, casting rainbows of light through the morning mist. Judith saddled her mare with practiced ease, then vaulted onto the horse's back. She urged the animal onto the road, the cool morning air stinging her cheeks as they picked up speed. The ribbons on her bonnet fluttered wildly in the breeze, and her cape flapped against her back, not as warm as she would have liked. But eventually, the sun would climb higher, warming the day and matching the heat inside her blooming in her chest at the thought of her new life with Alex, her soldier—and secret fiancé.

"Come, my sweet Pegasus," she cooed to the mare. "Take me swiftly, but quietly, to my new life."

With each powerful stride of the mare, she felt the distance between her and her old life stretching, the weight of her past lifting with every gallop. The countryside blurred around her, the wind carrying away her doubts and fears. Freedom and the promise of a future filled with love awaited her, just over the horizon, where Alex would be waiting with open arms.

She'd ridden about two miles when shouts echoed behind her in the distance. Her heart plummeted and she peeked over her shoulder. "No, please. You cannot find me."

Judith groaned, crouched lower, and kicked her legs against the mare's flanks. Noticing a different path off to one side, she urged her horse in that direction. Trees became thicker and the overhanging branches whipped at her face and tore off her bonnet, leaving it to fall to the ground. Her cape flew behind her as if she had wings. A few branches caught her riding habit, leaving tears in her sleeves and skirt. She didn't care. The further she traveled without being spotted, the better.

The woodsman's cottage came into view. Alex would be there waiting.

As she neared the cottage, Judith slowed the mare, her senses heightened and alert. Where was her beloved?

She patted the mare's neck, feeling the warmth and sweat beneath her hand, and urged the horse toward the structure. The ramshackle shelter loomed ahead, its worn timbers and sagging roof promising at least some respite.

"Alex, my love?" she called.

Several agonizing seconds passed, her heartbeat still hammering in her chest. Suddenly, distant shouts pierced the morning air, sending a jolt of fear through her. Panic surged like ice through her veins. She had no doubt now—they had discovered her absence.

From behind, a horse neighed and branches snapped. She whipped around, clutching tightly to the reins, preparing to flee. Through the thicket, two horses came her way. As they rode closer, she could see her beloved wasn't one of them. Both men wore black cloaks and knee boots as dark as midnight. Neither resembled nobility.

Please, Lord… Don't make them highwaymen!

Holding in her panic, she kicked her heels against the horse's sides, urging the mare into a run. The men behind her shouted, insisting she stop.

Judith slipped from one side of the saddle to the other, unaccustomed to the fast pace on a sidesaddle. The muscles in her thighs screamed from the strain of holding them against the horn, and her hands throbbed painfully from gripping the reins so tightly.

The thundering hooves grew closer, and she released a

whimper. She didn't dare look behind to see how close they were as the ground nearly shook from their approach.

Strong hands grabbed her around the waist, lifting her off the mare with a force that made her scream. Her fingers slipped from the reins as she was torn away from her horse. Immediately, she was pressed against the man holding her.

She had heard horror stories of what highwaymen did to women they held for ransom—tales that filled her with dread. Her mind raced, desperately searching for a way out as she struggled against their grip, her fear threatening to overwhelm her.

Judith's heart cried as she watched her horse ride into the wooded area without her. *Alex, where are you?*

The rider's horse stopped, which made it easier to struggle against him.

"Woman, cease. Do you wish to lame me?"

Without turning her head to look at the imbecile, she scrunched her forehead. Of course she wanted to lame him. Did he think she'd make this easy?

"Please stop, woman. I'm not going to hurt you."

Famous last words, she was certain.

Breathing heavily, she took a moment to study his face…and then sucked in a quick breath. Highwaymen weren't supposed to be this handsome. Windswept black hair waved around his head while brilliant blue eyes stared back at her. Didn't highwaymen wear masks? This one didn't.

His gaze skimmed over her in a lazy exploration, yet his mouth stretched in a melting grin before he met her eyes.

"Sir, I demand you unhand me." Her voice shook despite her efforts to sound commanding.

The second rider galloped up to them and pulled his horse to a stop. No doubt another thief, yet he didn't wear a mask, either. Perhaps these men were not as she expected. If so, what was their purpose?

The man holding her chuckled. "Hawthorne, the woman

demands I unhand her."

The man called Hawthorne shook his head, his gaze never leaving her. "I think you have found an uncooperative lass. I fear she'll be a handful for you."

The one holding her laughed as he pulled her closer. She screeched and slapped his hands, but he remained unaffected.

"Yes, Hawthorne, she's a handful to be sure, but a wench I can tame, nonetheless."

"Wench?" she shrieked. "Sir, I'm no wench. I'm a lady." Judith elbowed him in the chest, which was followed by his soft grunt. "And you had better unhand me this second or I'll injure you in the worst way."

Hawthorne threw his head back and howled with laughter.

"What's this?" The one holding her turned her head with his fingers, gripping her chin so she could look at him. Humor sparked in his dark blue eyes. "You proclaim yourself a lady, yet you are threatening me with bodily harm?"

She scowled. "Are you not still holding me prisoner? Therefore, you are no gentleman. Now let me go before I follow through with harming your person."

He grinned, and her heart did a foolish flip-flop. Those blasted dimples on his cheeks and his hypnotic eyes made her catch a breath. Though she still wondered about their purpose here, the initial fear began to fade, replaced by irritation.

"Pardon me," the man said, dripping with sarcasm. "I didn't know we were in the presence of such nobility." His gaze slid over her riding habit. "I wasn't aware that gentle-bred ladies adorned themselves in such a wicked fashion." He fingered the tears in her sleeves.

Once again, she slapped his hand. "You imbecile. My riding habit is ripped due to the ghastly trees and their branches."

"What are you doing traipsing through the forest by yourself? From what I understand, gentle-bred ladies are supposed to have an escort."

"That, sir, is none of your concern."

Hawthorne chuckled. "I think we have a runaway."

Her heart sank. They had deduced her purpose.

The handsome man holding Judith waggled his brows. "Will your father pay handsomely for your safe return?"

Her heart clenched at the mention of Pa. If he were alive at this moment, he would kill both rogues.

The thieves' purpose was now revealed: they wanted money. However, they dressed in finer clothes, not the rags a highwayman would wear. Even their boots were of the finest quality.

She forced down a hard swallow and lifted her chin. "No, my father will not. It would be utterly impossible to get one shilling from him, since he's buried six feet under."

The man holding her blinked. "He's dead?"

"I would hope so. I imagine a living person would find it difficult to breathe buried under the ground like that."

Silence, except for her quick breaths and horses' snorting, filled the air. The thief lost his smile yet kept his warm gaze on her.

"Please forgive me, my lady. I shall not amuse myself at your expense any further."

She nodded and adjusted herself on his lap. "Will you please let me down?"

"Not until you tell us what you're doing here. This is private land. You're trespassing."

Realizing now what their purpose was, she nearly sighed with relief. "Oh dear, forgive me. I did not know."

"Obviously, but you have not yet explained why you are here."

Shouts from down the road rang out, along with the crunching of leaves under horses' hooves. Squeezing her eyes closed, she gritted her teeth. *My servants found me.*

She met the thief's gaze again. "I beg you, sir, let me down. I cannot allow those people to locate me."

"Why?"

"Because they want to take me somewhere I do not wish to

go."

"And where might that be?" asked the other man.

Judith glanced at Hawthorne before looking back at the man holding her. Her vision grew blurred for a moment as dizziness assailed her. Why did she feel as if she would pass out? Perhaps she should have eaten this morning to give her body more strength.

She blinked to refocus. "I cannot explain now. They are coming upon us quickly."

"Then I suggest you give me some hint to your situation, my lady, because I'm the only one who can protect you."

Voices from the searchers grew nearer. She didn't have any other choice. "Sir, I'm the newly appointed ward of the Dowager Duchess of Kenbridge. There has been a terrible mistake, and I cannot be the dowager's ward. I'm here to meet my fiancé, a lieutenant in the King's Navy, so we can be married."

The handsome thief holding her hitched a breath, his arms loosening as if she'd suddenly burst into flames. Seizing the moment, Judith slid from his horse and quickly stepped away, putting some distance between them. Her heart raced with a mix of lingering fear and newfound determination as she prepared to face whatever came next.

"Thank you, sir. You don't know how much this means to me." Glancing around the glade, she searched for her horse.

The man jumped from his mount and took her by the elbow. "You are Miss Faraday? Lord and Lady Manderville's daughter?"

Her heart bounced to her throat as panic consumed her. "How—how do you know?"

He shook his head as he ran his fingers through his wavy black hair. "Oh, my dear Miss Faraday, this is certainly not your lucky day. Nor mine."

"Explain yourself, sir."

He released her arm and gave her a mock bow. "Lord Trey Worthington, at your service. We knew each other as children. The dowager duchess is my mother."

Oh, no! The fog thickened in her head as dizziness completely consumed her. Her chest tightened, making it impossible to breathe. Voices and sounds from all around grew dim as the ground rose up to meet her. Everything around her dissolved into darkness.

Chapter Two

TREY INSTINCTIVELY CAUGHT the unconscious woman before she hit the dirt, her limp body pressing against him, a stark reminder she was no longer a child. He closed his eyes and groaned, the weight of the situation sinking in. What had his mother done this time? No, it was his brother, Trevor, who should bear the blame, passing his ward to their mother for safekeeping without a second thought.

Trey looked at Hawthorne's wide-eyed stare and shook his head. "This cannot be happening."

A broad grin stretched across his friend's face, and his eyes twinkled with humor. "What a delightful day it has turned out to be, do you not agree?"

Trey grumbled under his breath, not wishing to voice how he truly felt. "What am I going to do about her now?"

Dominic Lawrence, Marquess of Hawthorne, shrugged. "I suggest you rouse the poor woman. Her search party is getting closer."

"Don't you see?" Trey growled. "If they think she has run away, her name will be ruined. In turn, my mother's reputation will be tarnished for accepting this girl as her ward."

"So, what do *you* suppose we do with her? As you want to avoid her search party's gossip if she's caught fleeing, I suggest we get her out of here." Hawthorne glanced at the shelter. "Or hide her in the woodsman's cottage."

Confusion swam in Trey's head. The others couldn't find her. His mother would have heart palpitations if she ever discovered her ward had run off.

Hawthorne nodded toward the structure. "Let me unlock the door. You can put her in there." He jumped off his horse and strode to the door. As he located the key above the doorframe, he glanced over his shoulder at Trey. "We cannot leave her in there alone."

"Why not?"

"Because this is the first place her search party will look."

Trey adjusted Miss Faraday against his chest as he glanced down at her delicate face, marred by a few scratches. Full lips drew his attention, and then her lush eyelashes as they brushed her cheeks. He couldn't remember her looking this pretty when she was a child. However, he did recall her stubbornness. The girl had been spoiled beyond reason.

He met his friend's stare. "So, what do you suggest?"

"You could stay inside with her."

Trey crinkled his forehead. "Why?"

"In case she comes to and makes a noise. I'll be out here to direct her searchers away."

"What if we are caught in the cottage together? You know as well as I how that will ruin her reputation."

Hawthorne tilted his head and smirked. "You forget, my good man, her reputation will still be intact because they will not know who is inside with you. I certainly will not tell them."

Trey dropped his jaw. "You must be insane to believe such nonsense…"

The voices and pounding of horses' hooves grew closer. Hawthorne motioned with his head to go inside. "Make haste. We have no time to argue."

Grumbling under his breath, Trey carried Miss Faraday to the bed and settled her gently upon the mattress. Hawthorne closed the door behind him with a resounding thud. Panic settled deep in the pit of Trey's stomach. Hawthorne's plan had better work, or they'd both be in trouble. Trey had spent the past ten years making certain women couldn't dig their claws into his life and trap him into marriage. All it would take was for one person to spot him with Judith Faraday, and Trey's future would be doomed.

He left her on the mattress and searched for a blanket to cover her. Outside, voices called out to Hawthorne in greeting. Trey's heart sank. What if the searchers wanted to see for themselves who was inside the cottage? Trey must hide under the blanket with her. There was no other way.

Beside the bed, folded on a chair, lay a blanket. He flipped it open as he crawled on the mattress. Adjusting himself, he pulled Miss Faraday closer. Unconscious, she was nothing but dead weight. Yet in his arms, she fit perfectly. He didn't want to examine why he felt this way, so he yanked the quilt over their heads and cuddled closer, resting his chin on her forehead.

Inhaling her jasmine scent, he smiled. He'd always loved women who smelled like heaven. Mentally, he scolded himself for thinking such a thing. And what made it worse was her warm breath blowing against his skin, creating shivers throughout him.

With much effort, he halted his improper thoughts. Strange she hadn't moved, other than her steady breathing. Was something wrong with her? His mother wouldn't be able to handle a sickly ward when the older woman battled with health issues herself.

The crowd of searchers gathered near the window, and Trey tried to pick up bits from their conversation. As he strained to hear, the woman next to him stirred and let out a small moan.

Silently, he grumbled. He knew exactly what she'd do when she regained her bearings. He tightened his arms around her body to keep her from lashing out. Although he had her arms pinned, he worried what he'd do if she screamed. And, most assuredly, she would.

Her eyelids fluttered open. A grimace pulled on her lips as she tried to move her arms. Blinking the haze of unconsciousness from her eyes, she looked at the blanket covering their heads before turning to meet his stare. Her eyes widened. Recognition must have struck, because panic lit her gaze, and she opened her mouth. Without thinking of the consequences, he covered her mouth with his, silencing the scream he knew was forthcoming. He couldn't let her go. Her reputation was at stake—not to mention his cherished bachelorhood.

"Shh," he mumbled against her mouth. "I'm not going to hurt you. We must be quiet." She jerked her head away and pummeled his chest with her fists. He yanked her hands above her head and held them with a strong grip. "A search party is after you. Please, I'm trying to hide you and save your reputation."

"I don't think kissing—"

"Now is not the time to *think!*" Using his free hand, Trey held her face while his mouth took over again. Though he only kissed her to shut her up, warmth spread throughout him this time, and he found he quite enjoyed this intimate embrace. Soon her lips softened, and he sensed her surrender. The kiss turned into something more tender.

Her mouth responded, the touch tentative and so sweetly naïve he was consumed by the need to show her his gentle side— a side he didn't normally show to women. As her lips matched his kisses, he slowly released her hands. Hesitantly, her palms slid over his arms to his shoulders and settled there.

What was he doing? And why, pray tell, was he enjoying it? He was more than enjoying it—thunder roared in his ears and pounded in his head. No woman had ever affected him thus.

Slowly, he realized the thunder he'd heard was the sound of the riders leaving. Nic's plan had worked. Judith was undiscovered. Trey stilled, hesitant to pull away, but nevertheless, he broke the kiss and lifted his head. Her glazed emerald eyes met his. Quick breaths fanned his face, but no words were spoken.

Trey swallowed the cotton collecting in his throat. "Miss Faraday, I hope you understand—"

"Augh!" She shoved him in the chest then glanced around the tent he'd made for them with the covers. "What do you think you are doing? Get off me, you big oaf!"

He hoped the riders were a good distance away as he threw off their cover and began to slip out of bed, but he didn't expect her foot to help him to the floor. He thought she'd be mad, but not enough to kick him.

She shrieked and leapt off the mattress. "I cannot believe you took such liberties. What in heaven's name were you thinking?"

Tilting his head, he met her eyes, waiting for her to shrivel under his intent glare. The stubborn woman didn't. "Well, obviously I wasn't doing what you *thought* I was doing."

Brilliant color stained her cheeks as she stood before him with fists on her hips. Her breaths released from her mouth at a fascinating speed. "How dare you speak to me in such a way?"

"Miss Faraday, if you'll be silent long enough, I can explain why we were lying on the mattress and under the blanket." He lifted himself off the floor and stood in front of her.

She pressed her mouth into a thin line. Her tirade stopped. Only the fire shooting from her eyes coupled with her heavy breathing betrayed her anger.

"After you swooned in my arms—"

"I did *not* swoon in your arms," she interrupted. "I hadn't eaten this morning, and I was weak from lack of nourishment."

"After you swooned in my arms," he repeated stubbornly, "I thought it best if we didn't let your searchers find you. Gossip alone can ruin a reputation, you know. Hawthorne suggested I bring you in here to hide. I didn't want them to spread rumors that you had fled from my mother's guardianship."

She gasped. "Instead, you would rather they think I was…was…" She pointed to the bed. "You know…compromised?"

"No, Miss Faraday. That's why we were both under the blanket. In case your searchers decided to peek in the window, they would not be able to see you. Or me, for that matter."

She lifted her chin. "They are unaware it was me?"

"I'm not certain what Hawthorne told them. However, I know he kept your name out of it. Your reputation won't be tarnished in any way."

Nodding, she wrung her hands against her middle. Her gaze darted around the room, and then rested upon him.

"Then why…why did you kiss me?" she asked softly.

Chapter Three

A GRIN PULLED at the corners of Trey's mouth, and he couldn't help but let it spread. The sight of her blushing, her cheeks tinged with a delicate shade of red, was simply too endearing. Those crimson hues highlighted her features in a way that made her look even more charming. He found himself captivated by the way the color deepened with her every reaction, an irresistible display of her genuine emotions.

He approached her with slow, deliberate steps. The closer he came, the wider her eyes grew, filled with a mix of surprise and anticipation. When he finally stood before her, he reached out and swept his fingers across her cheek in a soft, lingering caress, feeling the warmth of her skin beneath his touch.

"I find it strange how much I enjoyed the moment," he said. "But I kissed you to keep you quiet so you wouldn't scream and bring attention to us. My reputation was at stake as well, you know."

"Oh!" She slapped his hand away. "You are nothing but an uncaring, inconsiderate mule's...back end."

She stormed toward the door, and he chuckled. Even in her anger, she looked adorable.

He shook away the disturbing thought. She was his mother's ward. Thinking of her this way was *not* permissible. She had disrupted his carefree life enough already. He didn't need to add more complications.

Just as she reached the door, it opened and Hawthorne stood on the other side. His friend made an attempt to enter until he looked into Miss Faraday's face, and then he froze. She stopped in front of him and planted her hands on her hips.

"Well? Are you just going to stand there and keep me prisoner in this hut, or let me pass?"

Hawthorne swept his hand in front of him as he bowed mockingly. "After you, my lady."

Lifting her chin, she marched outside. Trey grabbed his cape and quickly followed. Hawthorne gave him a once-over, his gaze lingering longer on Trey's wrinkled shirt as he arched a brow.

Trey shook his head. "Don't ask."

Hawthorne pointed to her horse. "I found Miss Faraday's mare grazing close by."

"Thank you, sir," she said.

Once she reached her horse, she grasped the reins and ran her hand over the animal's mane. Softly, she cooed as she pressed her forehead against the horse. Trey took careful steps toward her, mainly to not upset her.

"Forgive me for frightening you," she said in a hushed tone. "I shall never let that happen again."

Trey knew she wasn't talking to him, and he found it strange to think she cared enough about the animal to treat the mare so kindly. Most women he knew never acted in such a way toward an animal.

He cleared his throat, and she stiffened. "Would you allow me to assist you?" He motioned to the horse.

She glanced at him long enough to give him a curt nod, and then presented her back to him as she prepared to mount. It surprised him when she allowed his hands to guide her up on the animal, but her rigid body proved her reluctance.

Once she was on the saddle, she glared down at him. "So, my lord, what do you plan to do with me?"

Trey smiled. "I'll return you to your home, where you shall

kindly gather your things so we might leave for my mother's estate."

"But you are not supposed to come get me until tomorrow."

"I'm here, so I might as well make the best out of it. Besides, if I leave you alone now, you will only try and run again."

She shot him another evil look. "What about the search party?"

Hawthorne chuckled as he mounted his own horse. "Actually, Miss Faraday, the riders weren't searching for you at all."

Swinging her head toward Nic, she gasped. "No?"

"They were looking for a missing lad who had wandered from their hunting party."

She groaned and buried her face in her hands.

Trey shook his head, grinning wider. "Just our luck, isn't it, Hawthorne?"

"No, old sport." Hawthorne smiled. "Just *your* luck."

Trey stepped to his horse and mounted. He glanced over his shoulder at the young woman who now sat ramrod straight with her chin held high. Stubborn to a fault. "My dear Miss Faraday, are you ready?"

She arched a brow. "I suppose I'm ready, although I doubt you have forgotten my thoughts on the subject. I feel you are leading me directly into Satan's lair."

"Splendid. Let's be off, then."

Miss Faraday threw daggers at him with her glare. Trey tried not to laugh. True, he knew how she felt, but she was now his mother's responsibility.

His thoughts came to an abrupt halt. Correction—Miss Faraday was soon to be *his* responsibility!

Trey grumbled under his breath. He'd promised his ailing mother he'd help with her ward.

Kicking the horse into a trot, he tightened the reins in his fists. He needed to get out of this mess as soon as possible. He loathed calculating women, and from what he'd observed thus far about Miss Faraday, he suspected she was one of these women.

As she rode ahead of them, Trey recalled bits and pieces of their conversation. She'd mentioned meeting her fiancé before she swooned. Yet no other man came to her aid. If she were truly engaged, why hadn't it been mentioned in her father's will? And, pray tell, why wasn't she already entrusted to her future husband? It must have been a lie. If she'd been betrothed, her parents would have known, therefore, she would have never been given to his mother as a ward. Miss Faraday held secrets, and he didn't want any part of it. Then again, he needed to protect his mother from entering into another scandal.

"Worthington?"

Trey turned to Hawthorne riding beside him. "Yes?"

"What are you going to do about her?"

He shrugged. "I wish I knew. She's too old for the plans I had."

"Which were?"

"Finding her a governess, of course."

Hawthorne chuckled. "So there's only one thing you can do."

"Pray, what would that be?" Trey cocked his head.

"You must marry her to the first benefactor who asks for her hand. She's a very hardheaded young woman, and most men find that abrasive. You need to betroth her to someone before they discover her flaws."

"As always, you are correct, Hawthorne. She's a handful, to be sure." Trey slid his gaze over her stiff posture. A wealthy, titled husband was her only hope—and Trey's. He needed to find one soon so he could wash his hands of the mess. His mother would understand when she realized the willful streak the girl possessed.

Girl? He chuckled softly. Not likely. The sooner she married, the better. No matter how he'd enjoyed her kiss, no woman was worth the risk of marriage. His parents' marriage had proved to him a long time ago that this was something he should stay away from. Far away. The late fourth Duke of Kenbridge had taught his son well. Love was a crippling emotion, one men should never be fool enough to possess.

Miss Faraday turned and glanced at him, then slowed her horse until he caught up. Hawthorne urged his faster and moved ahead.

"My lord?" She directed her question to Trey. "I wish to talk to you briefly, if I may."

"Certainly."

"What would it take to…well, to pay you off?"

Taken back, he gaped at her. "Pardon?"

"I have a lot of money from my inheritance that I cannot access, due to a stipulation in the will. I love my parents dearly and miss them every day, but I cannot understand why they would think I need a guardian. My father, especially, knew how self-sufficient I am. If you allow me to collect my inheritance, I could pay you well."

"Miss Faraday, I'm not pleased with the situation either, but it isn't customary for a young woman your age to be left to her own devices until she reaches her majority. You and I are stuck with each other until that time comes."

"I am in my second and twentieth year."

"But according to the law, you cannot collect your inheritance until you are five and twenty."

"I have no desire to be the ward of your mother. I'm certain she's an endearing woman, but I'm too old to have a guardian."

"Perhaps, but from what I understand about your situation, your parents never sponsored you into Society. My mother would be your ally in this endeavor."

Her face paled slightly, and he detected tears. Why would she act in such a way? Before he could comment, she blinked away the betraying moisture.

"I do not wish to be sponsored, my lord."

Through a narrowed gaze, he studied her. She must be addled. All the girls he'd ever met dreamed of having a wealthy, titled person sponsor them. Then again, because her parents were free-spirited people, they probably didn't educate her in the way she needed to be.

"I'm certain, Miss Faraday, your parents thought differently. From what I understand, it's the wish of every parent to have their daughter sponsored. Was your father not a viscount?"

Her jaw hardened as her lips thinned into a line. "Yes, he was, but you do not know my parents as well as I do, and you certainly do not know me. I'm not like most girls."

"Obviously." He ran his gaze over her once more. "Perhaps you should learn to be like them. I think, Miss Faraday, this is your very problem. A problem my mother and I intend to rectify."

Chapter Four

*P*ROBLEM, MY EYE!

Judith was not, nor ever would be, Lord Trey's *problem*. Unfortunately, she was stuck as their ward until she found a way out. Trey Worthington didn't even want to listen to her protests. Judith's parents may have raised her at their country estate, but she was far from being a country girl. They'd taught her everything she needed to know to enter Society.

That wasn't the reason she resisted. Before her parents' untimely death, her mother had started to plan Judith's coming-out ball. Once again, tears pricked her eyes and she blinked to dry them. How could she allow the dowager to plan her ball without wishing her mother was still alive to do it herself?

Knowing the best course of action was to keep her mouth shut so she didn't cry in front of Lord Trey, Judith spoke not a word until they reached her home. Before she could dismount, he jumped off his horse, hurried to her side, and helped her down.

Fool. Couldn't he tell she didn't want his touch? Her body still remembered his warm kiss, and she cursed her traitorous mind for being unfaithful to Alex—her secret fiancé.

He grinned. "Miss Faraday? Do you need me to escort you inside to collect your things and your servants?"

She bunched her hands into fists at her sides. "No, my lord. I'm quite capable of doing that by myself. However, if you would like to wait in the drawing room, I shall not be very long."

He gave her a nod. "Then you have exactly one hour to ready yourself and your belongings."

She marched inside. When the servants ran to greet her, she flipped her hand through the air. "My escort has arrived a day early. Please see to loading the trunks as soon as possible."

She didn't stop to see their expressions, but hurried up the stairs and to her room to change clothes. Mixed emotions swam in her head and tightened in her chest. Why hadn't Alex met her at the cottage? Had something happened to keep him away? Although she considered him her fiancé, their engagement wasn't legal in any way, shape, or form. So perhaps he didn't want to marry her any longer. Tears flooded her eyes. She couldn't let her servants see. They didn't know about Alex. Nobody did.

Since she didn't dare keep Lord Trey or his friend waiting for fear of what they'd do, she hurried with the organizing and met the pair outside not more than an hour later. Thankfully, the servants had spent the week packing, so they were ready. Lord Trey and the man he called Hawthorne instructed the servants with loading the carriages. One by one, she hugged the few servants who'd be staying, people she'd known as family for several years. Tears burned her eyes as they wished her well. She climbed in the coach, and moments later, it jerked into action, carrying her to her new prison as his lordship rode in front, leading the way.

Out the window of the departing coach, she watched as her childhood home became smaller and smaller. Sadness welled in her chest and tightened her throat. The pain of her parents' death was as real today as it had been when they were laid to rest two months ago. Tragic that their lives had been taken so quickly. When she remembered how much in love they were, her chest squeezed with emotion. She wanted to blame someone for their sudden deaths, but the authorities had told her it was an accident. Merely an act of God. After contemplation, she realized it was a true blessing they had died together.

She didn't know how long it would take to be free of the dowager's care, but Judith vowed to return home someday and keep the place the way her mother had had it. So many joyful memories were held within the walls, and Judith couldn't let anything happen to her home. This was where she wanted to live once she married Alex. Would that day ever happen now?

Leaning back in the seat, she squeezed her eyes closed. If Trey Worthington hadn't come to the cottage, she would not be sitting in a coach riding toward his home. Why couldn't she get it through *that man's* skull that she didn't need him? He must have forgotten how troublesome she could be…and she couldn't wait to remind him. A malicious smile tugged on her lips, and she looked out the window. He'd rue the day he interrupted her life.

Two uneventful hours passed, and the nearer they drew to the dowager's estate, the more restless Judith became. She needed to calm her agitation quickly, because snapping at the older woman and displaying her troubled disposition would not be a good way to begin a relationship with her guardian. Lord Trey was at fault for her temperament, and so she'd take it out on him. All she could do now was go along with the dowager's plans, but in the end, she'd make him sorry for upsetting her life. The smug man would soon realize she didn't take orders from anyone—especially arrogant men like him.

Beyond the window, the scenery changed. She leaned closer to look at the rolling, grassy lawns, obviously manicured by someone with a loving green thumb. Yellow and pink spring flowers blossomed along the pebbled drive all the way up to the manor, their green leaves swaying in the gentle wind. The two-story white and gray house with large columns circling the front conveyed an open welcome to guests.

Pursing her lips, she dug her fingernails into her palms. This would be her dungeon for the next little while until Alex rescued her. She sighed and relaxed in the coach, noticing the jarring of the vehicle was not as horrendous as it had been during the first portion of her trip.

Frowning, she thought about her beloved sailor—her lieutenant. What really happened to him this morning? His last letter mentioned he'd been under the weather lately, but he promised he'd be at the woodsman's cottage and they would elope. Loneliness gripped her heart and squeezed. She'd counted on him today, and he'd disappointed her.

The coach stopped, and within seconds, the door opened. Her family's footman reached in with a brown-gloved hand to assist. She hesitated before she let him help her from the vehicle. His sad eyes met hers, and the emotion tugged on her heart. Certainly, he knew what turmoil she felt.

The breeze blew the strands of hair not hidden by her bonnet against her cheeks, the scent of roses wafting all around her from the nearby bushes. She hadn't been this close to London in quite a while. Her parents brought her every year to enjoy the sights, but she was always happy to return home.

The manor loomed before her, looking much better than some of the estates she'd passed on her journey. Of course, she'd heard the dowager duchess's wealth far surpassed a lot of the nobility Judith had met in London. The fancy-dressed servants standing near the door attested to the truth of the rumors. Three stone archways led into a little alcove before reaching the main doors.

Within moments, Lord Trey stood by her side, offering his arm. She held in the unladylike snort she wanted to expel. Trey Worthington was far from being a gentleman, so why did he act like one now? Yet she couldn't ignore his chiseled, handsome features or the memory of him holding her in his strong embrace.

As they walked into the house, Judith held in a gasp. The great hall was filled with ancient statues and small tables that only held planters of flowers.

A short, thin man, wearing the black and white attire of the butler, hurried from out of a room and stopped in front of them. "Lord Trey. You are here."

"Why of course, Bentley. Where else would I be at a time like this?" The blackguard nodded toward Judith. "My mother is expecting Miss Judith Faraday."

"But not until tomorrow."

Lord Trey shrugged. "So we are here early. Please let my mother know."

"Yes, of course, my lord." Bentley bowed, turned, and hurried into the sitting room.

As Lord Trey led Judith into the sitting room, she moved her gaze over the beautifully carved windows, across the beige carpet, to the two fireplaces—one on each side of the room—before resting her eyes on the expensive vases and crystals used as decorations amongst the cushioned chairs and sofas.

A tall, slender woman rose from the nearest sofa, her smile wide. Isabelle Worthington, the Dowager Duchess of Kenbridge and Judith's mother's dearest friend, appeared far different than when Judith met her as a child. Then again, it had been at least ten years since she saw her last.

Silver ringlets threaded with blue ribbon framed the dowager's oblong, wrinkled face. Familiar eyes danced as she looked over Judith.

"Oh gracious, look at you. Overnight you have turned into a lady." The dowager duchess stopped in front of Judith and, with her knuckles, lifted her chin. "You look just like your mother in her younger days, God rest her soul." She grasped Judith's hands and squeezed. "But tell me, why are you not wearing the customary black mourning gown, my dear?"

Judith frowned. "I have been wearing the gown for two months, and although I know it's highly improper to do, I could not wear it one more day. Whenever I wear black, I think of my parents and feel as if I cannot go on another day."

"Oh, my dear." The dowager patted Judith's hand. "I truly understand your misery. Well, it's highly improper, but since you are now my ward, I think I shall forgo the year of mourning even if it raises some judgmental eyebrows." She winked. "Besides, nobody will be the wiser if they do not know. Correct?"

Judith sighed and nodded.

"It delights me to have you in my home," the dowager continued, "and I want to make you happy. Your mother was a wonderful woman. I promise to do all I can to finish raising you as a proper lady."

Judith offered a tentative smile as she boiled inside. Why did they seem to think that just because she wasn't associating with the *ton*, she wasn't a proper lady? "I appreciate everything, Your Grace, but my mother has raised me already."

"Of course, my dear." The dowager squeezed her hands again, turned, and led her into the drawing room. "But a girl can never receive too much education. Do you not agree, Trey?"

Doing a quick search, Judith found Lord Trey standing by the window. He glanced at her over his shoulder, humor glinting in his eyes.

"Indeed, Mother. Those ladies Miss Faraday's age always need something to occupy their time."

Judith's hackles rose. She'd show him how she'd love to spend her time—giving him a quick lesson in manners. She nodded, about to explain as kindly as she could that she required no further learning. However, the tears brimming in the older woman's eyes prevented Judith from speaking.

"I never had a daughter." The dowager's voice broke. "Having you here now will give me a privilege I missed out on."

Blast it all! Why did she have to say that? Guilt flooded Judith's mind, making her doubt her plans. She couldn't tell the dowager about Alex yet.

However, she didn't have to make it easy for Lord Trey. She looked at him still standing by the window, hand on his hip as it pulled his frock coat away from his waistcoat. Handsome as sin, he was the devil's own son, and she'd make him regret forcing her to come here.

Chapter Five

Trey and Hawthorne retreated to the study for drinks. As Trey paced the Persian rug in front of the fireplace, Dominic sprawled in a brown leather chair before the hearth, leisurely sipping his brandy. Trey passed his friend a scowl. How could Dominic act nonchalant at a time like this?

"Hawthorne, you are not relieving my frazzled nerves any."

A deep chuckle rattled from his friend's chest as he crossed one leg over the other. "My good man, I do believe Miss Faraday has gotten under your skin."

Trey stopped to face his friend. "That lady has certainly unnerved me, but it's only due to her circumstance. Pray tell, how can I find a wealthy husband for her if she's so adamant to marry this sailor I have yet to meet?"

Dominic shrugged as he took another sip. "Do not rely on me for answers. I have never been in this predicament before."

"Mother must start right away on getting Miss Faraday properly educated." Trey dragged his fingers through his hair.

"I thought your mother had entrusted that assignment to you."

Trey growled, wishing he hadn't taken the responsibility. The girl affected him entirely too much. He feared the only thing to relieve his problem would be to leave everything in his mother's hands—or try to find Miss Faraday a husband. Unfortunately, the girl's so-called fiancé was the problem.

Trey's thoughts came to a sudden halt. *The fiancé.*

He turned to his friend, grinning. "Hawthorne, I believe I have the solution."

His friend quirked a teasing brow. "You plan to marry the girl yourself?"

"Don't be absurd, Nic. Why would I do something so insane and ruin my life? The solution I refer to is to locate the girl's fiancé and marry her to him."

Nic straightened, eyes more alert now.

Trey chuckled, the idea taking shape in his mind. "I do not know why that thought never crossed my mind before. I shall find him so he can marry our dear Miss Faraday. Then my problems will be solved." He walked to the fireplace and rested his shoulder against the edge of the stone hearth.

"It sounds plausible, although I believe you have overlooked one thing."

"What's that?"

"What if your mother does not approve?" Nic leaned forward. "What if the man is as poor as a church mouse and seeks her inheritance? Your mother will not want some fortune-seeking oaf taking advantage of her ward."

Trey exhaled a deep breath. Why could nothing be simple? "I never thought of that. Perhaps we should have this man investigated first."

"And what if you discover something incriminating?"

"I will have no other choice but to hurry her lessons so we can find her a proper husband. After all, this is what her parents wanted when they awarded her to my mother." He rubbed his hands together. "First, I must learn the man's name."

Nic's snort of laughter stopped Trey. Hawthorne shook his head as he stood and moved toward Trey.

"I fear you have forgotten one thing, Worthington. That girl is not going to provide you with any information. She loathes the very ground you walk upon. In fact, it makes me wonder what kind of liberties you took with her in the woodsman's cottage to make her act this way."

Heat washed over Trey at the memory of holding and kissing her. He wasn't about to tell his friend about any of that. "She does not loathe me." The girl doth protest too much, and Trey knew firsthand how quickly she had succumbed to his kiss.

"I assume you are oblivious to her glares." Nic shrugged. "Then again, she probably only does that behind your back. My friend, I regret to tell you, I highly doubt you have made an admirer out of that particular woman."

"As that may be, I shall find the man's name and have him investigated." He grumbled as he started for the door to his study but stopped. Where were his manners to forget about his guest? "Hawthorne? Would you like the butler to show you to your room?"

Chuckling, Nic shook his head. "Why? It's still early and I can return home. It's only a few hours ride to my family's estate."

"I would greatly enjoy your company for dinner. I require help with Miss Faraday this evening. Besides, she needs the practice."

Nic cleared his throat, his eyes widening. "I beg your pardon. Practice in doing what, may I ask?"

"I need your help in assessing her educational background. For Mother's sake, we need to see what exactly the girl was taught about social graces."

"Fear not, my good man." Nic smiled wide. "I shall assist, but by tomorrow afternoon, I must leave."

"Splendid. See you at dinner."

"What are your plans now?"

"To pour a little sweetness on my mother's ward." Trey wagged his eyebrows. "I will prove to you, I have not lost my touch."

"Would you care to make a wager, Worthington? I never pass on an opportunity to make easy money."

Trey ignored Nic's comments, but as he walked out, Hawthorne's laughter rang through the room. Trey scowled. What did Nic know? His friend hadn't been lying next to Miss Faraday on the bed with the blanket pulled over their heads earlier this morning. Nic didn't know how fast her mouth had softened beneath Trey's, either. Ladies always enjoyed men fawning over them. He'd prove to Miss Faraday he was as gentlemanly as they came, since she had made it a point several times to tell him he wasn't.

In the corridor, his mother was discussing Miss Faraday's arrival with the servants. Kitchen maids wearing white aprons rushed in and out of the large dining room, carrying his mother's precious silverware. Her strong voice gave no indication of her weakened state. She had proclaimed to be ill in the letter she'd sent him a fortnight ago asking for his help. Was she indeed ill? If not, why did she pretend?

He bounded up the stairs two at a time before marching down the hallway to his chambers. As he turned the corner and neared one of the guest rooms, the door opened. Judith sashayed out, wearing a yellow and white day dress. Her chestnut hair had been re-styled—a tight bun at the back of her neck with only three ringlets by each ear. Now he saw more of her slender neck than he wanted to, even as a lace shawl draped over her shoulders.

Before she noticed him, Trey stopped and leaned against the wall to study her. Judith seemed preoccupied studying the lock and key. Was she trying to figure out how it worked? Perhaps she wanted to keep someone out. What were the odds he was the demon in her mind at this moment?

With her beauty, he suspected her parents must have fought off plenty of suitors before they died. Now, he and his mother would be the ones with the club in hand, turning away money-hungry men seeking to fatten their purses with her inheritance. And what about the poor besotted young pups who would fall madly in love at first sight?

He rolled his eyes. What a waste of life, in his opinion. Why would any man want to chain themselves to one woman? Raised by parents who couldn't stand each other, it was easy for Trey to discern what he wanted out of life. Love and marriage were not it.

His father warned him years ago that marriage was only for producing heirs. Falling in love was for fools and should be avoided. Obviously, the disastrous match between Trey's own parents proved that theory.

Without a doubt, he would wear the title of rogue for the remainder of his days without any regrets.

A deep sigh escaped Judith before she stopped fussing with the lock. She squared her shoulders and closed the door with a final resounding click. Trey remained against the wall, so when she turned, she nearly collided with him.

She shrieked, her hand flying to her mouth. Eyes wide, her gaze skimmed his face, then slowly down his cravat and shirt. It only took a moment before the fright in her expression disappeared. Her face relaxed as her eyes turned a deep emerald. He hitched a quiet breath, not prepared for how lovely she looked this way.

"Forgive me for startling you, Miss Faraday."

"I would hope so." Her voice shook.

He glanced behind her to the door before meeting her gaze. "Are you *safely* unpacked and *secure* in your room?"

"Indeed I am, my lord. I thank you for inquiring about my welfare."

"I suppose the lock works." He grinned and crossed his arms over his chest.

"It does." Her finely shaped eyebrow rose. "And I wish it to stay in working order throughout the duration of my stay."

"As it should." He pulled away from the wall, dropping his arms to his side. "I expected you to be resting. Are you not exhausted from your journey?"

"Unfortunately, there is too much on my mind for me to rest. I had hoped to take a stroll in your mother's flower gardens. I remember they were a sight to behold when I was a child."

He nodded. "Indeed, they are."

"Splendid. Now, if you will excuse me."

She stepped past him, but he moved with her, matching her quick stride perfectly. She looked lovely in the simple, high-waist gown. White ribbons threading through her ringlet hair made her look so innocent. His gaze trailed down to the folded paper in her hand. Perhaps a missive to her so-called fiancé? Could this be the reason she tried to leave his side in such haste?

She reached the stairs and took her time descending, not looking at all in his direction. He stayed beside her every inch of the way.

"My lord, do you not have a pressing engagement? I assure you, I can handle myself without your company."

"Nothing pressing at this moment, my dear. In fact, I had hoped you would allow me to accompany you outside to my mother's gardens."

She skidded to a halt, her gaze swinging to meet his. "Are you addled?"

He arched an eyebrow. "Of course not. Do I look it?"

Her teeth tugged on her bottom lip as if to keep her from speaking, but a twinkle lit in her eyes.

He chuckled. "Ridiculous question, I realize." With much tenderness, he placed his hand on her arm and she stiffened. He acted as if the contact didn't bother him when in reality, the heat emanating from her nearly knocked him off his feet.

"Actually, Miss Faraday, I would enjoy your company. It has been quite some time since we talked."

She blinked and her mouth gaped. "You *are* addled."

He scowled. "Why do you say such a thing? Just because I want to get to know you better?"

Shrugging off his touch, she continued down the stairs, faster this time as she tried to distance herself from his side. She crumbled the piece of paper and stuffed it in her reticule.

"The boy I remembered from childhood," she said over her

shoulder, "did not want to get to know me. He was a vicious, evil person, whom I could not stand to be around." She took a quick glance at him before putting her attention ahead of her, slowing her pace. "In fact, I'm quite certain you made the devil himself nervous."

Trey threw back his head and laughed. "Oh, what humor you possess. Tell me, Miss Faraday, why do you hold such ill feelings toward me?"

When he opened the door for her and they both walked outside, she stopped to face him. Humor left her beautiful face. Her eyes expressed the seriousness in the moment.

"Have you forgotten our childhood? Do you not recall burning my hair and blaming it on your brother?"

"Trevor? Why would I blame him?"

"No. You blamed your brother Tristan."

Laughter quickly left Trey as sadness filled his chest. Tristan was the one who did no wrong. Was it any wonder Trey had enjoyed blaming his sibling who was only a few years older? The reminder of his brother's tragic death two years ago sat heavy in his chest. His jaw tightened.

"Yes, I must have forgotten," he said in a quiet voice before turning away. He couldn't let Judith see his emotions. It took a lot of effort to bury them, and only seconds for them to resurface. Guilt suffocated him.

"My lord?" She touched his arm. "Did I say something wrong?"

He glanced at her slender fingers curled across his elbow. "You didn't say anything wrong, only because you probably don't know."

"Know what?"

Taking a deep breath, Trey barricaded his feelings behind the icy walls of his heart and faced her. "Tristan died two years ago."

She sucked in a quick breath as her hand flew to her mouth. "Oh, dear heavens, no!"

"I'm afraid it's true."

"What happened?"

Trey's heart fought his mind in a losing battle. He would not conjure feelings from the past that brought havoc to his life again. Tristan had allowed a woman to run his emotions, making him think of nothing else besides her, and there wasn't anything Trey could do to stop it from happening.

"Let's just say my brother was in the wrong place at the wrong time, and he was shot."

All because of me.

Chapter Six

JUDITH BLINKED, TRYING to keep the tears from building in her eyes. Tristan had been the only brother of the three who she'd grown close to. Fate had been cruel to claim a wonderful man's life.

She placed her hand on Trey's forearm. "Please accept my sympathy. I will always have fond memories of Tristan. He was a kind man and will indeed be missed."

A dark look passed over Trey's face. "I thank you. Your thoughtfulness is greatly appreciated."

He placed his hand over hers, his thumb gently stroking her knuckle in comfort. Heated shivers ran through her, making her heart hammer. What on earth was wrong with her? She certainly didn't agree with the pleasurable sensations dancing through her stomach.

Why did he look so handsome in his brown breeches and black knee-boots? But it was his cream-colored ruffled shirt, white cravat, and double-breasted brown tailcoat that made him appear majestic. He, in no way, resembled the highwayman she'd earlier thought him to be.

A trace of moisture formed in his eyes, but with a fast blink, it disappeared. An invisible tug pulled at her heartstrings. No. She mustn't feel pity for him. Not after everything he'd put her through as a child, and would probably put her through as an adult.

A lump formed in her throat, making it impossible to swallow. His hypnotic gaze had her under his spell, a place she didn't want to be. She firmly commanded herself to withdraw. Gathering her courage, she stepped away. His hand dropped to his side and relief poured through her.

The warmth in his eyes dwindled and within seconds was gone. His countenance suddenly became different from what it was a moment ago. Turning, he straightened his shoulders. When he walked ahead, she hurried to keep in step beside him.

Suddenly, she didn't want to be alone. The crushing pain over the loss of her parents would overwhelm her again. The worst part was knowing Trey had experienced the same devastation when his brother died. They could share this time and talk about their feelings. If Trey would only allow it. Then again, Trey wasn't the type of man who would share anything personal with a woman.

She studied his rugged features, from his square chin to his straight nose, and those irresistible lips. Again, she shook away the improper thoughts.

He cleared his throat. "So, I was a rotten boy, was I?"

Grateful he had steered them back to the topic she wished to discuss, she chuckled. "Rotten? What a polite word to describe you, my lord."

Tilting his head back, he laughed. "I was worse?"

"Oh, yes. I was frightened out of my mind when you came near. Of course, the only time I feared for my life was when you tried to burn my hair."

He turned his head to look at her. The melancholy in his eyes struck her as odd. Was he sorrowful for his past transgressions? She could only pray it was true.

"I did not mean to, Miss Faraday. It was an accident."

She slowed her pace and arched an eyebrow. "You had a burning stick in one hand and my hair in the other. Pray, how was that an accident?"

"I only wanted to threaten you. Believe it or not, you were quite obstinate, and stubborn girls only tried my patience. I wanted you to leave, so I threatened to burn your hair. I never intended to actually do it, but the wind had other ideas."

She reached up and patted her ringlets. "Indeed it had."

"Let's put all of that behind us now." He flipped his hand through the air. "I would enjoy beginning afresh with you."

Uncertainty filled her head, yet her heart did a silly flutter. "Why is that?"

"We are adults now. I promise not to singe your hair ever again."

She laughed. "I would like it very much if we could be friends. It might take a while to forget the past, but I'm willing to try."

"That is all I ask."

Silence lasted only a few seconds as they turned down the path leading to the dowager's flower garden. All around her, beautiful roses, lilacs, daisies and tulips decorated the grounds. It was as if the sun had poured golden light on the garden, infusing each flower with a heavenly scent. Closing her eyes, she took her time inhaling their sweetness. Her mother had a garden similar to this. The scent brought back pleasant memories.

When she opened her eyes, the gardener stood beside Trey, clipping a yellow rose. With a wide smile, he took the delicate blossom and offered it to her.

"Yellow is the color of friendship," she said softly. "Are you aware of that, my lord?"

"Indeed, I am, which is why I'm offering this to you. Please accept this rose as a truce."

Her heart leapt. Was he truly a gentleman? Did he indeed want to be friends or was this a ploy to trap her into doing something against her will?

HESITANTLY, SHE TOOK the rose and lifted it to her nose. The pleasing fragrance wafted around her, soothing her temper. "Thank you, my lord. I do enjoy flowers, roses especially."

"Why is that?"

"Because these were my mother's favorite flower as well, and their scent brings back happy memories."

"Then I'm pleased that you are pleased."

"I am, my lord."

His smile widened. "Please, call me Trey."

She nodded. "Then you must call me Judith."

"I shall."

Judith was the first to turn back to the path as she walked beside him. Why was it hard to trust him? He proclaimed himself a gentleman, yet he had stolen a kiss from her already. Hardly the actions of a true gentleman. How could she think of him as anything but a rogue?

He cleared his throat. "So, Judith, tell me about this young man of yours."

Panic gripped her throat as her heartbeat hammered in a quick rhythm. Should she tell him? She seriously considered doing the opposite and lying to him instead. She hesitated in answering. "Why do you wish to know?"

"I have been thinking …"

"That's a dangerous thing, my lord. I mean, Trey."

He grinned. "Perhaps, but earlier today I wondered why you were so dead set against allowing my mother to sponsor your coming out ball. I recalled you were to meet your fiancé at the woodsman's cottage, correct?"

"Yes." Her voice came out small.

"Why was he not there, may I ask?"

She shrugged as disappointment wrenched her heart. "That is a question that has been going through my mind all day."

"You mentioned he was in the Navy."

"Yes."

"Do you suppose his duty to the Crown detained him?"

"I had thought that." So she'd lie a little.

"Will you tell me about him? What is the name of this young man?"

The pebbled path took them farther into the colorful refuge of the garden. The fragrance of roses faded while lilacs and lilies became more predominant.

"I met Alexander Cutler before he joined the Royal Navy. He was a distant relative of our neighbors." Warmth crept up her cheeks. "He was such a charming man, and it didn't take long to realize we were meant for each other. We wanted the same things, but he knew he didn't earn enough to support a wife."

"What rank is he?"

"A lieutenant."

"You really believe he's the man for you?"

She grinned. "I *know* he is. We have so much in common, which is why we fell in love so fast."

He stopped short. "*Fell in love?* Oh, Judith. You are so young and innocent. Love is for fools."

Heat burned her face as anger snuck up on her. "Indeed, sir. Perhaps it's *you* who is so cynical. But yes, we are in love with each other."

"Is he young, like you?"

"He is four and twenty."

Judith waited for Trey to make a snide remark about Alex's age. Since Trey was against love, she figured he wouldn't hold his tongue. After a couple of moments of silence, she wondered what thoughts swam in his head.

He stopped near a lilac bush and bent to remove a dead leaf. "Judith? I know how anxious you are to meet up with your young man. Probably just as eager as my mother is to give you a coming out ball and fulfill her duty as your guardian."

She tightened her jaw. Where was this leading?

He stood and faced her. "Here is what I propose. You allow me to look for your fiancé to see what his true intentions are. Meanwhile, you let my mother do all she can to prepare your ball."

Chapter Seven

JUDITH SUCKED IN her breath. He was actually trying to compromise? Ridiculous! Yet, his proposal sounded genuine. Half of her wanted to agree, the other half didn't believe him. What choice did she have? The letter she hid from Trey not too long ago in her reticule was ready to send to Alex, only if Trey's servants would do the errand. But Trey's suggestion was better. He had more contacts than she did, so perhaps she should let him locate Alex. It wouldn't be too hard to pretend to let the dowager teach her, either. It might turn out to be entertaining.

She smiled. "Agreed."

A familiar look crossed his features, causing his eyes to darken again. She wished his mesmerizing gaze didn't affect her so. Why did it tickle her insides and make her heart flutter? Only Alex should do this to her.

Grinning, he nodded. "Agreed." He presented his elbow for her to take. "Shall we continue our walk?"

Before she could answer, he took her hand and draped it over his arm then led them further into the gardens.

"I do not think I have told you yet, but you have blossomed into a lovely lady, Judith." His gaze swept over her. "I'm pleased to see the years have been so kind."

Her heart skipped a beat. What was wrong with her? Why did her body react so quickly to him? Hadn't she just admitted how much she loved Alex? Yet, the harder she tried to picture his face, the deeper Trey's rugged good looks crept into her mind. Not only that, she had started to think of him as a decent person. A potential friend.

"Thank you for the compliment. I must admit, you turned out rather…um, different than I had expected, too."

He chuckled.

Suddenly, his appealing scent of spice and leather surrounded her, making her want to close her eyes and breathe in deeply. As she studied the side of his face, his mouth opened while he talked, but she didn't register what he was saying. Beyond her control, his baritone voice stirred something within her. Watching his lips move made memories of them kissing in the cottage return, along with the tingles that had soared through her.

What had come over her? His sudden kindness confused her. Either that or she must be in the hot sun, since she was melting all over. *Alex, where are you?* She tried to recall what it had been like in his arms, being kissed by the man she'd proclaimed to love, but it was useless. Trey held her interest completely.

The few times he gazed down at her, his crystal blue eyes captured her attention. Long thick lashes surrounded them. If she wasn't careful, she could stare at them forever.

Trey for certain knew how to make a woman swoon. Why else would she obediently walk alongside him with weak legs as he made his way toward the gazebo? A place where they could talk in private. Had his caring actions made her doubt his intentions?

Heaviness settled in her chest as her limbs grew shaky. Her heart beat with renewed excitement. Why did he want them to go somewhere so secluded? Worse, why did she want to go with him? He was a rogue no matter how much he dressed like a gentleman.

This was Trey Worthington, for goodness sake. Why did she trust him enough to be alone with him? Running far away would be the best course of action. Unfortunately, her legs weren't listening and matched his steps as they walked into the gazebo. Discreet shadows fell all around them. He faced her, keeping her close as his hands cupped her elbows.

Her breathing accelerated. Her heart would knock right out of her chest if she allowed it. Surprisingly, her wobbly knees kept her standing instead of collapsing to the ground.

A soft smile touched his handsome face. "Why are you looking at me like that?"

She couldn't breathe and tightness consumed her chest. She couldn't speak because her dry throat wouldn't work. Her parched lips refused to move.

His gaze dropped to her mouth. "You are breathtaking, Judith." His large hands cupped her face.

Would he kiss her? She mustn't allow it. Where was Alex when she needed him the most?

WHAT IS HAPPENING *to me?*

Trey was lost in Judith's emerald eyes. He couldn't believe how quickly she had fallen under his spell. To think he was sinking just as fast. He was a fool for wanting to hold and kiss her.

She grasped his elbows, eyes wide with wonder. Would she allow his kiss? The time in the cottage, she really had had no other choice, although she hadn't struggled. This time she did have a choice. He didn't understand why he wanted to kiss her so badly right now, but he hadn't the strength to pull away.

He leaned closer, and she followed his lead by bringing her face forward. Confusion swam in his head, but he couldn't stop himself. Before he could separate his thoughts, his mother's voice rang through the air from the gardens.

Judith jumped away. A flush bloomed brightly in her cheeks, her face reflecting honest bewilderment. In silence, he grumbled at his mother, fate, and for being utterly beguiled by Judith Faraday. He, too, felt a little off-center, and rightly so. To have been so close to kissing her, then to have the opportunity yanked from his grasp was almost more than he could bear.

She turned her back to him as her hands covered her cheeks. Straightening, he stepped out of the gazebo and inhaled deeply. Heat still soared through him. Try as he might, he couldn't lower the temperature.

Within moments, Judith stood by his side. They walked toward his mother, neither touching nor saying a word. He feared if she brushed against him accidentally, he'd be severely tempted to take her back to the gazebo whether his mother approved or not.

He hadn't noticed before, but now out here, the sun glinted off her hair, giving it a golden tone. Indeed, she was breathtaking, more than he wanted her to be.

The dowager still couldn't see them, so when she called again, he raised his hand, waved, and shouted, "Over here."

When her eyes fixed on him and Judith, she smiled and hurried toward them. Once she reached their side, she panted and color had disappeared from her face. Perhaps Trey had been too hasty in doubting her illness earlier, accepting her outward appearance of health as fact.

"Oh, there you two are." His mother placed her hand on her chest and rasped deeply.

"What do you need, Mother?"

She smiled at him. "The most exciting news, I must say." Then she turned her attention to Judith. "I wanted to let you know the dance instructor is coming tomorrow." She grasped Judith's hands, gave them a small, excited squeeze. "Is that not lovely?"

Judith nodded. "Just wonderful."

"Mother, I was thinking…" He waited until both women gazed his way before continuing. "I thought about having a mock dinner party tonight with Miss Faraday acting as our hostess."

"But—but she has not been properly instructed in how to be a hostess," the dowager said.

"I understand, but I would like to see how much education

she has acquired before we hire someone to tutor her."

"Well, I suppose." The duchess sighed. "But why tonight? I'm dreadfully exhausted and I had planned on having the evening meal in my room."

"The Marquess of Hawthorne is here and he guaranteed me he would allow Miss Faraday to practice being an exemplary hostess on him."

Beside him, Judith's gasp overrode his mother's. The younger woman scowled at him and bumped her elbow into his. "You neglected to tell me Hawthorne was a *marquess*."

He gave her a grin. "Does it matter? He's still my friend, and he's willing to let you be his hostess tonight, knowing you will certainly make a few mistakes."

Eyes that had once been a desirable green glimmered with intense malice. Trey certainly had enjoyed seeing her hot temper. She attempted to smile, although that too, was razor sharp.

"I suppose it matters not, my lord," she bit out.

"Good girl." He patted her shoulder then turned to his mother. "If you cannot make it to the evening meal, no harm will be done. This will only be a trial run for Miss Faraday. After tonight, I shall know what she requires as far as lessons go."

The dowager caressed Trey's cheek. "You are such a good son." She smiled at Judith. "We are going to have a lovely time. I'm giddy just thinking about it."

Judith forced another smile for her guardian. "Thank you, Your Grace. I'm looking forward to our adventures, as well."

If Trey wasn't mistaken, she geared that last part toward him. The gleam in her eyes when she glanced his way told him what vengeful thoughts simmered in her pretty head. Nonetheless, he'd made a bargain with her, and he'd stick to it. Just as he'd make certain she stuck to hers.

"I hope you two will excuse me. I feel a headache coming on." The dowager touched her forehead and frowned. "Oh, dear. I do believe it's here already." She turned and left.

Both Trey and Judith stood still until the dowager was out of sight, then Judith slapped his shoulder. "A dinner party? Tonight? With a marquess?"

Grinning, he crossed his arms over his chest. "Marvelous. You got all the details correct."

"You think being a hostess for a dinner party is beyond my capabilities?"

"Now, Judith, I didn't say that."

"You *implied* I was incompetent."

"I did not. I want to see where you are in your education."

She copied him and folded her arms. "You expect me to fail, and in front of a marquess, no less."

"You could not be more wrong."

Her lips pursed and her jaw tightened. Even the veins in her neck rose ever so slightly. "I know more than you think I do, my lord."

"I'm sure you do."

She scowled. "You still do not believe me. Ask me a question about the dinner party. Anything at all."

Was he trying to provoke her? Of course he was. Even though making her upset and seeing the heat in her eyes was quite exciting, perhaps he should continue to charm her and become her friend. How else would he win?

"Judith my dear, don't fret. I believe you. As I have mentioned before, this is just a trial run."

"Whom shall I expect for the evening meal tonight?" she asked with a stiff upper lip as anger remained evident in her eyes. "Will the marquess be escorting female company?"

"No."

"Will you?"

He chuckled. "No. Why do you ask?"

"What? You don't know?" She put on the dramatics by placing her hand at her neck and hitching a breath. "Why, my lord, are you not aware I will need to make a seating chart?"

"But of course."

"Then I need to know all the guests arriving tonight."

He rolled his eyes. She was impossible. "It will just be Hawthorne, you, and I."

She glared at him for a quiet moment. To be sure, the wheels in her head had to be churning as fast as a runaway horse. He wished he knew what vindictive thoughts charged around in there.

"Might I ask what happened to our bargain?"

Her voice remained calm, although he knew she was far from it.

He nodded. "It's still intact. You hold up your end, and I shall come through with mine."

"I had assumed you would find my Alex before you put me through this torture."

My Alex... The words rankled him. "Then you assumed wrong."

"Oh." She stomped her foot, and her hands bunched into fists by her side. "You had every intention of misleading me, didn't you?"

"My dear Judith, I have not the faintest notion of what you are talking about." He stroked her chin, but she slapped his hand away. "Let me give you some advice, my dear Judith. Well-bred ladies don't show their temper, and yours is mighty hot. To be quite blunt, it's highly ill-mannered. Even your fiancé would want you to be a gracious hostess."

She let out a loud grumble before spinning on her heels and marching back to the house. He grinned. He had her exactly where he wanted. Keeping her vexed with him was a good idea, also. The way she'd gazed at him in the gazebo—a moment more and he'd have been on his knees begging for her sweet kiss. He couldn't allow that to happen again, which meant he must make her upset with him at every turn.

Yet, the challenge energized him, too.

Chapter Eight

JUDITH MUMBLED EVERY curse she could think of as she hurried back to the house. That dirty, rotten…scoundrel. He'd swindled her into this, and now she was stuck. Her first instincts were correct. She shouldn't have trusted him for one minute.

And to think she almost lost her composure while in the gazebo. What in heaven's name caused her brain to stop functioning? She'd let her appreciation for Trey's assistance in finding Alex sway her in the worst way.

Growling, she shook her head. She couldn't let her curiosity get the better of her. Now she knew Trey's game, she would *not* play. Instead, she'd make him grovel for her forgiveness one way or another. She'd show him just how *hot* her temper could get.

She flung open the door and strode into the entryway. Immediately she was hit with an intoxicating aroma that made her stomach growl and her mouth water. While visiting the Worthingtons as a child, she always thought they had the best food around—thanks to their very friendly cook.

One of the times her family visited, they were served a dish. Lobster tails. A delicacy Judith loved. This particular time, she couldn't eat it because it burned her mouth. Nobody at the table could understand, but Judith couldn't eat for two more meals afterward due to her burned tongue. It was later that Betsy, the cook, discovered her sauce had been tampered with, especially the one served to Judith.

She walked to the kitchen and peeked inside. Betsy was busy with the servants, hurrying to prepare a wonderful feast. On the counter lay Lobster tails. How convenient they would have this dish. However, this time it wouldn't burn…

Judith puffed her chest as an idea sprang into her head. The day suddenly had meaning.

When Betsy saw her, she squealed and threw out her chubby arms, greeting Judith with an oversized hug. They chatted about the lost years, until Judith reminded her of the terrible meal that had caused Judith's mouth to burn.

The cook's eyes widened, and her pudgy cheeks grew dark pink. "Oh, Miss Faraday, I thought the Worthingtons would have dismissed me that night."

Judith smiled and patted the older woman's hands. "I'm relieved you discovered what happened."

A gray lock of hair fell into the older woman's eyes, and she blew it away before arching a brow. "I fear it was a certain *someone* who had tampered with my food. I cannot be certain, but I would put all my money on Lord Trey if I were a betting person. He was an extremely mischievous boy."

A laugh bubbled from Judith. "And I would bet my money with you, as well." She glanced down the hallway to make certain a particular person wasn't eavesdropping before she continued. "Do you happen to remember what it was that burned my mouth so badly?"

"Yes, Miss Faraday. It was an excessive amount of pimento spice mixed with black pepper."

"Would you like to help me get back at the person responsible for doing this to me?" she asked in a low voice.

Betsy glanced around as if she, too, wanted to keep their conversation private. The corners of her mouth lifted. "What do you have in mind?"

"The duchess will not be joining us for the evening meal, so I thought perhaps you could heat up dinner tonight for Lord Trey.

We both know how he loves his food *hot*, like a woman's temper."

The cook laughed until tears formed in her eyes. "I must say, it's a good thing the duchess will not be in attendance."

"A very good thing." Judith smiled.

Judith left Betsy to go about her preparations and wandered into one of the drawing rooms. Music lifted from the harpsichord in the corner of the room, causing her to turn in the direction of the lovely sound. The man she knew as Hawthorne sat on the bench, creating the beautiful melody.

As she listened to the music, she filled her gaze with the large room. Large tapestries occupied one wall, while portrait paintings crowded the other. The oak paneled ceiling made the room look darker even though the windows were opened to the sunlight.

The sunlight made the man at the piano stand out. She stared in awe at his muscular frame, and the wavy thick length of his hair as it swept the tops of his shoulders. Indeed, he looked very dashing when she thought he was a thief, but dressed in gentleman's clothing, he was spectacular.

Just like another man they knew.

She growled to herself. Why was she even thinking of Trey? Would thoughts of him ever leave her alone? Alex needed to replace Trey, but the longer she was away from the one she loved, the more the memory of his face faded. Trey had only kissed her once whilst Alex had kissed her a few times, yet it was Trey's kiss not the kisses of the man she loved that remained permanently branded on her lips—curse the devil.

As quietly as she possibly could, she walked closer to the marquess. He concluded the piece with a dramatic ending. She clapped and he swung around on the bench in her direction. He quickly stood and bowed.

She curtsied. "My lord, I must compliment you on your playing. I do not think I have heard anything so lovely."

"Thank you, Miss Faraday. Your compliment warms my heart."

She smiled and strolled toward the sofa. "I want to apologize for not addressing you properly before now." She sat, smoothing her dress around her legs. "I fear Lord Trey kept your title a secret from me."

He swiped his hand through the air and came toward her. "No harm done, I assure you. When we first met you by the woodsman's cottage, we were not ready for proper introductions, so it's no wonder you did not know."

"Well, it's nice to make your acquaintance, nonetheless."

He chuckled. "It would be if we were introduced properly."

She offered her hand which Hawthorne gladly took as he mocked a bow. "I'm Dominic Lawrence, Marquess of Hawthorne."

She grinned and nodded. "And I'm Miss Judith Faraday, daughter of the sixth Viscount of Manderville."

Dominic brought her hand to his lips and brushed a soft kiss across her knuckles. "Honored to finally meet you. My condolences for the death of your parents."

Her heart tugged painfully as she experienced again the mourning that had yet to relinquish her soul. "I thank you, my lord."

He released her hand and stepped back. Standing tall and straight, he looked every ounce of noble birth. She supposed Trey would look as dignified, too, if she didn't despise him so much.

"Lord Hawthorne, may I ask you a personal question?"

"Certainly."

"How long have you been friends with Lord Trey?"

He shrugged. "I have known him for as long as I can remember. We probably were introduced as young boys. Why do you ask?"

She studied the rose pattern lightly scattered on her dress. "I need to know where I stand with you since you are such good friends with him, and especially what I can and cannot say about him in your presence." Hawthorne's laughter snapped her attention back to him. "My lord, this is not humorous."

"I gather you are not fond of Lord Trey?" he asked.

"You assume correctly."

He stepped to the couch and sat on the edge, his knees brushed her dress. "Miss Faraday, do you know you are the only woman I have met who can say that? Most women think Trey is as dashing as he is charming."

She gave an unladylike snort. "Then they are nothing but twittering henwits in need of spectacles and a brain."

"Possibly." He chuckled again. "I fear you have only seen his bad side. He's normally not like this."

"I find him rude, crude, and socially unacceptable. Not only that, but he's demanding and very controlling. My lord, I do not need to see his good side. He is absolutely despicable."

"As it is, he's still my friend, and the most trustworthy person I know."

Judith pursed her lips. "I thank you for answering my question."

"And I thank you for entertaining me." He grinned. "Trey tells me you are going to be the hostess at dinner tonight."

"Yes."

"I'm looking forward to it."

"Let me inform you right now, however, that whatever I do tonight is not the real me, either. If Lord Trey can show me his other side, I shall, too."

Chapter Nine

LATER THAT EVENING, Trey stood near the hearth watching Judith and Nic carry on a conversation as they sat on the sofa. Trey didn't dare admit aloud that Judith did an exceptional job with conversing. She laughed easily at Nic's comments, yet it wasn't in a flirtatious manner at all. Trey had seen it often enough when women tried their wiles on men, but in this situation, Judith was being herself and not overly-flattering. Perhaps she did know more than he and his mother expected. That would make his responsibility for finding Judith a husband easier than anticipated.

While she chatted with Nic, her gaze periodically wandered to Trey. Anger and distrust still flickered in the green depths, but thankfully, she never voiced her thoughts. She didn't need to. He could read her mind already, and it wasn't good.

He knew it upset her how easily she melted into his arms. Stubborn as she was, Trey figured she didn't like feeling that weak. Although he shouldn't have taken her to the gazebo, he certainly enjoyed how she'd fallen for his charm. If his mother hadn't arrived when she did, the impending kiss would have been inevitable.

He shook off the indecent thought. Getting her out of his mind was essential to his plan. How could he find her a husband if he was infatuated with her himself? Their walk in the flower gardens hadn't helped his way of thinking, either. She'd mentioned roses were her favorite, and he couldn't believe how much that little confession had melted his heart. His favorite flower was the rose, as well. He enjoyed watching her smell the flower as the look of pure happiness spread over her expression. To be sure, that would be something he'd never forget.

Finally, a maid entered the room and announced dinner was ready. He stepped forward and offered his elbow to escort Judith inside, but she found Nic's extended arm first and hooked her hand around his elbow, instead. From over her shoulder, she gave Trey a triumphant grin and haughtily walked into the dining room with the marquess.

Trey boiled inside, balling his fists beside him as he followed like an obedient dog. Perhaps he should have invited more guests tonight—more female guests who actually wanted his company.

She indicated to where he and Nic would be seated then stood before her chair. Trey jumped to her side to pull the chair out for her, but once again, Dominic arrived first. Seething, Trey waited until she was seated before taking his appointed chair at the head of the table.

He watched her at the other end of the table, waiting for her to give the subtle signal to the servants to start serving, but she didn't. Maybe she didn't know how to host a dinner party.

When she lifted her hand, her pointy finger above the rest, Trey breathed in relief that she would start things now.

"We are ready," she yelled from across the room.

Startled by her loud voice, Trey nearly fell off his chair. After collecting his wits from her ill-mannered outburst, he glanced next to him at Nic, who bit his lip, appearing as if he tried very hard not to laugh. If his mother had been here, she would have swooned.

Trey groaned and rubbed his forehead. To think tonight was just getting started.

Once the food came, Judith dove into her meal like a starving person, leaning her elbows on the table and inhaling her food in an animal-like manner, using her hands and fingers more than the silverware.

Ashamed of her display, Trey shook his head and moved his gaze to stare at his own food. He definitely should have gone over instructions before letting her on her own. It was a very good thing his mother wasn't present, indeed!

Nic remained quiet as he picked at his food. Trey held in an agitated sigh. Apparently, Judith had ruined his friend's appetite, too.

When she was finished noisily slurping her soup, she pushed the bowl away from her and sat back. "Lord Trey?"

Trey raised his gaze and met hers. "Yes?"

"Are you ready for the second course?"

He shrugged. Might as well get this over with so he could retire to his room to ponder on her much-needed lessons. "Yes."

She cupped her hands around her mouth. "Bring in the next course," she shouted.

Once again, he groaned. Dominic covered his grin with a linen napkin.

When the food was served, she turned to Nic and started a conversation. Trey refused to speak for fear he'd snap at her for her improper decorum. But when he heard her garbling, he glanced up to find out why. The poor country girl talked with her mouth full of food!

Sighing in defeat, he rested his forehead in his hands. Oh, the embarrassment of it all. He'd never hear the end of this from Nic, that's for certain.

Trey picked a small piece of lobster tail and dipped it in the sauce. This had been his favorite meal, but because of Judith's manners, she'd ruined his appetite. Trying to ignore her outbursts of laughter, Trey slid the piece of lobster in his mouth and chewed. Immediately, his tongue burned, and the more he chewed, the hotter it became.

He reached for his glass of wine and quickly brought it to his mouth to sip, but the liquid only intensified the heat exploding on his tongue. In front of him on the table was a platter of bread, so he grabbed a piece, quickly shoving it in his mouth.

After the temperature in his mouth returned to normal, he took another bite of the lobster tail. Fire burned his tongue, more painfully than the first time. He shoved another chunk of bread in his mouth to take away the burn. His eyes watered and he blinked the moisture away.

Trey studied Dominic and Judith. They acted as if nothing terrible was happening at the table save for Judith's outrageous behavior, of course. Why didn't they act as if their food was spicy? How could only *his* food be hot and not theirs? Cautiously, he took a bite of the rice dish, but once again, the inferno in his mouth intensified.

Admitting defeat, he sat back in his chair and was content to eat bread, since that seemed to be the only food at the table that didn't burn his mouth. He watched Judith to see if she had any reaction to his discomfort, but she was engrossed in Nic's tale and didn't glance Trey's way.

Somehow, the situation seemed familiar. As if he'd been through this before. Yet he didn't ever remember eating anything so horribly hot. Suddenly a memory crashed through. He and Judith were younger. Her family had visited for the weekend. He didn't want to entertain her as his parents had forced him to do. Instead, he wanted to push her away from him. From his family. That evening, he tampered with the meal by pouring pimento and black pepper in her lobster sauce.

Coincidence?

He thought not. That little minx had planned this. He'd bet money on it.

Finally, she glanced his way. He gave her a knowing grin.

Confusion crossed her face, but soon it cleared and she smiled pleasantly.

Curse her. He still couldn't tell if she'd planned this. But if she had, he'd get her to confess. Tonight, if possible. Strange thing was he looked forward to the confrontation, especially her temper afterwards.

A movement from the doorway yanked his attention away from Judith. His mother walked in the room, her eyes wide as she focused on the girl. Trey inhaled sharply. His mother would realize Judith didn't know a thing about entertaining. Trey and Hawthorne rose to their feet.

"Mother? What are you doing here?"

The older woman smiled as she smoothed her palms down her dress. "I wondered how Judith was faring."

"Uh…well, I don't think Miss Faraday is quite ready—"

"Your Grace, please come in and join us," Judith interrupted.

Trey swung his gaze to her. Instead of hunched shoulders and elbows on the table, the young woman sat with a straight back as she patted her linen napkin to her lips.

"How is your headache, Your Grace?" Judith inquired sweetly.

"Much better, thank you."

Trey pulled out a chair for his mother. "Are you hungry?"

"Just a bit."

Holding his breath, he waited for Judith's holler for service. Instead, she subtly motioned for the servant to bring his mother a plate. *What the devil?*

Aghast, he watched the next little while as a different Judith emerged. Instead of the uneducated girl he'd witnessed since they'd entered the room, Judith was doing everything perfectly. After the servant brought his mother's plate, Judith picked at her food like a proper young lady, and never once spoke with food in her mouth.

What was her game? Was she purposely trying to make a fool out of him?

Obviously. But he was on to her now.

He grinned. Taming her would be a chore, but an enjoyable one, he was certain.

Chapter Ten

JUDITH SMILED WITH triumph as she climbed the stairs, her steps light and confident, heading toward her bedroom. Tonight had been a resounding success, and she reveled in the satisfaction of her splendid performance. After dinner, the marquess had even remarked that it had been quite some time since he had been so thoroughly entertained. The evening had indeed been amusing, even if she had to admit it to herself.

The thought of her own antics brought a chuckle to her lips. She hadn't been able to watch Trey the entire time, which was probably for the best. If she had, she might have lost her nerve and faltered in her performance. Several times, she caught Lord Hawthorne trying to stifle his laughter, his eyes twinkling with mirth. She was certain Trey had been mortified, his expression a mix of embarrassment and exasperation. She could almost feel the heat of his glare, knowing full well he was likely cursing her under his breath.

Despite this, Judith couldn't help but feel a surge of victory. She had managed to captivate the audience and, more important-ly, to unsettle Trey just enough to keep him on his toes. It had been a night to remember, and as she reached her bedroom, she felt a thrill of excitement for what the future might hold.

When the dowager arrived, Judith had to change her initial plan to prove how well she could host a dinner party. It had been worth it. The few times she'd glanced at Trey, he resembled a large mouth bass while he stared dumbfounded at her. Things couldn't have gone better.

Chuckling, she reached her room and opened the door. By the number of pieces of bread Trey had shoved in his mouth, she knew the amount of pain he suffered. She stepped inside, and as she pushed the door closed, it swung open and smacked her knuckles. Surprised, she grabbed her throbbing fingers and gasped.

Trey strolled in. His waistcoat was absent as well as his cravat, and his high collar white shirt lay unbuttoned at the throat. Within seconds, her palms became clammy while her heartbeat sped up a notch.

"Trey, what are you doing barging into my room without an invitation?"

He arched a brow. "Would you have offered me one?"

"Absolutely not. It's improper."

"Then forgive me for entering, regardless. What I have to discuss with you is highly important, and I felt it needed to be aired in private. Unless of course, you want my mother to hear about the wicked plans you had concocted for tonight's entertainment."

Instead of giving him a verbal answer, she glared at him.

He closed the door with his boot heel before leaning against the hard wood. He folded his arms across his wide chest.

"Speak, then leave," she snapped.

His gaze skimmed over her, from the top of her ringlet hair down to her slippered feet. The corner of his mouth lifted in a mock grin. "I must say, you were quite entertaining tonight."

"I thank you for noticing."

"But I must know what you thought to gain by that little performance?"

She chuckled as she walked to her vanity table that sat by the far window, slipping off her elbow-length white gloves before laying them on the table. "I wanted to show you exactly what I do know about hosting a dinner party." She gave him a glare over her shoulder. "I do *not* need instructions or a tutor."

Trey pushed away from the door and inched toward her. With each step, her heartbeat knocked harder, nearly shaking her corset loose. Suffocation threatened to make her swoon. She pushed aside that thought. *I must be strong.*

"All you showed me tonight was the ill-mannered girl I recalled from our childhood." He ran his fingers through his hair and grinned. "You were unruly as a child. From what I have observed, you have not changed a bit."

When he stopped beside her, he grasped one of her hands and brought it closer to his face, studying her fingernails. "I half expected to see claws."

She yanked her hand away and glared. "Keep goading my temper and you will, my lord."

Shaking his head, he tsked. "My dear Judith, have you not realized who holds the key to your future? You have been entrusted to my mother's care whether you like it or not. She has asked for my help with your education, which I will do, but you are not making it easy."

She gave a forced laugh. "I do not plan on it."

"I thought we had made a bargain this afternoon in the flower garden."

"As did I, but you swindled me into signing my soul to the devil."

"Miss Faraday, you wound me. I'm not the devil." His voice dropped, low and smoldering. "If you let me, I can be your salvation. I truly wish to locate your fiancé, but you are making it difficult for me to be pleasant."

Anger shot through her, and she wanted to scream. Instead, she faced him, hands bunched at her sides. "You have not done anything yet."

"I have hardly had the time, Miss Faraday. Tomorrow afternoon, come to my study and we shall pen a letter to the Navy. Will that please you?"

She held her breath. The last time she relied on him, he'd made her look incompetent. Obviously, he didn't want her company any more than she wanted his. To end this ruse, they had to work together, even as disgusting as the idea sounded.

"Yes, that will please me. What time shall I come to your study?"

"After the noon meal."

"Splendid. I shall be there." She stepped closer until she nearly touched her nose to his. Trey's eyes widened but he didn't retreat. Shoulders back, she held her ground and wouldn't cower. "This time, I shall be on guard. I cannot trust you, my lord. You say one thing and mean another, which you have proven to me thus far. If you do not come through with your side of the bargain, I shan't either. Agreed?"

Every second that passed, his ragged breaths blew against her face. A hint of brandy wafted through the air along with the pimento. His gaze lowered to her lips, and soon his hardened expression softened.

"You are a hard woman to resist, Judith. If you graced me with that lovely smile you bestowed upon Lord Hawthorne this evening I might be lost forever under your control."

He slid slowly away from her and left the room. With the contact broken, she grew cold inside. She reasoned she had built an ice-wall to keep him out. That was the only good explanation she could come up with right now.

Chapter Eleven

TREY DRUMMED HIS fingers on his oak desk, staring out the window. Judith's letter couldn't be put off another day. His solicitor needed this information quickly in order to look into Lieutenant Alexander Cutler's past. Finding out about the man was of utmost importance.

Since last night's dinner, and especially the heated exchange he'd shared with Judith in her room, his thoughts kept straying to the young woman and her beau.

Trey arched a brow. Exactly how close had Judith and her officer gotten before her parents died? A sour taste invaded his senses. Could this be the reason she fought Trey's help in finding her alternative suitors? He'd have to ask her about it. Innocence was key in the art of husband hunting and if she'd been compromised... Trey groaned. Could the girl be in a family way? When had she last seen Alex?

Trey rubbed his forehead. If Judith wasn't the maid his mother had expected her to be, Trey would have no choice but to dismiss her from his family's house. Another scandal would be more than his mother could endure. What a disaster this was turning out to be.

A light hum from the hall drew his attention to the opened door. The swishing of skirts grew louder before his mother passed his study. Quickly, he stood. "Mother? Might I have a word?"

Seconds later, her head of silver ringlets peeked around the doorway. "You wish to speak with me?"

"Yes. Could you come in, please?"

She nodded and, ever the picture of grace and decorum, floated inside, smiling. "What is on your mind, son?"

He motioned to the cushioned chair near his desk. "Have a seat. I do not wish to exhaust you by making you stand."

She sat and folded her hands on her lap before he took his seat.

"Mother, I have not yet had a chance to speak with you about your letter."

"Beg pardon? What letter?"

"The letter you sent me a couple weeks ago, requesting my assistance with your newly appointed ward."

She smiled. "Oh, that letter. What is it you wish to discuss?"

He drew his finger across the corner of the blank piece of paper in front of him. "I want to know why you asked for my help. If you needed someone to assist you in instructing the poor girl, why did you not hire a professional tutor?"

Even as regal as his mother always appeared, she grimaced, her lips thinning into a line.

"I'm appalled you would ask such a question. Judith is the daughter of my dearest friend. As a child, you knew the girl well. It's not as if she's a stranger to us."

"Are you saying you expected me to help because I had known her as a child?"

"Why, certainly," she said as though the situation should be perfectly obvious. "You know very well how important her parents were to your father and me. Judith needs people she can love and trust and who love and trust her at this very difficult time in her life."

In silence, he growled. How often as a young man had his mother made him feel guilty? Apparently, she'd not given up this ability no matter his age. "Why did Trevor not do this himself?

After all, it's his responsibility as the duke."

She arched a brow. "Your brother is married with a pregnant wife to care for. Trevor has other responsibilities and does not have the time to cater to me like you do."

The truth came out. Finally. He groaned and rubbed his forehead. "Forgive me, Mother, but do you not believe I have responsibilities, too?"

Her mouth pursed, eyes flashing. "The only responsibilities you claim are those of ill-repute." She arched a brow. "Do you think I do not know? Rumors spread quickly, Trey."

Bunching his hands into fists, he held his breath, trying to calm his ire. "Mother, the activities you mention are merely sport. I do have other responsibilities and business dealings requiring a great deal of time and attention."

"Oh!" She stood and glared at him. "Trey, we have had this talk many times. I'm quite certain you are tired of hearing it, as I grow weary of telling. Your life is slipping away, and you do not have a thing to show for it. Do you want to be like your father, dishonorable as he was, embarrassing the family while causing scandal after scandal? Why can you not be more like Trevor? Even Tristan had been a good example of a decent nobleman."

Trey's heart clenched. Tristan had been the perfect example. Indeed their father's curse flowed through Trey alone, and it was the very reason for Tristan's death.

"Mother, if you will excuse me." Trey turned his attention to the quill and ink on his desk. "I have pressing matters to attend."

She huffed. "You cannot dismiss me that easily."

"I must." He glanced up briefly. "Due to my new responsibilities with *your* ward, I have arrangements to make on her behalf. Or have you decided against sponsoring her coming out ball?"

"Of course not."

He stood. "Then if you will excuse me, I have schedules to maintain."

With her back ramrod straight and chin lifted, his mother exited the study. Trey sank into his chair, picked up his quill, and dipped it in the ink-bottle before writing a list. He jotted down everything to accomplish before Judith's ball. With each new sentence, his concentration faltered. His penmanship worsened until he merely scribbled.

In distaste, he threw down the quill and pushed away from his desk. He paced the Persian carpet like a caged tiger, his chest tightening with each step. Why did his mother have to bring up the past? She knew how much he'd loved Tristan. Although Trey might be following in his father's footsteps, at least Trey stayed away from the kind of scandal his old man enjoyed creating.

Out of everything Trey's sire had taught him about life—good, bad or otherwise—the most important lesson was in love. His father instructed him countless times not to give his heart to a woman. The pain could never be worth it. And it was a lesson Trey hadn't needed to be told. He'd seen it every day of his childhood, watching the bitterness between his parents. They loathed one another. Over and over again, Trey's mother reminded him of how much he was like his father. Not just now, even as a boy she'd chastised him for the similarities.

Even now it was difficult for him to ignore his mother's wishes. He knew she loved him, but he couldn't let her shape him into something he was not...and as much as she wished it, he'd never be a younger version of Trevor.

A soft knock interrupted his thoughts. He swung around, half-expecting to see his mother. Instead, Judith stood in the light of the hallway, angelic in her cream-colored day dress. Her chestnut hair was swept up in a stylish chignon with wisps of curls lining her forehead and around her ears. He almost wished they were outside again, just so he could see the golden touches from the sun.

Chapter Twelve

"My Lord? Is this a bad time?" she asked meekly.

Trey motioned with his hand. "No. Do come in, please."

"Yesterday, you did say to meet you here after the noon meal, but you and your mother were not at the table, so I worried our meeting had been postponed."

"No need to fret, my dear. You are right on time." He grabbed the cushioned-chair his mother had occupied earlier and pushed it closer to his desk. "Have a seat and we shall begin."

After she settled herself, he took the other chair. Her sweet fragrance wafted around her and on impulse, he leaned closer to get a better whiff. Inwardly, he groaned. He'd always been a fool for women who smelled like flowers. Her scent enticed him to bury his face in her neck and never leave.

"My lord?" She withdrew as confusion creased her face.

He straightened, realizing he'd been caught in his fantasy. "Forgive me, Judith. I was just enjoying your pleasing fragrance."

Her face flamed a brilliant red. She lifted her chin higher, her hands clasped in her lap. "I thank you. I think."

"Now, where were we?" He scooted away, knowing the closer they were, the more tempted he'd become.

He picked up a blank piece of paper and set it between them on the desk. He dipped his quill into the ink-bottle then began writing: *To whom it may concern.* Then stopped and looked at her. "Do you know who we should address this to?"

"I do not."

"Hmm…" He tapped the other end of the pen against his chin. "Perhaps then, we should just address it to: *Lieutenant Alexander Cutler's Superior.*"

"That sounds very professional. I believe it will work."

Keeping his penmanship precise, he proceeded to write the letter. He introduced himself, along with the dowager, as Miss Faraday's guardians. When a thought crossed his mind, he stopped again. Earlier, he'd wondered just how close she and Mr. Cutler had been. Now would be a good time to ask her before finishing the missive.

He turned abruptly toward her, bumping against her in the process. He hadn't realized she leaned quite so far into him. A gasp escaped her throat. Once again, her face reddened and her eyes widened.

"Forgive me," he said. "I didn't know—"

"Oh, no. It was my fault entirely."

Silence hung in the air as he met her emerald gaze. He studied her shocked expression, but mainly her parted lips and the breaths rushing forth, breezing against his face.

"Why did you stop writing?" she asked.

How could he ask such a personal question without flaring her temper? Although he loved watching heat spark in her eyes when anger consumed her, this was not the time. Their discussion must be on a serious level.

He set the quill down, leaned back in his chair, and folded his arms across his chest. "Judith, before I continue, I need to know something."

"What?"

"Tell me more about you and Mr. Cutler."

She arched an eyebrow. "I thought I had."

"Not entirely. There are still a few questions left unanswered."

"Such as?"

He cleared his throat. "You had mentioned earlier your parents did not know about your engagement."

She lowered her gaze. "Alex and I kept it a secret. We were going to tell them after he had earned enough money to support me." She shrugged. "However, before that could happen, my parents died in a carriage accident."

He leaned forward and patted her clasped hands. "Judith, forgive me for bringing up bad memories about your parents." It was a pain he knew all too well.

Her eyes flew up to meet his and she nodded.

"Tell me more about Alex. How *well* did you know him?"

She pulled her hands away from his touch. "After we realized we were in love, we met once a week for two months. At first our rendezvous were at my neighbor's house, since Alex was related to them, but later in our relationship we met in secret."

Taking a deep breath, he prepared for the next question. "What exactly did you two…um…*do* during your meetings?"

Her forehead creased as she narrowed her gaze. "Mainly we planned the rest of our lives as husband and wife, discussing our dreams and goals."

Sighing heavily, he pinched the bridge of his nose. "Judith, I don't need to tell you how scandalous it is to meet a man in private, or how it can ruin a girl's reputation."

The corner of her mouth quirked. "Of course not. Did I not blame you for trying to do that when we were at the woodsman's cottage?"

"If you knew, then why did you continue to meet Mr. Cutler in private?"

She blew out a ragged breath. "Because I loved him, and I knew my parents would not approve. I knew it would take a while before I could convince them I wanted to marry him and it did not matter if we were caught alone because we were—and still are—engaged."

"But only in secret, correct?"

"Correct. We do not have anything in writing."

Facing her, he took hold of her hands once again. Moisture from her palms coated his fingertips. Nervous? Of course she was. She had every right to be with the questions he threw at her. Especially if she were guilty.

"You mentioned both of you were in love. So now my question is, how much did you love him?"

"I don't understand."

"Did he…did you…" Good grief, why did this have to be such torture? Her hands were stiff and he tried to relax her by rubbing his thumbs along her knuckles. "Judith, I might as well come right out and say it."

"I wish you would."

"Judith." He held her gaze. "Did you…give yourself to him?"

She gasped, yanked her hands away from his, and jumped to her feet. The quick motion scooted the chair back, which put distance between them.

"How dare you!"

He stood. "Now, Judith. I have every right to ask."

"You certainly do not."

"My mother is sponsoring you. She is spending money on your coming out ball. If you are already um…deflowered, then she has the right to know. Why should she spend money on instructing you for a ball you do not need?"

Tears glinted in her eyes, but she blinked the moisture away. "Just because you took liberties and kissed me in the woodsman's cottage, does not mean I'm the kind of woman who gives them freely."

He admired her courage to stand up to him, and—he believed her. She could be lying, but deep down inside, he didn't think so. Relief poured through him, and he nearly sighed aloud.

"I'm relieved to hear that, Judith." He reached for her, but she took another step backward. "Now that we have that out of the way, would you like to finish writing this letter?"

Several minutes passed as they stared at each other. She stood straight with her arms at her side, her hands fisted. Lines of anger marred her beauty, and he wanted to stroke the skin and make them disappear.

Finally, she nodded and walked to her chair. As he settled in his seat, he picked up the quill. "Now, let us continue."

As Trey wrote, he asked for suggestions, which she responded to coldly. His heart twisted, knowing he was responsible for humiliating her. But he had to know. Not only for his mother's sake, but because he needed to know for his own peace of mind.

It surprised him that Lieutenant Cutler was such a gentleman. That man must have been immune, because Trey found it almost impossible to be near Judith without wanting to take her intimately in his arms. Even now as he glanced at her, regret for making her feel this way wrung his heart and he wanted to hold and comfort her.

Once the letter was written and sealed with his family's crest, he leaned back in his chair and smiled. Still, her expression remained impassive, her attention remaining on the missive.

"Now what happens?" she asked.

"I will have this delivered to my solicitor. Then we wait."

She bobbed her head, but stayed in her chair. Silence stretched through the room. In the hallway, the grandfather clock struck two. There was no light in her eyes. No lift to her mouth. It was as if the life had been sucked right out of her.

His throat tightened. What had he done? "Judith?"

Slowly, she moved her gaze to meet his. "Yes?"

"I can tell you are still put out about that question. Please forgive me for asking. I just needed to know."

"I understand." Her bottom lip quivered before her tongue darted out and swept across it. "But what I don't understand is why…why…"

He leaned forward, linking his fingers across his knees. "Why I needed to know? I thought I had explained that."

She shook her head. "No, what I want to know is why Alex didn't try to take advantage of me when he had the chance."

Her answer was so very soft, he wondered if he misunderstood. The tears forming in her eyes confirmed her statement. She actually thought this was her fault?

He took hold of her clasped hands again. Instead of being moist, they were cold. He rubbed his thumbs over her skin, hoping to warm her up. "My dear Judith, what are you saying? Did you want him to compromise you?"

She hiccupped a laugh. "I never thought of this until now, but Alex could have compromised me several times. He was not raised with noble parents, yet he was very proper around me." She blinked as the tears continued to build. "In fact, you have touched me more than he has."

Trey groaned. Why did she have to say that? More importantly, why did excitement leap in his chest from her confession? Seeing her emotional like this made him want to gather her in his arms, more so than he'd wanted to before. Who was he kidding? He wanted to kiss her like the dolt, Lieutenant Cutler, hadn't been able to accomplish.

A tear streaked down her cheek and he caught it with his finger. "Judith, you should not think this way."

"How else am I supposed to think? He didn't even try. What's wrong with me, Trey?"

If only she knew how much he wanted to show her nothing was wrong, that she was a very desirable woman, she'd certainly box his ears.

"No, my pet." He cupped her face, which brought her liquid gaze to him. "Nothing is wrong with you. However, I have serious doubts about your fiancé. What man in his right mind could resist your charm?"

"Stop lying."

He barked a laugh. "Lie? No, my dear, I'm not lying. Have you forgotten the kiss we shared at the woodsman's cottage?" His voice lowered. "Or the walk in the flower garden? The gazebo?" He shook his head. "On my word, I'm telling you the truth, Judith. You are a very charming and irresistible woman."

She blinked several times, which dried her tears. Her hands covered his still holding her face. "So why could Alex resist me?"

Trey couldn't believe how their conversation had turned. If he didn't put a stop to this now, he'd take her in his arms like he'd thought about doing. "I'm a rogue, Judith. I'm drawn to beautiful women. Cutler is probably more of a gentleman than I will ever be."

Her face flamed, heating the skin under his palms. A smile wavered as she pulled away. She swiped the wetness from under her eyes.

"Forgive me for my emotional outburst. It will not happen again."

"Judith." He took her hand, brought it to his mouth and kissed her knuckles. "There's nothing to forgive. You can count on me to help you in any way."

What had he said? Good heavens, had a roaring fire been lit in the room? A window needed to be opened, and quickly to cool his ardor.

Judith pulled away from him then stood. "I thank you, Trey, for the letter you have written. I hope we hear something soon."

"As do I."

As she walked out of the study, he seriously prayed his solicitor found something disagreeable about Lieutenant Cutler. There was no way her fiancé deserved a woman such as the very lovely Judith Faraday.

Trey frowned. He didn't deserve her, either. She wanted a husband, and he definitely wasn't looking for a wife. Finding her a man to marry and getting her out of the house was top priority. He couldn't have her under his roof any longer.

His reputation was at stake, as was hers.

Chapter Thirteen

JUDITH RUSHED OUTSIDE. Spring's warm wind caressed her heated face, making her stop and close her eyes. Breathing deeply, she calmed her rapid heartbeat. What a fool she'd been. Why did she allow her emotions to take over, especially in front of Trey? Now he knew her insecurities. Knowing him, he'd use them against her one day.

Just now he'd been so wonderful and caring, which was not like Trey Worthington at all. He said the right things and made her feel like a real woman. Tingles erupted throughout her from his words and his heated touch. She'd soaked it in like a withered flower yearning for water and sunlight. Those feelings should be saved for Alex. After all, she loved him, didn't she? Only moments ago, doubts had filled her head. Her fiancé had never made her feel like Trey had.

She opened her eyes then squinted against the brightness of the sun. Had she been chasing a dream that would never come true? Had she been in love with love, instead of the man himself?

After a few cleansing breaths, she turned and strolled back inside the house. From down the corridor, the dowager stepped out of a room, spotted her and waved.

"Judith? Come quickly."

Forcing herself to smile, she hurried to the older woman. "What is it, Your Grace?"

"Your dance instructor is here. Is that not exciting?"

"Extremely." Judith tried not to dampen the dowager's enthusiasm, although Judith had been taught by her mother and father how to dance.

The reed-thin man in the center of the ballroom stood a good two-heads taller than her. His long face, and equally long nose, would be hard not to stare at. She bit her bottom lip, forcing herself not to laugh. He reminded her of a pelican.

"Judith dear, this is Mr. Henry Teethers. He's one of the best to instruct young ladies in dance. I'm quite certain you will learn much from him."

Judith curtsied slightly. "Pleased to meet you, Mr. Teethers."

When the man spoke, his voice squeaked like a young boy's in the years before becoming a man. Once again, she tried not to giggle. Instead, she followed his instructions, pretending this was the first time she'd been shown the dance steps.

The dowager duchess sat on a cushioned chair against the wall, carefully poking the needle through the cloth sampler before pulling it out. Would she notice how quickly Judith caught on?

"Splendid, Miss Faraday. Now, let me put some music to it and try again," her instructor said.

Judith scanned the room, wondering where the music would come from since there was no orchestra much less a harpsichord on the premises. Within seconds, Mr. Teethers cleared his throat and began humming a tune. His squeaks and squawks were worse than birds outside in a fierce hailstorm.

Since she didn't have to concentrate on her steps, she looked around the room again, noting the size and grandness, and especially the many chandeliers that hung from the ceiling. A few tapestries hung on the wall to give it more decoration. The dowager still looked engrossed in her sewing with her creased forehead and narrowed eyes. When Judith moved her glance toward the doorway, a familiar figure caught her attention and held it.

Trey.

He leaned his shoulder against the frame, his arms crossed over his muscular chest. Dreamy eyes followed her around the ballroom, and she couldn't stop from looking at him. Shivers of delight cascaded over her, making her limbs weak. She couldn't understand the effect he had on her.

Heavens, he was handsome. Why couldn't she think of him as the swine she'd met that first day? Was it because he'd admitted he was attracted to her? She couldn't allow that to enter her mind. Her head was already full of doubts about Alex.

Instead of listening to her instructor, she kept her attention on Trey, recalling every time he'd touched her and made her tingle. Would Alex be able to accomplish such a feat? And why in the world was she comparing Trey to the man she was going to marry?

Her mind was in such a whirlwind of confusion that she didn't notice she'd stepped on Mr. Teethers' foot until he yelped and stopped humming. She snapped out of the spell Trey's mesmerizing gaze had put her under. She focused instead on the man making hissing noises under his breath. "Please forgive me, Mr. Teethers. I should have been more aware."

A deep chuckle came from the doorway as Trey walked in, slowly clapping. "I see your pupil has learned quickly, Mr. Teethers. Indeed you are an excellent instructor."

The older man bowed. "Thank you for the compliment, my lord."

"Oh, Trey." The duchess put her sampler aside and stood. "I'm thrilled to see you here. Now Judith will have someone else to practice with instead of Mr. Teethers."

"What?"

"Pardon me?"

Both Judith and Trey exclaimed their surprise at the same time. The dowager wanted Judith to dance with *him?* Her heartbeat quickened and her mouth turned dry. No. She couldn't get that close. Not now.

The older woman motioned Trey closer. "Come dance with Judith to see if she's ready for her ball."

Panic gushed through her, yet Trey's tight lip and wide-eye expression mirrored how she felt. Didn't he want to touch her, even after what he'd told her earlier? Had he indeed, lied?

His gaze darted between her and his mother, but finally he smiled and stepped closer to Judith and held out his hand.

"Would you do me the honor, Miss Faraday?" He mocked a bow.

She swallowed the cotton that had formed in her throat before curtsying. "Yes, my lord."

The moment he clasped her hand in his, heat consumed her very being. Her heartbeat pounded as excitement shot through her. She held his stare, and nothing could tear her away from his amazing blue eyes.

His eyes darkened. Although he might have panicked a moment ago, his gaze now told a different story—that he indeed enjoyed this as well as she.

Mr. Teethers hummed another tune, but the sound faded quickly, only leaving the beat of her heart as it tapped the rhythm she and Trey were dancing. Every nerve in her body came alive and spun out of control, especially when his thumb rubbed her skin.

"You are a remarkable student, Judith." Trey's deep voice caressed each word.

"Thank you, my lord."

"Trey," he encouraged. "I wish you to call me by my given name."

"Trey." Oh dear, had she sighed his name? Hopefully, her ears were playing tricks on her—as well as her breathing.

He grinned. "You shall make my mother proud when she presents you at your ball."

"That's the plan, is it not?"

"Indeed, it is."

"When is the special day? I do not believe you have told me."

"Friday after next."

She nodded. "I shall be ready."

His arm tightened around her waist, drawing her closer to his chest. She feared he'd be able to hear her pulse beating from her bosom.

"My mother is planning to take you to the dress makers in Town and have your wardrobe made. Unless…"

"Unless what?"

"Unless you'd like *me* to take you."

Her heart jumped to her throat. "That's not necessary. My parents saw to my welfare before they died."

He squeezed her hand. "You are forgetting my mother wants to do this. She never had a daughter. Pray, do not spoil her excitement."

"As you wish."

Silence stretched between them, but Judith never lost eye contact. She couldn't no matter how hard she tried. Once again, his entrancing spell had pulled her in.

It wasn't until the clapping from the dowager and Mr. Teethers rang through the ballroom that Judith realized the older man had stopped humming, yet she and Trey still danced. He seemed rattled, too, as he stopped and quickly stepped away. Finally, the spell had been broken. She was almost relieved.

Almost.

If it weren't for the cold emptiness seeping through her body, she would have been extremely grateful for the interruption.

"Trey my boy, you and Judith dance perfectly together." The dowager beamed.

Mr. Teethers nodded. "Excellent form, indeed."

Trey chuckled, then lifted Judith's hand and kissed her knuckles. "The pleasure was entirely mine." He winked, then turned and left the ballroom.

It was all she could do not to call him back. But she wouldn't. He wasn't the man she professed to love—the man she *should* have on her mind.

She quickly made her excuses to the dance instructor and the dowager, and quit the room not much longer after Trey had. The dance left her disturbed and very much confused. Being in Trey's arms as he swung her around the ballroom filled her with a sense of belonging. Of peace and security.

She snorted a laugh and shook her head, quickening her steps as she took a brisk walk away from the manor toward the wooded area. Being outdoors always cleared her head, and if there was any time she needed to think straight, it was now.

The more she thought about Alex, the more anger consumed her. Earlier when she'd met with Trey to write that letter, many issues were brought up. Those she'd never even considered. Did Alex even want to marry her? Had she been fooling herself all this time with fantasies of wedded bliss?

Nearby a gurgling brook captured her attention. She followed the sound until she entered the wooded area. Down the slope a bit was the brook. She stopped near the edge and peered into the clear water rushing over rocks of all sizes. Memories of her childhood flowed into her mind. Her father had taken her fishing, taught her how to swim, and as she grew older, he gave her instructions on how to maneuver a rowboat. How she missed those special days.

Quickly, another memory rushed through, involving this very stream and the boy who tormented her as a child. Once when her parents were visiting, Judith had come to this section of the estate, hoping to have privacy. Instead, she'd had a run-in with Trey.

As a young girl, she enjoyed taking off her stockings and shoes, wading through the water without anyone knowing. On this particular day, she'd followed her urges. This was where Trey had found her. By this time in her life, she was leery of trusting him, and rightly so since he went out of his way to tease her.

He'd convinced her to continue wading through the stream, because he and his brothers had done this many times. Soon, she'd realized her mistake in trusting him since he led her to a section in the water that was deeper. She'd fallen, twisted her ankle, and ruined a new gown.

Judith shook her head, chuckling over the memory. Strange how different they both were now. Although, she still had a hard time trusting him not to lead her into deep water in all aspects of her life.

She sat on the grassy spot near the water and stared at the stream. A slight wind rustled through the leaves on the tall oaks, and in the distance chirping birds relaxed her. If only real life could be as serene. Unfortunately, Trey wouldn't let it.

She pulled her knees to her chest and rested her forehead against them as she wrapped her arms around her legs. Closing her eyes, she breathed deeply, allowing the soft sounds around her to put her into another world where she could dream to her heart's content.

"Ah, I see you have found my favorite spot."

The deep timbre of Trey's voice jerked her alert. She snapped her head up and met his twinkling eyes. The sun created a halo around his head until he walked into the shade near her. His rugged appearance nearly stole the breath right from her throat, as did his charming smile.

This was *not* good at all!

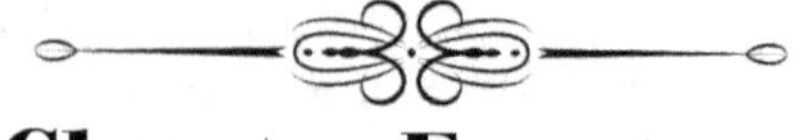

Chapter Fourteen

HE MOTIONED TO the grass beside her. "May I sit?"

Judith nodded, not knowing what to say since words had left her mind. All she wanted to do was stare at his handsome profile, content to study him.

Once he sat, he bent his knees up like she had hers, then looked at her. "It's so peaceful here, don't you agree?"

Her throat had turned dry, so she swallowed. "Indeed, I do."

"As a lad, I used to come here with Tristan quite a bit. Especially in the summer months."

"Why the summer?"

Trey chuckled and moved his stare to the water. He picked up a rock and tossed it in. "Because boys do a lot of adventurous things, and he and I used to wrestle. We would wrestle in the water, just to see who could get soaked the quickest. The heat was horrendous, and getting wet made it bearable."

Her heart softened from his confession. "I'm certain you ruined a lot of clothes that way."

"Not really. They dried quickly enough, so Mother never knew what mischief kept us from our studies."

She laughed. "I love being outdoors, especially when it's quiet. I find it easier to think that way."

He nodded. "Very true." His focus came back to her. "Would you like to be alone now? I will leave if you wish."

"That's all right. I do not mind your company." Once she said it, she wondered why. She did mind his company, especially when it made her so confused.

He raised his brows. "Indeed? When did this turn of events happen? I thought you abhorred my presence."

She couldn't stop the tug pulling up one corner of her mouth. "Only when you insist on being wicked, my lord."

A loud laugh came from deep in his chest, making his body shake. The color of his eyes softened. "Oh, but I think you enjoy that, my sweet. More than you let on."

"I shall never tell." Although she wanted to stop smiling, she couldn't. She turned her head and tried not to look at him, but focused on the water, instead.

Silence lasted a few minutes as she snuck peeks at him. What could he be thinking now? His wandering gaze slid over her in a slow perusal, heating her up quickly. If he didn't say something soon, she might scream with frustration. Perhaps she should leave. Being this close was not good for her health.

Suddenly, a chuckle came from him, making him turn to meet her stare. "Do you remember that time when you and your parents stayed the night, and my brothers and I snuck in through the bedroom window and pretended to be ghosts?"

It only took a few seconds before the memory hit her full force. Laughing, she nodded. "I do recall that time. You had me frightened to death and I didn't want to come out of the covers." She arched an eyebrow and cocked her head. "Do you know I could not sleep without a candle in my room for a month afterwards?"

Trey tilted back his head and roared with laughter. "Oh, dearest Judith. You knew it was us, so why had it scared you so badly?"

"I think it was because I realized if you could all three climb through my bedroom window, then other kinds of goblins would do the same."

He shook his head, still grinning. "We were little devils back then, were we not?"

"Tell me, whose idea was it to climb through the window and scare me that night?"

Humor slowly left his face. "Mine."

She nodded. "Exactly. I believe *you* were the devil and not your brothers."

He shrugged. "However, they followed my lead on most adventures I went through as a child."

"I'm sure they did."

He looked back at the water and silence stretched between them once again. Finally, after several minutes passed, he moved, but only to pull off his boot. She hitched a breath and dared to look into his face. He grinned at her as he yanked off the other.

"What are you doing?" she asked.

"I just realized how long it's been since I waded in the stream. And you know what? I miss it." He pulled off his socks and stood. "Join me?"

Her heart leapt nearly to her throat, it seemed. *Join him?* Preposterous. Didn't he remember the last time he persuaded her to join him in the stream? But that was many years ago. He wouldn't be foolish enough to try that stunt again, would he? Then again, she wasn't naïve any longer and wouldn't allow herself to be pulled in by his deceitfulness.

He walked to the water and stepped in. "Ah, nice and cool. The perfect temperature."

Her feet itched to slide in the water and feel the coolness against her skin. They were adults now. Surely he wouldn't return to his childhood methods of callousness.

After a few seconds of watching him swish through the ankle-deep water, she sighed and gave in. It'd been a while since she'd done this, too. Quickly, before she changed her mind, she slipped off her shoes and rolled her stockings down her legs. Just as she discarded the last one, she realized she'd just given him a peek of her calves. Sucking in a breath, she looked his way to see if he'd been watching, praying he hadn't.

He had. The rake!

His eyes darkened, and his expression transformed from playfulness to something entirely different. He stood frozen, staring at her legs. Instead of being embarrassed, a feeling of power came over her, knowing she had made him this way. Earlier, he'd confessed she tempted him. Now she believed and had new understanding of his words.

Trey lifted his gaze to hers and smiled. Slowly he walked out of the water toward her. When he reached her side, he held out a hand. Without a second thought, she slid trembling fingers into his and let him pull her to her feet.

Judith watched his face, especially his dark blue eyes. Closely, they stood in front of each other content to stare. He kept her hand in his, stroking a thumb over her fingers. When his attention dropped to her mouth, she held her breath. Would he kiss her? Half of her wanted him to, and the other half argued how wrong it was. This was Trey Worthington, she reminded herself, a man not to be trusted.

Stepping away from her toward the water, a smile stretched his lips. He tugged on her arm and she obeyed his silent command and walked into the water with him. Once the cool liquid covered her feet, she gasped, then laughed. He dropped her hand and joined the merriment. The spell was broken, and she breathed easier. Trey turned away from her and cautiously moved down the watery path.

"When I was a boy," he said, "I would come out here by myself to reflect on my life. Being the youngest, I didn't appreciate the way I was treated compared to my brother, Trevor."

She lifted her dress just enough not to get the bottom wet. "Why? You knew Trevor would eventually inherit the title."

"Yes, but it was as if my parents looked down on me. For years, they tried to compare me to my brother, bringing out my faults and telling me what I should be doing to be more like him."

"How dreadful. I think that would be a hard life."

"Extremely." He shrugged. "Perhaps that's why I became a

mischievous boy."

"To get attention."

He glanced over his shoulder at her and nodded. "Exactly."

"Being the only child, I did not have to worry about such things."

"True. At times in my life I wondered what it would have been like to be the only child. Then I realized I would have been bored to tears."

"Why? Nobody to tease?" She giggled.

He swung around and planted his hands on his hips as he stared at her. His grin let her know not to take him seriously.

"You think you know me well, do you?"

"Am I correct?"

He dropped his arms to his side and winked. "I shall never tell."

Trey turned back around and proceeded down the stream. She took cautious steps, enjoying listening to him talk about his life. It comforted her to know he would say such things. It softened her heart as well.

Suddenly, he stopped and raised his hand to keep her from going any further.

"What is it?" she asked.

"There's a hole somewhere around in this area. I need to find it to keep you from stepping there. I would hate for you to soil your lovely gown."

She hitched a breath, and placed her hand on her chest for fear her heart would jump out. He'd actually remembered the hole. Did he remember leading her to it when they were children? Certainly he didn't act as if he did.

"Ah, there it is." He turned to her and held out his arms. "Allow me, fair maiden, to play the gallant warrior and carry you through the trepid waters."

A laugh bubbled from her throat. "Are you jesting?"

"No." He pointed to the water. "There's a hole, and if you step in it, you will sink to your waist, I'm sure. If I carry you across, you will not be harmed."

He couldn't be serious. Yet his warm gaze told her he was. Apparently, he didn't remember the time when they were small. Now the question was—could she trust him? Would he indeed carry her to safety or would he turn back into the person she'd known him to be? She hesitated, arguing with her mind once again.

Confusion crossed his features and he tilted his head. "Don't you trust me?"

Once again, his words caused her to laugh, which made him grin. "Oh, Trey. I believe you know that answer already."

He nodded. "I wish you would learn to trust me. We are becoming friends, are we not?"

She shrugged. "I would like to think so."

"I promise not to let you fall. Please believe me."

Why was her heart softening, and why was she giving him her hand? He pulled her closer then swept her up into his arms. Up this close, his nearness stirred quivers inside her belly. Hesitantly, she hooked her arms around his neck and looked at his lips.

Trey tightened his arms around her as he stepped into the hole. The rhythm of her heartbeat shook her chest, increased her breathing, and caused her mouth to turn dry. Heat from his body blended into hers and threatened to melt her this very second. She must stay strong.

After he had stepped out of the hole, he stopped and let her legs drop. Slowly, she slid down the front of his body until her feet touched the gravelly bottom. His arms still held her against him while his fingers drew circles along her back. He studied her mouth just as she'd looked at his a few moments ago. Being up so close against his chest, she felt the beat of his heart hammering quickly with hers. She swallowed to moisten her throat, wishing he'd release her, and at the same time, hoping he didn't.

Suddenly, he dropped his arms and stepped back. His eyes widened as his mouth pulled into a line. He turned and walked out of the water toward his shoes.

"Trey?" Her voice whispered the plea. "Is something amiss?"

"I just remembered a meeting I had this afternoon. Please forgive me, but I must go."

She hurried out of the water and collected her stockings and shoes. "Of course. I understand."

After he was fully dressed, he looked at her. "Judith, I had a pleasant time with you just now. We shall have to wade through the water again."

"I agree."

Without another word, he walked away. Her tight chest finally relaxed, letting her breathe normally again. Why had she acted in such a way? And why did her body have to burn the way it did?

Yet, she realized he had established a bond between them. He actually gave her reason to trust him, which is something she never thought would ever happen.

JUDITH PUSHED HER mare faster, clutching the reins and tightening her knee around the horn of the sidesaddle. The sun began its descent in the sky, but there was still enough light to ride. This afternoon had been a challenge, mentally and physically. She'd never felt so much frustration than she had in Trey's presence, but being in his arms was purely sensual. Every last second of it.

Obviously, there was an attraction between them. Strange, since they didn't like each other as children. Now, however, they were both matured. Never did she think Trey would be as handsome, or charming. Every time she looked upon him, she couldn't help but admire the man he'd turned into.

Earlier this evening, she had tried to visit with the dowager, but Trey was always lurking—watching her with heated eyes. She even tried hiding in the library, but she'd bumped into him there, as well. Now she needed to think without anyone around, so she saddled a mare and rode farther onto the estate. Perhaps she would be free of Trey for at least a few hours.

Another stream caught her eye, and she slowed her horse to a trot as she neared the water. Was this an extension from the same one she and Trey had waded through earlier today? If it was, the water appeared deeper here. Wading was definitely out of the question this evening.

She stopped her horse, dismounted then tied the animal to a tree. As she lifted off her bonnet, she breathed deeply. The heavenly aroma floating through the air from a nearby lilac bush made her smile. Her father had loved this smell, and even had perfumes and soaps made to match the scent for his wife and daughter.

Yearning for a time long gone crept upon her as tears gathered in her eyes. If her parents had lived, what would they be doing now? Certainly, she wouldn't be standing here in the glade wondering about her future with Alex.

Or was he really meant to be in her life?

Situations happening lately spoke of a different turn of events. With her sudden attraction to Trey, she wondered if he was the man for her instead.

A laugh sprang from her throat. What a vivid imagination. Trey had tormented her endlessly as a child, and she feared for her life most of the time. Even now, he tormented her, but in a stimulating way. That emotion was so very different, yet she enjoyed the rush of heated tingles fluttering in her belly.

So was Trey supposed to be the man she fell in love with?

She rolled her eyes and kicked a pebble into the water. Men like Trey would never settle down. Their sole purpose in life was to woo every maiden that came in their path. Judith didn't want a man like that. She wanted one who would love and shower her with affection. One who wanted to raise and support a family. Like her father had done. Men like Trey would not fit into this category.

The thundering of horse's hooves pulled her attention away from the water and to the rider barreling down upon her. Gasping, she clutched the high-neck collar of her Spencer jacket and moved toward her mare. Good heavens, the rider would trample her any second now…

Chapter Fifteen

CLOSER THE RIDER came through the shadows of the evening, but she couldn't see his face. Just as he was upon her, the outline of his body seemed familiar, and she breathed a heavy sigh of relief. What was Trey doing here? Could she be alone with him without those betraying tremors making her body warm and soft at the same time? Today while they played in the water, she'd grown close to him. Emotionally. He'd proven to her that she could finally trust him. He'd also proven to her that he enjoyed her nearness. While he'd held her so close, she'd felt his ragged breaths upon her face and the uneven rhythm of his heart.

He stopped his horse short and jumped down. This evening he wore brown riding breeches and black boots. A cravat was absent, but his white lawn shirt and brown waist jacket emphasized his perfect skin color, and made his blue eyes nearly shine. Relief was the best way to explain his expression and his wide smile as he walked toward her.

"There you are." He tied his horse near hers. "I wondered what became of you."

"Why?"

He faced her and his attention slid over her body. As each second passed, his smile widened and his eyes darkened. Her heartbeat knocked faster against her ribs.

"You seemed to have disappeared. Mother said she thought

she saw you taking Bluebell out to ride." He shrugged. "I could not help but worry about you riding through the estate with shadows all around."

She arched a brow. "Why? Do you think the only time I can ride is during the daylight hours? I assure you, I have had riding lessons since I was old enough to sit on a horse."

Chuckling, he drew closer. "I have seen firsthand how you can ride when the sun is not fully in the sky, my dear."

Thinking of their meeting at the woodsman's cottage caused her to blush. "Then why were you worried tonight?"

He stopped only a few feet in front of her. "I worried because I know how easily it is for you to sneak off without being noticed." He winked.

Judith laughed. "Then I forgive you this time."

His gaze boldly caressed her again, only slower. On impulse, she folded her arms and found the courage to raise her stubborn chin, facing him instead of cowering.

"I needed to be by myself for a while. That's why I went riding." She turned toward the stream, walking toward the edge. "It's such a lovely evening. I could not let it pass without a short outing."

"Indeed, it's a perfect evening for being outdoors, but—" He grasped her elbow. "I fear because of the shadows, if you get any closer to that water, you will slip on the moist ground. This water is much deeper than what we had waded in earlier. I would hate for you to soil your dress."

Warmth spread from his touch like wild fingers of comfort racing through her. She sucked in a breath and looked at him over her shoulder. Had the bolt of energy passed through him, also?

"No, Trey. I definitely don't want to soil my dress. I do know how to handle myself in these circumstances. After all, I was raised in the country, or have you forgotten?"

"My dear, how could I forget something you remind me about every time we talk?"

"Yet you still insist on treating me like a child you have to keep an eye on." She arched her brow. "Like now."

"A child?"

This time when Trey's attention skimmed over her, he lingered longer in his observation. Every place his gaze touched, her skin ignited. She was certain he meant to do this, to upset her. The rogue!

He must have known what he'd done to her this afternoon. Every time he came near her, she couldn't breathe. He'd watched her closely, too. In fact, she was willing to bet he hadn't had a meeting earlier, and his quick departure had something to do with the strange attraction happening between them.

"No, my sweet. You are not a child." He rested his hands on her shoulders and turned her to face him fully. "If you were a child, I would not fret about you so."

Her throat tightened. "What do you mean?" she croaked without meaning to.

"Now that you are a woman you have become a temptation to men, my sweet Judith. I must keep watch over you for as long as you are in my mother's care."

Once again, she couldn't breathe. He was too close but she couldn't push him away. She didn't want to. "When we were writing that letter earlier, you mentioned that I tempt you. If that's indeed true, then why are you with me now? And why did you join me at the stream?"

As his grin widened, his blue eyes twinkled. "You do tempt me." He gently twined the wisp of hair by her ear around his finger. "But I fear I cannot stay away. I enjoy your company. When I thought you had escaped this evening, I dreaded what I might discover. Now I know you have not left and I find myself relieved...and very much pleased you are still here."

Gingerly, he cupped her face, his thumbs caressing her skin.

"And who will protect me from you, my lord?"

His fingers slid down her throat and all proper thoughts and words ceased to exist. She fought for control, even while she wanted to sigh his name and close her eyes.

Clinging to his arms, she held herself from melting to the ground. "Trey, why are you doing this?"

His smile wasn't as wide, and his eyes darkened while his lips parted. Heaven help her, she wanted to kiss him, even as her mind argued that fact.

"Pray, my dear. What am I doing?" With a slight tug of his hands, he'd pulled her against him. He dipped his head to her neck and brushed his lips across her ear.

She bit her bottom lip, trying hard not to sigh aloud. Her breathing became ragged, and she tilted her head back to give him better access to her neck.

"You are making me…" She stopped herself before confessing. No, she couldn't tell him how much she wanted him right now. "I'm not supposed to…I cannot feel this way, Trey."

"Why? Are you not enjoying it?"

She dissolved against him and closed her eyes. "Oh, yes. Heaven forgive me, because I am."

Groaning, he tightened his hold as his mouth searched for hers. Judith couldn't hold back. She needed to feel his lips, and turned her head to meet his in a searing kiss. The heat strumming through her was a long awaited pleasure. She wrapped her arms around his waist, returning his kiss with great urgency.

Large hands wandered over her back, holding her in place. She didn't want to think of why she enjoyed his kiss so much, but the longer his lips melded to hers, the further away reality drifted, and all she cared about was being held by Trey.

As Trey continued to kiss her, she couldn't stop thinking about being with him. Forever. Dreams she'd had with—oh, what's his name—disappeared and all she wanted was to be with this exciting man holding her. The first man who made her feel like a real, desirable woman. She wanted more. Wanted to be his wife, to have his children. Wanted only the attention he could give her. She wanted him, and only him.

The realization brought her alert and out of her dream world. Trey was not the kind of man she could have. He wasn't the loving family man like her father.

Her heart sank to the pit of her stomach. What had she done?

Pushing her hands against Trey's chest, she broke the contact and stepped back. Deep breaths rushed out of her and kept pace with his. She placed hands over her burning cheeks, still not believing what she let him do. He raked his fingers through his hair.

"Trey, we cannot do this."

He nodded, turning a frustrated circle. "You are correct."

The wild beat of her heart took a long time to slow, and during this time, all she could do was stare at Trey. Confusion creased his brow for a few minutes, then finally the lines disappeared and he smiled.

"Forgive me, Judith. I got carried away in the moment."

She forced a chuckle. "I understand completely."

He scrubbed his hands over his face and straightened. "Do you wish me to escort you home?"

"No. I shall be fine."

"Then I shall be off. Once again, please forgive me for taking such liberties."

A cold draft seemed to come out of nowhere and chilled her, so she folded her arms. "There's nothing to forgive. I...I allowed it, although I should not have."

He nodded and strode to his horse. In one swift movement, he swung atop the steed, and without another look, he urged his horse into a run and was gone.

Emptiness filled her chest and she wanted to cry. In Trey's arms she experienced things she'd never known existed. But she could never allow that to happen again. He wasn't husband material, and she could never change him.

A small smile tugged at her lips. Strange thing was, she didn't want to. His charm was what made him the man she desired. Was it the role of a rogue? Possibly, but it went further. All she knew was if Alex didn't come for her, she'd have to find a husband soon, because the longer she stayed here, the more she wanted Trey.

Chapter Sixteen

THE MORNING SUN on Judith's face stirred her out of a deep sleep. With a yawn, she stretched her arms above her head. After blinking to clear her vision, she glanced around the room. Her mind rolled from the rapid change to her life. She pulled the blankets to her chin as she curled beneath them. Even as uncertainty dominated most of her thoughts, she smiled. How could she not? Trey's attention had given her something to ponder.

Not once had a man stirred flutters in her belly and made her heart beat with such wild palpitations. Not once had a man's kiss made her mind go blank, only to fill with thoughts of him. Alex had never made her toes curl or her mind blank, yet last night while kissing Trey, she couldn't even remember her fiancé's name. How could Trey make her feel so desirable when Alex hadn't come close to inspiring that kind of feeling inside her?

She rolled on her side and stared out the window. Last night before she came to bed, she'd left the drapes open, staring at the moon while making silly wishes. Now in the light of day, she wondered if her wishes could become reality.

Was Alex really the man for her?

Or was Trey?

If, by some great chance, Trey's thoughts turned to marriage and family, would he make a good husband? She closed her eyes and cuddled her head against the pillow. Would it be so terrible to fall in love with Trey? They were adults now. She didn't need to fear him as she'd done as a child.

A growl rumbled through her stomach, reminding her of the need to eat. She climbed from the bed and rang for her maid to help her prepare for the day. With each stroke of the brush through her hair, her thoughts were on the man who disturbed her in more ways than one. By the time she was dressed and ready to leave her room, she anticipated seeing Trey this morning.

Telling him about her thoughts was out of the question, mainly because she was uncertain of them herself. Besides, she didn't want to frighten the poor man. She needed to test the waters first. Did he have the same confused feelings about her?

Judith strolled into the dining room for the morning meal eager to follow through on her decision, but Trey's absence gave her pause. The dowager ate alone. Heaviness sank in Judith's chest. Something must be wrong.

The older woman smiled and motioned for her to enter. "Do come in, child. I welcome your company."

Straightening her shoulders, Judith walked to the chair beside the dowager and sat. "Where is Lord Trey this morning? Usually he's here and halfway finished with his meal before I arrive."

"Oh, he will not be joining us for a few days. Business called him out of town, unfortunately."

Disappointment crept into Judith's heart, although she tried to usher it out. There was no reason for her to feel this way. He was a free man and could come and go as he pleased.

Why did he have to pick today to go out of town? He'd kissed her so passionately yesterday, leading her to believe there could be more moments like that. Now guilt washed over her like a turbulent wave hitting against jagged rocks. She had indeed frightened him away. Her first instincts about him had been correct. He didn't want a wife. Just a scandalous liaison. He knew Judith looked for a husband and nothing less.

A footman brought her a plate of assorted fruits with scones and honey butter. She picked up an apple slice and nibbled. Her appetite vanished and all she wanted to do was return to her room and sulk. Silently she scolded herself. What made her think he'd change? Naturally, pigs don't lose their bothersome scent. And Trey would always be a rake of the worst kind.

Isabelle Worthington sipped her tea then patted her mouth with the linen napkin. "I have decided you are ready to plan a real dinner party."

Judith gasped and swung her head toward the dowager. "Are you certain?"

"Of course. I know an adept pupil when I see one. Mind you, it shan't be a large gathering, just ten or twelve friends. How does that sound?"

Planning a social gathering didn't worry Judith. She'd done it several times while her parents were alive. Could she accomplish hosting a successful gathering without Trey there to tease? For some odd reason, he'd been her sole motivation lately. Perhaps his absence was a good thing.

"That sounds wonderful, Your Grace. I would be pleased to host a dinner party."

Isabelle clapped her hands. "Splendid. We shall have it in four days. Since you are not familiar with those who live nearby, I will send out the invitations."

Judith forced a smile. "Wonderful. Please be certain to invite the Marquess of Hawthorne. I'm acquainted with him."

"As you wish, my dear. His family is very close to ours. I, too, would like to visit with him again. I heard his cousin from France is visiting. I shall invite her, as well."

Isabelle chatted about the guests she intended to invite while Judith picked at her food. It would be enjoyable to see Dominic again, but could she talk to him without wanting Trey nearby? She silently cursed that man, then herself for not being able to stop thinking about him.

After the meal, both she and the dowager walked into the

drawing room. Judith stood by the window, gazing into the flower garden. The bright sun colored rainbows above the beautiful plants and beckoned her to venture out and enjoy their loveliness. It wouldn't happen today. Not with her sour mood. She'd wilt the petals if she strolled too close.

"Judith, I hope you do not mind, but I would like us to travel into London to Bond Street this afternoon. I feel it's time to outfit you in the latest fashion."

She yanked her attention away from the window and focused on her guardian. "Why? I'm not in need of anything. I have plenty of gowns."

Isabelle flipped her hand in the air. "Humor an old woman, please. I would very much like to take you shopping. Besides, women can never have enough gowns and accessories in my opinion."

Strange how being raised a country girl was so different than how Isabelle lived her life. Judith nodded. "Then I would enjoy an outing with you."

Her guardian walked to her before clasping their hands. "We shall have a fabulous time. Go now and ready yourself. I would like to leave shortly."

"As you wish."

As Judith hurried to her room, her thoughts turned to Trey once again. Not too long ago he'd offered to take her shopping, but she declined. What would have happened if she hadn't turned him down? A thrill shot through her and made her stomach flutter. Going alone with him would certainly cause a scandal, especially since she couldn't keep away from him. Instead, she'd have to imagine what it would have been like in secret, knowing it would never happen in real life. Unfortunately, reality was not as sweet and left her heart flat, without emotion.

It didn't take long to get ready for the trip, and soon she sat across from the dowager in the black coach trimmed with silver; the family's crest painted on the door. The coach bumped them around on the seat, more than Judith would like.

"Your Grace? Would you mind if I asked you something personal?"

The older woman's eyebrows rose. "What is it, my dear?"

"I sincerely hope I'm not dredging up bad memories, but—" she swallowed hard—"Lord Trey briefly mentioned Lord Tristan had died. If you are up to it, could you tell me what happened?"

Isabelle's smile faded and her eyes ceased sparkling. She wrung her hands in her lap as she switched her attention to the landscape passing outside the window.

Judith's heart sank. Perhaps she shouldn't have said anything, but she desperately wanted to know the fate of her childhood friend. It was obvious Trey was troubled by his brother's death and refused to talk.

Several minutes passed. The only sound came from the clip-clop of the horse's hoofs, and the coach's wheels crunching on the road. Finally, the dowager turned as her eyes met Judith's stare.

"I suppose I could speak about it. I have not said anything for so long, hoping the pain would disappear." She shook her head. "It has not."

"It might never leave," Judith whispered. "I will always mourn the death of my parents, but I choose to remember the good times instead of the bad."

"You are correct of course, my dear." The older woman pulled herself a little straighter. "The truth is I really do not know every detail of his death, just what Trey has related."

Judith wrinkled her brow. "Lord Trey was with him?"

"Oh, yes. They were traveling abroad, somewhere near the North Sea. Trey said they came upon bandits who were being chased by the local military regiment, and they were caught in the crossfire. Tristan was shot, and the blow knocked him off his horse. Apparently, they were near a cliff, and Tristan fell a great distance into the water below." The dowager's bottom lip trembled. "Trey tried to find his brother. Searched night and day, and had others helping, but they finally came to the conclusion the sea had taken Tristan's body."

The dowager dabbed her finger at the moisture sliding down her cheek. A knot formed in Judith's throat. What a tragic death.

Isabelle sniffled. "Trey was beside himself for months afterward. He stayed in his room or his study, drinking himself into oblivion. I feared for his mental state. He would not talk about it. When he did, he blamed himself."

Tears gathered in Judith's eyes as her heart broke.

"If it was not for Lord Hawthorne, I don't know what would have become of my son."

"What did Lord Hawthorne do?"

The duchess shrugged. "I never learned exactly what he had accomplished, but Dominic stayed in Trey's study for forty-eight hours straight talking and sobering my son. After that, Trey took things day by day. He was never the same. For some reason, he had hardened his heart against everything he had cherished."

"And Lord Trey has never talked about what happened?"

The older woman shook her head. "Never. Every time I ask him, he changes the conversation."

"Was that when his lifestyle became…um…less than admirable?"

The dowager chuckled. "That's a very nice way to say it." She wiped her tears. "But the answer is yes, in a sense. Trey had always been a wayward child and young man, but after Tristan's death, Trey's attitude toward everything changed, especially his taste in female companionship. As hard as Trevor and I tried, we could not persuade Trey to think differently."

"I suppose he will never change," Judith said hesitantly as sadness hung in her chest.

"That's yet to be decided. I think all people can alter their lifestyles, especially men. Trey needs to find the right woman, I believe. Once he loses his heart to the perfect lady, he will change. I'm certain of it."

Judith's heart wrenched. The older woman had such high hopes. How well did she know her own son? Was there a chance he would change? Deep inside, Judith wanted to be the woman to transform him into a better man. Inwardly, she chuckled. Why did she think that? Of all people, *she* was certainly not the woman for Trey.

Yet why did the idea take root in her mind, and especially her heart? She wanted to ignore common sense and at least try to help.

Chapter Seventeen

TREY SAT ACROSS from his solicitor and tapped his fingers on the desk. Mr. Lewis gathered his papers and set them on the corner of the dark oak top, pushing them until they touched Trey's fingers.

"It's all there, my lord. I still have a few more leads to follow, but that shouldn't take much time."

Nodding, Trey picked up the first page and glanced at the words, not letting anything register in his head. He really didn't need to. Mr. Lewis had told Trey what he needed to know.

Alexander Cutler was a deceiver and poor as a church mouse.

Maybe poorer.

"As you will see on page two," the solicitor added, "Mr. Cutler had never been a part of the Royal Navy. If he continues portraying an officer, the Royal Navy will have him arrested."

"Sounds as though arresting the man is the wisest decision regardless of his impersonation," Trey muttered. "I sincerely hope this man is found and judged for his crimes."

Originally, he'd hired a solicitor to find Mr. Cutler so Judith could be married and out of his hair as quickly as possible, but the more he grew to know her, the more he hoped Mr. Cutler would fade from her life.

Fortune smiled upon Trey once again. This was the very thing he needed to keep the man away from Judith. Now Trey would have to tell her that her dear beloved officer wasn't whom he proclaimed. She'd be devastated, and rightly so. Her hopes and dreams of marriage would crash around her, putting her into the pit of despair. Trey would be right by her side to comfort of course. She'd cry in his arms, and he'd soothe her the only way he knew how. The idea excited him, and he almost looked forward to the prospect.

Groaning silently, he shifted in his chair and looked at Mr. Lewis. "Have you found where Mr. Cutler is hiding?"

"No. I asked around and a few people have spotted him, but the man certainly doesn't want to be found, my lord."

Trey pushed his fingers through his hair. "Makes me wonder if Mr. Cutler even knows how much Miss Faraday's inheritance is worth. Now I think the man does not. If he knew how wealthy the young lady was, Mr. Cutler would have been sniffing at her heels the day after her parents were buried."

"It makes sense, my lord. I think when Mr. Cutler finally discovers her wealth, he will return to claim her."

"You are thinking as I am, Mr. Lewis. Greedy lowlifes like Cutler always resurface when they believe their prey most vulnerable." Thoughts of Judith disappearing without a word to meet Cutler again raced through his mind, churning his stomach.

"Not to fret, my lord. I shall stay on the case until he's found, I assure you."

"Splendid." Trey stood, as did the solicitor, and they shook hands. "I hope to hear from you soon."

"You will, my lord."

As Mr. Lewis left, Trey began planning when he'd give Judith the information about her dear fiancé. Trey would take Judith somewhere secluded, so they wouldn't be disturbed—somewhere he could hold her comfortably while cuddling the sobbing woman in his arms and shower her with kisses. As always, she'd melt in his embrace and quickly respond. The moment would definitely be enjoyable. He couldn't wait to experience that out-of-control emotion while kissing her. Just like what happened yesterday evening. He'd enjoyed their private moment in the glade more than he should, because now he wanted more.

Smiling, he grabbed his coat and hat as he hurried out of the office, closing the door behind him. As he practically skipped down the stairs two at a time, he nearly ran into a wide form stopped at the doorway. His friend, Nic, peered over his shoulder at someone outside, his forehead creased in close scrutiny.

"Hawthorne, old sport," Trey greeted. "What are you about this afternoon?"

"I do believe your brother is in town this morning. I have not seen him for quite some time." He glanced at Trey before looking outside again.

"Trevor's here? Are you certain?" Trey stepped to the opened doorway and peered out. As Nic mentioned, the duke's coach stood in front of the tailor shop. "How remarkable! He has come out of hiding."

Nic chuckled. "Why was he in hiding to begin with?"

Trey stepped out on the boardwalk as he shrugged on his over-coat. "He was not really trying to hide. He just needed time to get to know his new wife. Their marriage was arranged, you know."

"I had heard that rumor." Nic kept in step beside Trey. "I don't know how any man could let someone else govern their life and tell them who to marry."

Trey placed the hat on his head before turning to meet Nic's stare. "Although I'm not planning to marry, if something were to happen to Trevor, leaving me the next in line, I would have to find a wife and create heirs. But I have been thinking a lot since Trevor's nuptials. If I have to marry, I will choose a woman who compliments my lifestyle and is beautiful and passionate beyond reason."

Nic snorted. "And one that will not argue with you, correct?"

"Absolutely." Trey nodded. "Why should I marry a woman I cannot come to terms with? My parents were not satisfied with that kind of arrangement, so why should I be?"

"Very true."

"Besides that, I know firsthand how a controlling woman can ruin a man's life. Look at my poor brother, Tristan, rest his soul.

If he had not met up with Lady Diana, he might still be alive today." Trey's heart sank. And if he had responded quicker, Tristan would definitely be alive.

Nic clapped his hand on Trey's shoulder. "I had forgotten about her, but you are quite right. She was a crafty woman for certain."

Together, they stepped onto the cobblestone street and crossed to the other side, heading toward the nearest drinking establishment. Many carriages and buggies blocked their way, and Trey had to quicken his step to keep from getting hit. Lords and Ladies clustered the side paths, and especially in front of the stores. Gossip ran thick through London, especially this part of Town.

"So tell me, my good man," Trey began, "what kind of wife do you plan to settle down with?"

Nic threw back his head and laughed. "What makes you think I'm going to settle?"

"We all will eventually, to have heirs, of course."

"I don't believe *settle* is the correct word. The woman I marry is someone whom I can talk easily to, and one that can fulfill my deepest desires. I can only hope she thinks the way I do, and enjoys the occasional sport."

Trey nodded. "Ah, yes. One who's not uneventful. I understand."

Nic scrubbed his chin. "Actually, Worthington, I'm surprised you brought up this conversation."

"Why is that?"

"Because, ever since I met your mother's ward, I have been thinking about her quite a bit. I might be interested in getting to know her on a more personal level."

Trey stumbled but quickly righted himself, hoping Nic hadn't noticed. Irritation and a twinge of jealousy shot through Trey. Dominic could not possibly have feelings for Judith. Trey wouldn't allow it!

Chapter Eighteen

TREY STOPPED AND glared at his friend, balling his hands into fists behind his back. Anger and confusion poured through him and he wanted to take his friend by the cravat and shake him. Trey shoved his fists into his pockets. "Miss Faraday? You think you have feelings for Judith?"

Nic tossed him an indifferent glance before resuming his stroll. "I said I *might* be interested in courting her. The night of her mock dinner party, she kept me thoroughly entertained. She has a quick wit, that's for certain."

"Indeed, she does, and whether you know it or not, she was trying to make a fool out of me in the process."

Hawthorne laughed again. "Exactly. That's what I found very entertaining about her."

Growling, Trey marched ahead and into the pub in front of Nic. They walked to a table and sat. Trey needed a strong drink quickly to drown out the frustration flowing through him. Within seconds a barmaid stood by their side with two cups of ale in her hands, placing them on the table. Once she was gone, Trey wanted to change the subject, because discussing Dominic courting Judith was definitely out of the question.

"Worthington? What ails you? Don't you think Judith is a breath of fresh air? From what I have observed about her thus far, she's unlike any woman I have ever met."

The anger level in Trey kicked up a notch. He did not want to discuss this. Yet, he couldn't make a scene. Nic might get the wrong impression about his feelings.

Trey paused in thought. What exactly were his feelings for Judith? True, she tempted him as no other woman had done before, but perhaps it was because she was forbidden? Her kisses ignited a fire deep inside him he'd never experienced.

"I have to admit, Miss Faraday is certainly different. She has me confused most of the time," Trey mumbled.

"Confused about what?" Nic leaned forward and wrapped his fingers around the cup, but didn't drink.

Staring at his ale, Trey tried to think of an intelligent answer. He didn't want Nic to know Judith made him insane with desire. His friend knew there hadn't been a woman to accomplish this. It was hard enough for Trey to admit it now. "I'm confused about what kind of woman she is. She says her parents have schooled her, yet sometimes she says or does something that contradicts her words. I want to find the best husband for her, but heaven help me, I don't know how to go about looking because just when I think I have her figured out, she changes. She's a wild-cat one minute and a sweet, purring kitten the next."

Nic finally sipped his drink. "Have you heard anything from your solicitor?"

"Oh, yes." Trey quickly dismissed the doubt sneaking into his mind about Judith and told Nic the exciting news.

Hawthorne's eyes widened. "Cutler is impersonating a lieutenant?"

"Indeed, which means the Royal Navy is also looking for him."

"Well, that's one black mark against him. Is that all?"

"For now." Trey took another gulp of his ale. "Apparently, Mr. Cutler is hiding from someone or something, because all the leads given to my solicitor come up dead."

"Interesting. Does make me wonder what else the man is trying to hide."

"Indeed, it does. I can only speculate, and it's not good."

"How do you think Miss Faraday is going to take this?" Nic asked.

Little by little, excitement built in Trey's chest, and the fantasy he'd imagined earlier resurfaced. He knew she'd be devastated, but he also planned to give comfort in any way he could.

Nic shook his head. "I think she will not be very thrilled about the news. Perhaps I should be the one to tell her."

Once again, jealous anger shot through Trey. Instead of lashing out physically, he clutched his cup in a death-like grip, holding in his disgruntled thoughts. No! Nic was not going to comfort her. Trey knew what comfort his friend had in mind. Very similar to the kind Trey wanted to give. His friend wouldn't be allowed such privileges.

"Actually, Hawthorne," Trey mumbled between clenched teeth, "I was not going to tell her just yet, but wait until I have the whole sordid story of her dear fiancé first."

"Excellent idea." Nic raised his drink in a salute before gulping the rest down in one swallow. He set the empty cup on the table then relaxed back in his chair. "So Worthington, when do you suggest I call upon Miss Faraday?"

Trey had lifted his drink to his lips and sipped when Nic's question came out. Trey choked on the burning liquid as it stung his eyes and nose. "You cannot be serious. You really intend to court Judith?"

His friend shrugged. "Like I mentioned before, I think she will be quite entertaining. She has so much passion in her when she's vexed with you, I cannot help but imagine how much passion she would have if the right man were to take her in his arms and shower her with affection."

Trey seethed until his lungs blazed with heavy breaths. He wouldn't allow Nic to court Judith. His friend couldn't know how correct he was in assuming the depths of passion lurking inside the woman. Perhaps the way to deal with this situation would be to ignore Nic's request. Clearly, the Marquess of Hawthorne was the wrong man for Judith.

Slowly, the anger inside Trey diminished. That's what he'd do. Hopefully, Judith would listen to his advice without argument. Although, he sure enjoyed arguing with her and seeing the light in her eyes sparkle.

"Well, certainly you have to wait until her coming out ball. But as I said before, Hawthorne, I think you should wait until after she learns about Mr. Cutler." Trey threw his money on the table before pushing away and standing. "I hope you don't mind, but I must get back to business matters. I told Mother I would only be gone for a few days, which does not leave me that long to put everything in order."

"I understand." Nic stood and he, too, put down money for the barmaid.

As the two men made their way outside, Trey ran head-on into a strapping man who came through the door. Preparing to apologize, Trey looked up into a set of familiar eyes. Before he had a chance to collect his thoughts, the man arched a brow, giving Trey that big brother demeaning glare.

"What is this I hear about you and my ward?" Trevor demanded in a deep, booming voice that nearly rattled the windows on the building.

Trey narrowed his eyes toward his big brother. What had his older brother heard now? Nobody could possibly know how Trey thought of nothing but Judith.

Or could they?

He forced himself to smile at Trevor and clapped him on the back. "Trevor. What a surprise to see you in town."

His brother's eyes darkened as he narrowed his gaze on Trey. "I'm quite certain it is a surprise."

"Would you like to walk with me as I head back to my office? I fear I cannot chat long since my business ventures are waiting."

Trevor nodded. "Certainly."

Nic cleared his throat and stepped ahead of them. "If you will excuse me, I shall leave you two alone to catch up on old times."

He bowed slightly to Trevor. "Your Grace, it's a delight to see you again."

"As it is you, Hawthorne." Trevor smiled as Nic walked out the door.

With Trey's heartbeat knocking against his ribs, he led his brother outside in the direction of his office. What did his older sibling know about Trey's feelings toward Judith? And worse, how many others knew it, too? Could rumors about him and Judith be circling London without his knowledge?

He glanced at his older brother. Straight back, chin erect, clutching the walking stick and looking as much like a duke than Trey had ever seen. Still, there was something in his brother's eyes that made him suspicious. The way Trevor's mouth sloped into a frown hinted of a deep sadness. Perhaps Trey's mother had been correct when she said Trevor was not able to handle a ward at this particular time.

"Are you going to answer my question, Trey?"

Trey grimaced, not liking the sharp tone of Trevor's voice. Before Trey answered his brother, he needed to discover what Trevor knew. "Of course I will answer your question. So you have heard something about Miss Faraday? What would you like me to tell you, Trevor?"

Trevor's glare pierced through Trey. "Why are you interfering with my ward?"

"*Your* ward?" Trey snorted a laugh. "The last I had heard, you turned that responsibility over to Mother."

"Trey." His brother's voice grew harsh. "Cease this foolishness. We both know why I turned Miss Faraday to Mother's care. Now tell me why you are interfering."

"Pardon me?" Trey stopped and looked at his brother. "Pray, what are you talking about? I'm not interfering at all. Mother requested my help."

"Oh, come now. You don't expect me to believe that, do you?"

Trey scowled. "I don't give a wit what you believe. I'm only doing what our mother asked of me." He grumbled and marched toward his office again.

"Why would she want your help?" Trevor continued to harass. "You are a scoundrel, Trey. Why would any mother ask their son with your reputation, to assist with a young, innocent beauty?"

Trey's steps slowed as his mind unscrambled the doubt creeping into his head. Trevor was correct. Why would his mother ask for Trey's help? Was she playing matchmaker and trying to hook him up with Judith? Impossible. His mother knew what kind of man Trey was and how he followed so closely in his father's footsteps. So why would she plan such a ridiculous scheme?

He quickly dismissed the doubt Trevor had lodged in his head and flipped his hand in the air. "She asked for my help because she's ill." Over his shoulder, he tossed his brother a scowl. "And because she does not dare disappoint you. What other choice did she have?"

Trevor shook his head. "Mother has certainly lost leave of her senses then." He grabbed Trey's elbow and stopped him. "Tell me, is Miss Faraday still innocent?"

Anger consumed Trey, different than what he'd felt with Hawthorne. He wanted to give his brother a good pounding for that comment. "Obviously, you have little faith in me."

Finally, a grin tugged on the corners of Trevor's mouth. "Tell me a time when I have been wrong about your character, brother dear." He arched an all-knowing eyebrow. "What have you done in your life thus far to make me think I should trust you?"

Trey grumbled under his breath. Trevor knew him well.

Hesitating to give an answer, Trey scrambled through the cobwebs of his mind to think of something… "I have it." He smiled. "I have managed your bets at Whites, and you have never lost. Whenever I have one of those *hair-brained* schemes—as you so call them—I have never led you astray. Have my money ventures not turned out positive?"

Nodding, Trevor folded his arms. "Indeed, I commend you

on that. So let me rephrase my previous question. What have you done thus far in your life where it concerns a woman that hasn't turned out scandalous?"

Trey muttered a curse. "Judith is innocent, you fool. She is Mother's ward. I will not compromise her. She's safe with me."

"She's *safe* with you, eh?" Tilting his head back, he released a loud laugh that droned on for many seconds. When he met Trey's gaze, Trevor's eyes sparkled with mirth. The dimple both brothers shared appeared on Trevor's chin—something Trey hadn't seen for quite a while.

Trevor shook his head. "For some reason, that sounds more like a contradiction, don't you think?"

Indeed, his brother was correct. Trey hated how Trevor's *holier-than-thou* attitude always surfaced whenever they argued.

"As it is, Miss Faraday is protected while under Mother's care. Rest assured, I shall guard her from men like me." Trey quickly turned. Obviously, Trevor didn't have much faith in his younger brother. Then again, Trey had never given him reason to have faith.

They walked a few more streets in silence. Finally, Trey glanced over his shoulder. "You never told me what you are about this fine afternoon."

"I needed some clothes repaired, so I took them to the tailor."

His brother's answer was too quick and sharp for Trey to believe him. Besides that, Trevor's servants could have run the errand for him. Something was definitely amiss with his brother. Trey wanted to ask, but he and Trevor had never been one to share their thoughts and feelings, even as young boys. For some reason, they'd never been close.

"How is Gwendolyn?" Trey asked. "Is she well and blissfully satisfied in her marriage to a stranger?"

Trevor shrugged. "We are still getting to know each other, so I have not a clue as to how happy she is. But she's not doing very well with her pregnancy. The doctor has told her to stay in bed for a while."

Trey stopped in front of his office. Worried lines added a deeper level of seriousness to his brother's grave expression. "That doesn't sound good at all. Does the doctor give hope for a normal pregnancy?"

"Yes. His words are still very encouraging."

"Splendid. I shall relay the information to Mother, unless you would like to do it."

Trevor shrugged. "I don't know when I will see her next."

"Certainly you will see her at Judith's coming out ball, Friday after next."

Trevor's eyebrows rose. "That soon?"

"The girl is ready, so why not get it over and done with? Personally, I cannot wait to find her a husband so I can return to my own life."

Trevor laughed. "Always thinking about your well-being, I see. Glad to know you have not changed." He bumped his elbow into Trey's arm.

Rage burned through him like a torch. His brother had always made Trey feel inferior. Obviously, the titled brother hadn't changed, either, but the reason he gave Trevor was far from the truth. Trey didn't want to give Judith to another man. He wanted to be the one to kiss those sweet lips. Him and none other.

Unfortunately, that was the very thing he couldn't do, which was why finding her a husband was so essential. Especially now that her former beloved had turned out to be a scandalous man. Trevor would never understand how Trey felt. Trevor had always been a saint who did and acted the way their parents expected of him. Which was why the older brother let his parents arrange his wedding to a woman he'd never met.

"Well, I must be off." Trevor adjusted his hat on his head. "I shall attend Miss Faraday's ball, only to see how well you have taken care of my ward."

Trey nodded. "And when you see how well she turned out, will I hear an apology?"

Laughter rang through the air as Trevor turned. "Only time

will tell, brother."

Yes, time would certainly tell. Trey seethed. He couldn't wait to hear his brother grovel when Judith turned out a splendid performance. He was confident she would amaze everyone, including his mother. She would have beaus lined up at the door, just as every girl her age dreamed of having.

He growled and hurried inside his office. How could he deal with this sudden feeling of possessiveness? Finding a titled, wealthy man for Judith was exactly what her parents would want, God rest their souls. Yet, how could Trey give her away so easily when he wanted her himself?

He mustn't give into temptation. He needed to remain strong. Judith would not be compromised by him. Her husband would be very pleased.

For some reason, that thought left a disgusting taste in Trey's mouth, and an ache in his chest. The ale he'd sipped must have been bad, he reasoned.

Chapter Nineteen

I T HAD BEEN quite a while since Judith took the time to visit the shops along Bond Street. As a young girl, she'd gone with her mother, excited to be holding her parent's hand as they strolled from venue to venue. Although she wasn't with her mother now, the thrill returned as enthusiasm bubbled in her chest.

When Trey had first mentioned training her for her ball, she'd found the mere idea distasteful. She didn't want another person besides her mother doing that. Even though she missed her mother greatly, deep inside her heart Judith knew this was what her parents wanted for her, to enjoy herself to the fullest.

So perhaps going shopping was indeed a wise idea.

The dowager giggled like a schoolgirl at the hustle and bustle of the shops. Judith smiled and hid her laugh from the older woman. Remarkable what an outing would do for someone's spirits.

A cluster of the king's sailors stood in front of a shop, and Judith's heartbeat raced with anticipation. Would Alex be here? She eyed each one carefully, their red coats with silver buttons shining in the sunlight. When Alex wasn't among the men, her hopes plummeted. Thankfully, the dowager didn't remark on the way Judith studied each one, because she didn't know how to explain Alex to her yet.

The first establishment they entered was the dress shop

where the owner, Mrs. André greeted them by shaking both Judith and Isabelle Worthington's hands. One of the helpers insisted Judith remain firmly on a stool while she draped colorful silks over her to see which colors Judith would look best in. Standing still, she had nothing better to do than gaze through the mirror as each silk lay across her shoulders and bosom. Isabelle and the shop owner stood behind her nodding their approval or the negative shake of their head. If the dowager had her way—which she would—Judith would receive only the best gown for her ball.

Judith heaved a disheartening sigh. *My coming out ball.* She'd made a deal with Trey. She held up her end, but would he? Would he be able to find Alex before she made her debut into society?

Boredom overcame Judith quickly, and her gaze wandered out the window at the people walking by, and the fancy dressed horses pulling the elaborate carriages up and down the cobbled streets of London. With a frown, she sighed heavily in defeat. Coming out balls were for girls who sought marriage. She already had an agreement, so why did she continue with this farce? Until she knew for certain why Alex hadn't come to the woodsman's cottage, she must have faith he still wanted to marry her.

For the past few months, she'd dreamed of marrying only one man, Lieutenant Alexander Cutler. Even if Trey's actions confused her and his kisses set her on fire, she would remain steadfast in her decision to marry Alex. It wasn't fair to give up on him so soon. After all, he wanted her for herself, and not for her inheritance. Once her worth became known, every fortune hunter around would be sniffing her skirts like animals in heat.

Alex was different. He'd fallen in love with her before her parents died, never knowing how much her inheritance was really worth. She smiled. That put him at the top of her list.

Judith convinced herself that once she was in Alex's arms, he would make her forget Trey completely. Alex would erase all the limb-trembling times she'd been in Trey's embrace, and especially all the heated times he'd kissed her. She closed her eyes and let her mind wander back to yesterday afternoon, a place where she shouldn't be. Yet staying away was out of the question. How could she ever forget the way Trey had made her feel?

Shaking away the pleasurable memory, she reminded herself Trey wasn't interested in marriage. She was a pathetic fool for believing he would change. She opened her eyes and forced herself to pay attention to what was happening around her. Isabelle and the shop owner giggled over the sketches, and the young girl continued to drape Judith with colors. She switched her gaze to the window again as people scurried along the walkway. She glanced across the street, resting her eyes on a familiar figure as he crept between two buildings.

Her heart paused then sprang to life. "Alex," she screamed and jumped off the stool, knocking the seamstress over to fall on her buttocks.

Judith pushed past the other patrons entering the building and ran outside. Two women stopped short of bumping into Judith as she scampered toward the spot she'd seen Alex. Several carriages and coaches were in her way, but she didn't have time to wait until they passed. She must get across now.

On tiptoes, she tried to peek above the conveyances. A flash of brown from his jacket caught her eyes. For a moment she wondered why he wasn't in uniform. "Alex," she shrieked louder.

He turned and looked right at her. She waved madly and screamed his name again, but a carriage moved in front of her, blocking her vision. Without thinking what might happen, she ran into the street. Horses neighed and rose on their hind legs as drivers cursed, swerving to keep from hitting her.

From behind, the panicked cry from the dowager sliced through the air. Judith couldn't stop to explain her actions to the older woman. Not yet.

Judith zigzagged between two more carriages before reaching the other side. The alley where she'd seen Alex was empty. Her heart plummeted and tears stung her eyes. Quickly, she scanned up and down the street again, looking, searching in panic. Where was he? He did see her, so why didn't he answer her call?

Elbowing past the crowd of people on the walkway, she hurried in one direction, praying it would take her to Alex. Up the street, more shouting from drivers arose along with the neighing of horses. Without looking to see, she hoped her carelessness hadn't caused the commotion.

She ran as fast as she could, clutching her dress in her fists as she held it up to her ankles, trying to keep her feet free. Strands of hair clung to her moist face, and she didn't care that she'd left the shop without her bonnet. This was more important.

Ahead of her, another passageway approached fast. She turned and hurried into the alley, hoping this was the way Alex had gone. On the boardwalk, heavy footsteps clamored behind her mere seconds before someone grasped her elbow, bringing her to a stop.

"No." She sobbed, trying to yank her arm away. "Let me go."

"Judith, cease this improper display immediately."

Trey's voice calmed her frazzled nerves only slightly. She swung her head and gazed into his worried eyes. A scowl darkened his face as his lips pulled tight in a straight line.

"Trey, you must let me go." Her voice broke and more tears filled her eyes. "I saw Alex."

His eyes widened, and he glanced up and down the alley. "Where?"

"I saw him across the street from the dress shop first," she said, pointing, "but then he ran in a different direction. I don't know which way he went." She clasped his hands with hers. "Trey, he looked right at me. He knows I'm here. Please, help me find him."

He shook his head. "I don't know what he looks like."

"He's wearing a brown coat and tan breeches with black riding boots."

Trey's head swung toward the road. Worry creased his brows. "Judith, my sweet, that describes most of the men I see."

Another sob came from her as she pulled away. "No, you have to do this for me. He's very close, I can feel it."

He pulled her in his arms. "My darling, I cannot."

Panic surged through her. They had to keep looking. But even as she struggled in Trey's arms, he wouldn't let her go. "Please, Trey. You have to find him. Maybe he went behind these buildings—"

"My sweet, you are not listening to me. I told you, I don't know what he looks like."

"His hair is brown and curly, his eyes are brown," she said with a shaky voice, but soon her cries wracked her body. She buried her face in Trey's chest and let out her fury. This couldn't be happening. So close, and yet so far, and to think Alex slipped right through her fingers.

"Shhh…" Trey stroked her back and shoulders. "If he's this close, then I'm certain my solicitor will find him."

Pain sliced through her heart, making her ache just like when she thought she'd first lost Alex. Yet, anger rose in her chest, because she had screamed his name. Why hadn't he stopped when she called out to him? He looked right at her mere seconds before the carriage had blocked his path.

He had definitely seen her, yet ran in the opposite direction. Doubt clouded her thinking, wrenching her heart. The answer was plain and simple. He hadn't gone to the woodsman's cottage to meet her because he didn't love her any longer. And just now he'd avoided her, which told her he was too much of a coward to explain.

She pressed closer to Trey and his arms tightened around her. Warmth from his body blended quickly with hers, soothing her, and comforting her more than she expected. His scent of spice and leather clung to his clothes, and she resisted the urge to bury her face in his neck and be swept away.

"There she is!"

The call from the dowager duchess brought Judith from her momentary safe haven.

"Oh, good heavens child. What happened to you?"

Judith tried to pull away from Trey, but he continued to hold her in his strong arms, so she stopped struggling and settled against him, content to remain there. She pushed back the strands of hair hanging in her vision, wiped her eyes and looked into the worried face of the dowager. "Please forgive me, Your Grace, but—"

"Mother," Trey interrupted. "She thought she saw a childhood friend, but she must have been mistaken, because I cannot see him, either. Seeing this person reminded her of home and when her parents were still alive."

Judith's throat choked with emotion. Trey was trying to protect her secret. Her heart melted.

"Oh, no wonder you are so distraught." Isabelle stroked Judith's moist cheek.

Judith nodded. "When I realized I only imagined seeing him, all the grief and pain I have experienced of late came gushing forth." She sniffed and wiped her eyes again. "I'm truly sorry for ruining your afternoon."

"Nonsense, my dear. You didn't ruin it. I'm just relieved you're all right. The way you dodged in and out of those moving carriages had me swooning with fear. Then when I saw Trey run in the street after you and he was nearly run over, I thought my heart would fail for sure."

"Again, please forgive me for worrying you so."

The dowager patted Trey's arm. "Son, will you please escort us back to the dress shop? Mrs. André still requires measuring for Judith's gown."

"Yes, Mother."

The older woman looked back at Judith. "Can you manage to walk by yourself?"

Judith nodded. "I shall be fine, thank you."

Trey stepped away from her but hooked her hand over his arm, keeping her close as they walked back to the shop. She didn't mind. She didn't even care about the raised eyebrows people threw her way as they passed. But if they had seen her display a few minutes ago, they would have thought she'd gone insane for a brief time. Maybe she had.

Trey brushed his fingers along her arm. "How are you faring? Better?" he whispered.

Familiar tingles swept through her from the soft timbre of his voice. Heaven help her, but she wanted to be back in his strong embrace.

"Yes, I'm better. Thank you for...for being there. I didn't know you were in London."

"Did Mother not tell you?"

"She just said you were away on business."

"I am. I will be in London for a couple more days." He grinned. "Try not to miss me, all right?"

A laugh erupted out of nowhere, and she covered her hand over her mouth. He chuckled too as his eyes twinkled.

"Your mother wants me to plan another dinner party. Will you be able to attend?"

He raised his brow. "That all depends."

"On what?"

"On if you decide to make the food spicy again."

She smiled. "I promise to have Betsy prepare the blandest food you have ever tasted."

"When is it?"

"In two days."

He nodded. "I shall certainly try to be there."

The beat of her heart knocked crazily against her ribs. "You had better come. I will not know a soul other than your mother and Lord Hawthorne."

"Oh, I'm quite certain you will mingle just fine." He winked.

"But, I would really like you there, nonetheless."

"Indeed?"

"Yes. Will you promise to come?"

"I promise," he whispered deeply, which sent excitement through her, kicking up her heartbeat another notch.

They reached the dress shop and when they entered, he released her hand. Emptiness consumed her, and she wanted to return to his side, to look closely into his intoxicating eyes. But she couldn't. It wasn't wise to become so close to him, especially in public.

Timidly, she walked to the mirror where the young seamstress waited, assuming her position. Trey leaned against the wall with his arms folded across his chest as he watched Judith. A lazy grin stayed on his handsome face, even all the while Mrs. André chatted beside him. From time to time, he nodded at what the shop owner said, but he didn't take his gaze off Judith.

Her breath caught in her throat, making her mouth dry, yet her body became consumed with an ache she couldn't describe. All she knew was that she needed to be next to him while he comforted her. Plain and simple, it was torture, and she longed for that kind of pleasure. Even now, while everyone stood around them.

Hours passed, yet time didn't seem that long. Soon they were done and leaving the shop. Trey took her hand and placed it over his arm as he escorted her outside, with the dowager ahead of them. He walked them to their coach then turned, took Judith's gloved hand and placed a kiss on her knuckles. His eyes darkened even more as his lips lingered in a soft caress.

"Please forgive me, but I must return to my office."

Words were stuck in her throat and all she could do was nod as he straightened.

"Thank you, Trey, for coming to dear Judith's rescue." Isabelle patted his cheek. "You are such a kind-hearted man."

"You are too free with your compliments, Mother." He kissed her cheek. "Do not hesitate to contact me if you need something."

"Of course, my dear. I believe we are done here today. You will, I presume, be home for Judith's dinner party."

"I shall certainly try."

"Splendid." The dowager held out her hand for Trey to help

her into the coach.

He turned to Judith and took her hand, too. His fingers caressed her palm gently, sending shooting sparks of fire through her body. When he cupped her elbow, her skin nearly burned with fervor.

As she settled in her seat and watched him until the footman closed the door, her heart sang with gladness. Would she always feel this way about him? Heaven help her if she did. She couldn't fawn over a man who would never settle down and marry. If she did, she was only inviting pain and heartbreak.

But stopping her thoughts from heading his way, and her body from quivering whenever he touched her was beyond her control. Indeed, she would suffer, and learn to deal with this torture.

Chapter Twenty

ANTICIPATION PUMPED THROUGH Trey as he paced the study, holding a cut crystal glass of Bourbon. Judith's dinner party was tonight. He could hardly stand the wait, and it wasn't because of his hungry stomach. Tonight, a different kind of craving surged through him.

For the past few days, he'd stayed away from the estate, making more investments with Dominic, which promised to double both their bank accounts. The time was spent wisely, yet being away that long made him anxious. It nearly killed him when he had to tell Judith good-bye at the dress shop.

Now he couldn't wait to see her again. Would he act like a smitten schoolboy? All he could think about these past few days was kissing her endlessly. The only thing stopping him was the scandal and subsequent disgrace it would cause his sickly mother.

Besides, Judith wanted a husband, Trey reminded himself. Since he had no desire to obtain a wife, he must stay far away from her no matter how hard the struggle. She tempted him beyond reason. Once he found her the perfect husband, he couldn't touch her again.

The bell at the front door announced more guests, which the butler would show into the drawing room where his mother and Judith would undoubtedly greet them. Behind the closed door of his study, he didn't want to see her yet. Couldn't until he had a hold over his uncontrolled emotions.

He sat on his cushioned chair and took another swig of his drink, realizing his performance tonight needed to be better than Judith's. It wouldn't be good if his mother's guests noticed how Judith's nearness affected him. Tongues would wag as the gossipmongers went to work. Once again, the Worthington family would be at the center of a scandal, and Trey couldn't allow that to happen.

From out of nowhere, a memory slammed into him of when Judith and he were younger. This was probably one of the last times he saw her, and her body had started to grow and mature. His mother was having a weekend party at their estate, and Trey had noticed how the boys his age were giving Judith more attention than Trey thought she should have.

Closing his eyes, he drifted back to yesteryear...a place he didn't like to visit very often.

Trey stood behind a tree and spied across the yard. Why had Judith and her parents come to this event? Couldn't he get away from the little nuisance just one summer?

Yet this summer seemed different for some reason. Her hair was browner. Longer and prettier. She wasn't as chubby as she'd been last year. In fact, without walking up to stand by her and measure her height, he would guess she had grown since he'd seen her last year. And her dress...

He shook his head and blinked, not believing what he saw. Good heavens, but she actually filled out her bodice a little better. Then again, she was in her twelfth year if memory served him correctly, and that was about the age girls started blossoming.

Two of Trey's friends stood by her. Their eyes twinkled with mirth as they laughed over something she said. Trey rolled his eyes. What in heaven's name could they find so humorous? Judith's personality was as dry as a day-old piece of bread. Yet these boys seem to think this country girl was something special. Trey knew differently.

Within seconds, a third boy joined the little group as he brought her a glass of punch. She smiled sweetly and lowered her gaze as if shy. Trey snorted. She was definitely not that shy.

He moved his focus from her to the other families gathering for the weekend party. How could he enjoy himself with his friends with Judith here? It was bad enough her family came to his family's estate once a year, but Trey never told his friends he and his brothers had to entertain the girl. Now... Inwardly, he groaned. His friends would certainly laugh at him if they knew.

Hopefully, she wouldn't want to talk to him during the weekend.

As soon as the thought crossed his mind, he chuckled. For the past few years Trey had been doing everything in his power to push the girl away. So then why now would she even dare approach him? The only reason he remotely enjoyed her visits was so he could tease her and make her cry to her mommy.

Although—come to think about it, Judith never really did go crying to her mother. Brave little girl.

From the corner of his eyes, he saw Tommy Little—the second son of the Earl of Cornwell, dash toward Judith. She couldn't see Tommy because her back was to him. But if Trey knew Tommy—and he did— that boy was up to no good. Tommy's stunts sometimes made Trey's look amateurish.

But Tommy wasn't slowing down. In fact, he was gaining speed and heading directly toward Judith. Although Trey shouldn't care what the other boy was going to do, Trey suddenly felt defensive. Judith was his scapegoat. Nobody could tease her but him!

Tommy neared Judith and pushed her as he ran by. She stumbled into Edward Fraser, spilling her punch down her lavender and white dress, getting some of the drink on Edward.

Trey grumbled. That was it? That's the best Tommy could come up with? Well, Trey would show the dolt how it was done...

He marched to Judith who was now trying her best to smile under the uncomfortable situation as she swiped the excess liquid off the material. The boys spoke words of encouragement as if they were trying to keep her spirits up. When Trey stopped in front of Judith, her eyes widened, and for a moment, malice flashed in their emerald depths. He didn't know why, but he enjoyed riling her...seeing anger—and irritation—shine in her eyes.

The other boys greeted Trey, but he didn't reply, just content to stare at her while his thoughts scrambled to think of what he could do to top Tommy.

Suddenly, she straightened her shoulders and arched an eyebrow. Was she challenging him? Well...he was certainly up for the task. Before he could think of something to say—or how to act—a sweet fragrance drifted from her and enveloped him. Flowers...

He couldn't stop his attention from dropping to her lips. Good grief, they were fuller than he remembered, and oh, so tempting!

Before he could stop himself, he stepped right up to her, grasped her shoulders and kissed her soundly on the lips. Her body stiffened. The boys in back of him gasped.

Warning bells clanged loudly in Trey's head, startling him like never before. He quickly withdrew. Of all the things to go through his mind right now, why did it have to be that he'd beat Tommy?

Grinning in victory, Trey strolled away from the group, realizing nobody could top him now...

A hard knock came upon the door to his study, yanking Trey out of his memory.

"Worthington? Are you there?"

Trey blinked and glanced around the room to get his bearings. Oh yes, the dinner party—and Judith. He opened the door and smiled at his friend. The marquess stood in front of him, grinning like the cat that had swallowed a canary.

"My good man, what are you doing holed up in your study when you should be greeting guests with your mother and Miss Faraday?"

"I'd rather not take on that responsibility right now, thank you very much." With his hand, Trey motioned for his friend to enter. "Would you like a pre-dinner drink? I have Bourbon or Brandy."

Nic chuckled. "Are you purposely trying to get sloshed?"

"No, I just need something to steady my nerves."

Dominic eyed him closely then leaned closer and took a deep sniff. "Well, you are almost there. I fear if you drink anymore, you will make a fool out of yourself falling on your face as you enter the dining room. We don't wish to embarrass Miss Faraday, do we?"

"What makes you think I will embarrass Miss Faraday?"

"You forget, I have seen you drunk."

"I'm not drunk. Yet." He took another sip then set the snifter on the tray. "But you are quite right. It's time to stop while I'm still in an upright position."

"So, Worthington? What has you so upset?"

Trey shrugged, walked to his brown leather chair and sat. "What makes you think I'm upset?"

"You have been out of sorts for a few days. Now I see you drinking before the evening meal." Nic shook his head. "That's not like you." He sat on the sofa and crossed one leg over the other. "Tell me. Why has Miss Faraday set you on edge?"

Chuckling, Trey massaged his forehead. "Why do you suspect Miss Faraday?"

"You have not been the same since we met her at the woodsman's cottage."

Trey cursed under his breath. Dominic noticed his change. Did that mean everyone had? "I suppose I'm anxious to get her married so I can get on with my life."

"Have you heard from your solicitor yet?"

"Not since the other day. Hopefully, I will hear soon. That too, would ease my burden some."

"I agree. Then you will be able to concentrate more on money matters."

Trey lifted his brows. "Have there been any new developments in my stocks?"

Nic laughed. "Only that they keep rising."

"Ah, very good news indeed." He glanced at his empty hand. "If I had a drink, I would make a toast."

"Save it for later."

From the doorway, the butler cleared his throat. "Excuse me, my lord, but Her Grace requests your presence in the blue drawing room, along with the Marquess of Hawthorne, of course."

Trey nodded. "We are coming." He stood and straightened, trying to appear calmer than he felt. When he walked, he tried not to rush to the room where Judith awaited. They had only been apart for a few days. So why then did it seem like weeks?

As Trey stepped inside, he braced himself as he searched for her. Near the large hearth, Judith stood by his mother's side looking more beautiful than any woman had a right to be. A forest green high-waist gown trimmed with gold practically clung to her, making his mouth dry. Her white elbow-gloves emphasized slim arms, the color matched the pearls around her neck and at her ears. Green ribbons wove through her chestnut hair piled on her head, very fashionable, and very alluring. He groaned. Tonight would be pure torture to be sure. Hopefully he sat far enough away from her during the meal that she wouldn't notice him drooling.

From across the room, her gaze met his. Immediately, a sparkle lit her eyes and she graced him with a smile. His heart flipped. Now why did he have to react like that? And why were his feet taking him toward her? No! He had to stay away.

When he stopped in front of her, he lifted her hand and kissed her knuckles. "You look ravishing tonight, Miss Faraday."

Her cheeks reddened. "And you, my lord, are devilishly handsome."

He chuckled and kept her hand in his, gently caressing her with his fingers. Curse him, but he couldn't let go. Beside him, Nic nudged his elbow and brought Trey out of his dreams.

"You remember the Marquess of Hawthorne?" Trey asked between clenched teeth.

"Why of course."

She withdrew her hand and gave it to Nic, who bestowed a customary kiss on her knuckles. Jealousy ignited in Trey's chest and made it difficult to breathe. Would he act this possessive when every man kissed her hand? Probably. Although...this was Nic. The very man who admitted he found Judith interesting.

The man who wanted to court her.

The compliment Nic gave her didn't register in Trey's mind. He was too busy devouring her beauty to hear anything, yet he knew every time she smiled, laughed, and moved her lips. She was simply lovely, taking his breath away by the minute.

He was a besotted fool, but at this point, he didn't care. Perhaps the liquor was working.

Time passed quickly, and soon the guests were seated for dinner. To his horror—yet greatest delight—he sat across the table from Judith. Jealousy reared its ugly head when Nic took the chair beside her. Did she do this on purpose? After all, she had previously arranged the seating chart.

Inwardly, Trey seethed. During the meal, he had to watch as his best friend made Judith laugh. Several times Nic whispered something in her ear, their heads bent too close together. It was all Trey could do not to jump across the table and separate them. Why would the marquess go against Trey's wishes for wanting to court her? Obviously, Nic was in the beginning stages.

On a few occasions, she glanced at Trey and smiled. His heart melted from this gesture, until she started talking with Nic again. Trey gripped his glass as he lifted it to his mouth. He'd have to reprimand Nic for his bold actions toward Judith, and without Trey's consent.

A woman to his left leaned toward him, forcing him to tear his gaze from Judith and focus on her. He hadn't even realized Nic's cousin, Emma, from Paris sat next to him. He smiled as politely and charmingly as he could, since deep down inside he was ready to explode with frustration.

"My lord, I have been trying to get your attention for the last few minutes."

Awkwardly, he laughed. "Forgive me, Mrs. Pettengill. I was distracted."

She glanced across the table at her cousin and Judith. "I see Miss Faraday has distracted most of the men tonight. She's a very lovely woman." She looked back at Trey. "Or is it my cousin, Nic, who has you so vexed?"

Her brows arched, one higher than the other, as she gazed into Trey's eyes. He couldn't fool her. Then again, he had to. It really was none of her business who held his attention this evening.

"Hawthorne is always upsetting me in one form or another." Trey winked. "But enough about that, what have you been doing since the last time we talked? How is your painting coming along?"

He had to mentally pat himself on the back for remembering her favorite pastime. Mrs. Pettengill's eyes lit up like stars as she talked, and he was thankful she had taken his mind off Judith.

As he visited with Mrs. Pettengill, he noticed the resemblance between Nic and her. Both had hair and lashes the color of midnight. In fact, Emma was quite a handsome woman, if he dared admit. Of course, he wouldn't think of dallying with the young widow since she was off limits, being Nic's cousin, but one lucky man would find her a treasure, indeed. Lately, the only woman who occupied Trey's mind was the woman he could never have.

His heart ached with the realization. He had to give Judith to another man when the time came. She was never going to be his. It surprised him that it mattered since most of the women Trey met in his life were certainly not worth his time. So why did he think Judith was so different?

Forcing himself to relax in his chair, Trey kept his attention on Emma and conversed with her. She laughed at his comments and occasionally touched his hand. Nothing too forward. On impulse, he glanced across the table at Judith. She'd fixed her stare on him as she cut her meat. By the whiteness of her fingers as she gripped her knife and fork, he received the impression she wasn't pleased with him.

He grinned. She was jealous, just as he was envious of Nic. The knowledge filled his chest with excitement.

After the meal, the few men gathered in the drawing room

for cigars and brandy. Trey didn't want to mingle, yet constantly mulling over something he could never have didn't sound pleasing, either. Nic stood beside him near the hearth as they sipped their drinks. Trey doubted this was the place to talk about Nic's flirtation with Judith, but he'd let his friend know his feelings soon.

Nic chuckled, breaking the silence between them. "Miss Faraday is certainly one intoxicating woman. She's very easy to talk with, and she made me laugh more times than I could count."

Trey held in his anger as he gripped the glass tighter. Perhaps now was indeed a good time to talk about Nic's actions. "Good to hear she's performing well. Mother worried her ward would not be able to carry on a good conversation with nobility."

Dominic raised his drink to his lips. "I believe she has mastered that goal. Why, she nearly had me hypnotized this evening. I could not get enough of her."

Trey gulped down the remaining liquid, then motioned to the servant for another. "I noticed." He rested his glare on Nic. "But I thought we had already discussed this."

"Discussed what?"

"That you would not pursue your feelings for her until we learned more about Alexander Cutler."

Nic threw back his head and laughed. "Oh, Worthington, old boy. Be careful. The green monster of jealousy inside you is baring its hideous, sharp teeth."

The servant brought Trey another drink, which he quickly tossed down. "You are talking nonsense. I'm not envious in the least. I just don't think you should begin your pursuit until we find out more about Mr. Cutler."

"Well, if you don't find him, rest assured, Miss Faraday will win every man's heart at her ball."

Trey clenched his teeth. "It relieves me to know she will do so well."

"Oh, yes. Your drawing room will be filled with many callers after the event, I can assure you. You will have her married in no time."

Married and away from me.

That had been Trey's goal since learning his mother had a ward. Now he couldn't imagine her with another man. Didn't want to. When Trey thought of her in a man's arms, it was with *him* and no other. His chest constricted and he took another long gulp. Why couldn't he get her out of his head? The best thing for her was to find a good husband who would take care of her. Unfortunately, Nic was not that man either, since he and Trey were titled rogues with the best of them.

All around him, the walls closed in, and suffocated him. Dizziness swam through his head, warning him he might have drank too much tonight.

"Hawthorne? I need to step outside for a moment. Please excuse me."

Without waiting for his friend's answer, Trey rushed to the side doors and hurried out. He walked down the path toward the stone bench near his mother's flower garden, taking deep breaths as he tried to clear his head. So perhaps he did have too much to drink. He dismissed that thought. If so, he wouldn't be thinking about Judith and caring that she would marry another man.

He reached the bench and plopped down, holding his head as he closed his eyes. The night air helped clear his head, but still thoughts of Judith wouldn't disappear. At least the ground wasn't tilting any longer.

Several minutes passed and he stayed in this position, elbows resting on his knees while his palms cradled his head. Songs from the evening's insects hummed around him, but it didn't override the laughter from inside the house. A few times, he detected Judith's voice, and he smiled. Strange how he knew her sound so personally. Not only that, but he knew the tilt of her head and creased brow as confusion filled her. He knew the exact part of her lips when she breathed heavily, especially the heady twinkle in her eyes right after they kissed.

Her flowery fragrance would continue to stay on his mind, reminding him how wonderful she smelled. Even now, he detected the scent of flowers, and his hands itched to wrap around her as he buried his face in her neck. The soft click of shoes brought him out of his thoughts as the scent became stronger.

"Trey? Are you ill?"

He snapped his head up and met the wide eyes of his fantasy.

Tonight was going to be pure hell, to be sure.

Chapter Twenty-One

JUDITH BREATHED A sigh of relief. Trey was all right. She worried when Nic had mentioned Trey had stepped outside to inhale some fresh air due to his intoxicated state. Not very often did she run across a man who'd consumed so much alcohol. Even now, she couldn't tell if Trey had or not.

"Ah, Judith, my love. You are a sight for these tired eyes tonight."

Her heart flipped. He'd called her *my love*. Did it mean what she had hoped? Or did that only happen in her silly dreams?

"Lord Hawthorne told me you had come outside for some air. I worried you were ill."

"Why did you fret over me?"

He cocked his head, peering at her through squinted, glassy eyes. Perhaps he was intoxicated after all. Obviously, it was a challenge for him to look at her.

She smiled. "I didn't want you to think I had the food tampered with again."

Chuckling, he took her hands in his and pulled her closer. Her heartbeat drummed quicker, making her breathing ragged. Although the house was full of guests, they were alone outside where they could be discovered at any moment. How much longer did she have with him like this?

"Ah, dear Judith." He kissed her knuckles. "I know you didn't poison the food. Instead, I poisoned myself with liquor without thinking of the consequences."

"May I ask why?"

He lifted his head. His eyes opened wider, and shined in the full moonlight. "Many problems weigh on my mind, and I required some help sorting through them."

"Has it worked? Has the liquor helped you at all?"

He rolled his eyes and frowned. "Not yet."

She pulled one of her hands from his only to brush her fingers through his hair. He closed his eyes and let his head fall back. The urge to kiss him overwhelmed her, but even worse was the desire to trail her lips down his neck. Indeed, he had put her under a spell, a hex she had no wish to have removed. She hungered for him as a starved person does for food, wanting his touch, his arms around her more fervently than ever before.

She licked her suddenly dry lips. "Trey, I missed you while you were away," she whispered. Silently, she scolded herself. Why did she tell him that? What was the use of having feelings for someone who'll never return them?

Slowly, he opened his eyes and met her stare. A grin stretched across his tempting mouth. "I doubt it was anywhere near how much I missed you."

Her heartbeat accelerated, yet at the same time, she wondered about her weak mind. She wanted to stay mad at him, mainly so she wouldn't daydream about him. "You have a strange way of showing it," she mumbled.

He arched a brow. "Pray, how do you wish me to act, my love?" He stood, and his jacket brushed against her gown. "Were you expecting me to take you in my arms and devour you with kisses?" His hands slipped around her waist, keeping her in a loose hold. "Or did you want me to sweep you off your feet and carry you to a private glade on the estate where nobody could find us?"

Heaven help her, both sounded pleasing. But no. She must remain put out with him. That was the only way to keep a level head.

She shrugged. "Although you have described some intimate situations, my lord, I think not flirting with another woman would be the perfect way to act as if you missed me."

He blinked with wide eyes. "Pray, what are you talking about?"

"At the table tonight you flirted with Nic's cousin, Mrs. Pettengill. I would think if you missed me as you proclaimed, you would not have carried on with her as much as you did."

His stare stayed on her for a few silent moments, then a slow chuckle rumbled in his throat. Within minutes, it had turned into a full-fledged bout of laughter. Irritation grew inside her, but she waited for his fit to subside. Tilting her head as she narrowed her glare on him.

"Oh, Judith, what a humorous woman you are." He cupped her face. "We are similar creatures, you know."

"No, I'm not aware of this."

"I, too, had the same jealous feelings tonight as I watched you and Hawthorne converse with your heads close together. Every time you laughed at something he said, the vile monster of envy wrapped his long claws around my heart and squeezed."

Huffing, she pushed his hands away. "I'm not a jealous person, Trey."

He grinned. "Yes, you are, and it pleases me beyond words."

Strange, but hearing his confession delighted her, also. "So, are you admitting you were flirting with Mrs. Pettengill just to vex me?"

"I'm not admitting any such thing, love."

She growled. "Oh, you're impossible!"

Judith wanted to stay angry at him, but the wider his smile stretched, the more those adorable dimples in his cheeks flashed at her, making her want to kiss him and never stop. As she stared, the lines of laughter on his face disappeared until his expression turned serious. His gaze dropped to her mouth, and her heart leapt. Were they far enough away from the house that they couldn't be seen? Did she dare to step closer and let him take the lead?

His hands brushed down her arms and sent trickles of warmth through her body. As his fingers retraced the path, she closed her eyes and tilted her head back in silent encouragement. But heavy footsteps on the bricked pathway jerked her to awareness.

"There you are." Dominic stopped beside her.

Trey withdrew his touch so quickly she wondered if she imagined his fingers igniting a fire inside her.

"Yes, here we are," Trey answered. "Is there something amiss, Hawthorne?"

Judith collected her composure and faced Nic, forcing herself to smile, even though she wanted to scold him for the interruption. "I hope I didn't worry you, my lord."

Nic took her hand and patted it. "On the contrary. I had suspected you were searching for Worthington. However, the dowager is looking for you both. It seems some of the guests are about to depart."

"Oh, dear," she replied. "I cannot believe I forgot my hostess duties. I need to get back."

"Indeed, that's the proper decorum." Nic offered her his elbow. "Shall I escort you, my dear?"

Nibbling on her bottom lip, she switched her attention briefly to Trey. His creased forehead and drawn brows presented his jealousy.

Almost as a reflex reaction, her heart melted. "My lord, please come in and join the party. I think the fresh air has cleared your head enough, do you not agree?"

He arched a brow and the corner of his mouth lifted. "Indeed it has, my sweet." He looked at Nic. "Hawthorne, lead the way, my good man."

Judith kept her hand on Nic's elbow, but it was Trey's body she felt as he walked on the other side of her. The occasional brush of his arm made her heart skip and her skin burn. She knew he did this on purpose, since he'd admitted earlier of his jealousy.

Tomorrow, she'd ask Trey if he had heard any word from his solicitor about Alex. If the solicitor hadn't found anything, she'd take it into her own hands. One way or the other, she had to find the truth about the man who promised to marry her then left without a trace.

Staying at the Worthington estate was not good for her mental—or physical—state. It was time she stopped letting others make her decisions for her and take control once again.

Chapter Twenty-Two

J UDITH SMOOTHED HER hands down the cream colored day dress she'd donned that morning, hoping her moist palms wouldn't mark the material. She stood in front of the door to Trey's study, the very room he'd been in since before breakfast. No voices were heard on the other side of the thick door, but his fascinating scent of spice and leather wafted around her, reminding her how his very aroma could make her an emotional mess.

Last night had ended terribly, especially after the guests left. The dinner party itself had turned out splendid, but Judith was anxious to talk to Trey, yet somehow he'd disappeared once the last guest departed. After that, the dowager kept Judith busy so she couldn't search him out before retiring for bed.

However, this was a new day, and she felt like a new woman. No longer would she allow herself to melt when he was near. She wasn't going to waste her time longing for a man who couldn't commit to a marriage.

Swallowing hard, she raised her hand to knock, but quick footsteps down the hall made her hesitate.

"Miss Faraday?" the butler called.

She dropped her hand and turned toward the servant. "Yes?"

"You have a visitor in the drawing room."

"A visitor?" She lifted an eyebrow. "Pray, who could be calling upon me this early in the morning?"

"Lord Hawthorne, Miss."

Dominic? What is he doing here? Could something dreadful be wrong? "Thank you. I shall not keep him waiting a moment longer."

She hurried down the hallway to the drawing room, curious to see what could bring the marquess to visit her this early in the day. When she entered, Dominic sat on the sofa sipping a cup of tea. His gaze lifted to her mere seconds before he set the cup on the side tray and rose.

"Good morning, Miss Faraday." He grinned and bowed.

"A good day to you, Lord Hawthorne." She curtsied then swept her gaze over his attire, black riding boots, black breeches and a double-breasted brown riding over-jacket. "What are you about this early in the morning?"

"I thought to invite you to go riding with me."

She blinked with wide eyes. "With *you*, my lord?"

"I know what an excellent horsewoman you are, and I would love some company during my ride."

A chuckle escaped her before she could stop it. "Surely you jest."

"No, Miss Faraday. I would enjoy your company, if you don't mind."

His gray eyes sparkled with mischief. That's the only word she could think of to describe them. He didn't appear to be a man bent on wooing a lady. So what was his purpose? There was only one way to find out.

She shrugged. "If you will give me a few minutes, my lord, I will change into my riding clothes."

"Take all the time you need."

As she hurried to her bedroom, questions swam through her head. Why was he really here? He didn't want to court her, did he? Dominic would indeed make a fine husband as long as the right woman could reform him. Judith wasn't that woman. Although Dominic was charming, handsome, and wealthy, she didn't have any feelings for him but those of a friend.

It took her only forty-five minutes to change before she met him outside by the stables. He held the reins of his horse as he visited with the stable boy who held her mare. Acting the gentleman, Dominic helped her mount before he climbed on the back of his horse.

During the first few minutes, she studied him, but still didn't feel that his main purpose here was to court her. Indeed, he acted as if he just wanted her company. She supposed it could happen that way. They were friends, after all.

As they trotted their horses side by side, she cleared her throat. She'd make use of this time alone with him. "Tell me, my lord, how did you and Trey meet?"

"Our mothers are distant cousins. However, I have never really thought of Trey as a relation, and we have always been friends."

When Dominic talked about his childhood, his face relaxed and a twinkle lit his eyes. Indeed, she knew he thought a lot of Trey and would always defend him. It softened her heart to know Trey had a friend like this.

"Trey has always had a stubborn streak to him," Dominic continued, "as I'm certain you well know."

She laughed. "More than I would like."

"I remember when we were in our nineteenth year. I thought his mother would disinherit him for good when he was seen in the company of some...shall we say, unorthodox-minded women. He was certainly causing more scandal than the dowager could handle."

Judith tilted her head, studying Nic's profile. The man genuinely cared about the dowager, too. "Why would Trey think that? Scandal happens all the time, especially in wealthy families. I believe their money gives society more to gossip about."

"Very true, Miss Faraday, but the dowager has had her share, and none of it was her doing."

"Why do you say that?"

He pulled on the reins and stopped his horse. Judith halted

her mare, as well.

"Have you ever met Trey's father?"

She nodded. "Yes, when I was younger."

"And you didn't *know* about him?"

"I'm not certain what you are referring to, my lord."

Dominic scrubbed his hand over his chin. "It's quite difficult to talk about in front of a lady." He chuckled. "If I were at the gentleman's club, I would find this topic easier."

"Please tell. I promise not to tell anyone you broke the rules. And I promise not to swoon from the delicate matter."

He laughed. "But Miss Faraday, do you not remember swooning when you first met Trey and myself?"

She grumbled. "I did *not* swoon in Trey's arms. I was weak from nourishment, and combined with the news Trey had just presented me—"

Dominic held up his hand. "Yes, I know. I was just jesting with you. But to continue, I don't believe you are the type of woman who swoons over such controversies. Besides, it's going to be a pleasure breaking the rules with you." He winked. "Trey's father was a man who flaunted his mistresses everywhere he went. The dowager wasn't ignorant about her husband's affairs, but neither could she stop him. On several occasions, he dueled over these unfortunate women, injuring their husband or lover, and then weeks later he found another woman to shower his attention on."

Heat surged to Judith's face, both from embarrassment over the subject, and from anger. How could that man do such a thing? Poor Isabelle for having to put up with such a man. "Oh, how terrible."

"So you see," Dominic continued, "the family has had its share of gossip. It was not until after Tristan died, when Trey hardened his heart to a lot of things and acted like he didn't have a care in the world."

Her heart clenched. "Tell me, my lord, why would Trey continue to lead such a life of ill-repute when his father did, making them a topic of gossip within the best circles?"

"Trey has always been told he's like his father. Perhaps Trey feels it cannot be helped. At least he's not causing scandal like he did in his younger years."

Judith urged her horse forward in a slow walk, Dominic keeping up beside her. Many questions still swam in her head, but her heavy heart couldn't stop feeling sorrow for the boy Trey once was and the man he was today.

"Can you tell me something else, my lord?"

"What?"

She glanced at Nic. "Will Trey ever change?"

"How do you mean?"

"Will he ever want to settle down and find a good woman to marry, and stay faithful to?"

Dominic shrugged. "I want to believe all of us rakes will eventually find a woman to marry and to have heirs." He grinned. "As for Trey, I cannot be certain. I think deep in his heart, he does not want to end up like his father. I believe Trey longs to find the woman who will change him."

"He would certainly have a miserable life if he continues to live like he's doing now."

"Many women have tried to change Trey."

She arched her brows. "Indeed?"

"Oh yes, but they are going about it the wrong way."

Chuckling, she shook her head. "My lord, is there a *right* way?"

"Every man is different, mind you, but Trey needs a woman who will get to know him and love him for himself. She also needs to be patient and give him the time to fall in love." Dominic ran his fingers through his hair as he adjusted himself on the saddle. "Most women want to trap Trey quickly without going through the other steps."

She shook her head. "I think, my lord, you are the romantic one out of the two. Trey told me once that loving someone was foolish."

"I suppose it can be, but only if you fall in love with the wrong person."

"And pray, who is the wrong kind of woman?"

"I believe Trey has met many women who are like the kind his father visited frequently. Trey does not want someone who falls easily into another man's arms."

"Most women do not want a man who falls easily into another woman's arms, either."

"Exactly." He winked. "Although Trey may not realize it yet, he's hoping to find a woman he can trust, not only with his name, but with his heart. When he finally falls in love, it will be forever."

Emotion squeezed her chest and tears burned her eyes. Quickly, before Dominic could see, she pushed her horse faster. She couldn't explain to him about her tears. Too many times over the past few days she had hoped for a way into Trey's heart. Although she still questioned her feelings for him, she yearned for his nearness.

Trey was so different from Alex, and it surprised her to think she could have such feelings. She had thought Alex was the kind of man who'd make the perfect husband and father. Trey was far from that, yet he would certainly know how to kiss her to oblivion, making her think of nothing else.

Regretfully, putting him out of her head was the best thing— and finding answers about Alex was the second best.

Chapter Twenty-Three

B Y THE END of the day, Judith was ready to strangle someone. Mainly Trey. He had managed to disappear from the estate, even though the servants admitted they saw him earlier. If Judith didn't know better, she would think he was purposely hiding from her. She needed answers about Alex. And now. She would go insane if she had to wait another day.

After the evening meal where Trey was suspiciously absent, she excused herself and told the dowager she had a terrific headache. When Judith reached her room and closed the door behind her, she marched to her vanity table. Slumping on her stool, she stared at herself in the mirror and pulled out the pins holding the knot at the back of her head. She picked up the brush and punished her locks by yanking the bristles through each curl. Soon her ringlets were gone and thick hair fell over her shoulders and down her back.

She wasn't ready to retire to bed. Her mind wouldn't let her rest. The only way she would be able to set her jumbled thoughts in order was to deal with Trey. Even if she had to become a bloodhound to do it, she'd search this house from one side to the other until she found the rotten coward. What other word could she call him besides coward? Obviously, he didn't want to confront her for some unknown reason, which was why he hid.

She pushed away from the vanity and hurried out of her

room. The hallway was quiet, as were the rooms below. The dowager must have gone to bed early, as well.

Judith first tried the study. She knocked, waited a few seconds then opened the door slowly. A strong cigar scent hung thick in the air, combined with ale. She waved her hand in front of her nose. Had he been here holed up all day? From the smell, it would seem he had.

"Trey?" She peeked her head inside. The heavy velvet curtains had been drawn, and the room held many shadows.

Unfortunately, the room didn't hold him as she'd hoped.

Throughout the lower floor, she looked in every room before rushing upstairs to his bedchambers. When she stood in front of his room, her hands moistened and her heartbeat quickened. Certainly, this was not proper, but she couldn't put off talking to him a minute longer. If he were inside, she would just invite him to come out and take a walk with her through the flower garden.

On second thought, outside would be dark and they would only have the moon to guide their stroll. Not a good choice when she hadn't convinced her body to stop desiring him. If only her mind could control her body's reactions whenever he was around, she would have no need to fret.

Making her decision, she knocked on the door and waited. She listened intently for any sounds on the other side, but detected none. She turned the knob and opened the door. A few lamps dimly lit the wide opened space, but so far, no sign of Trey. However, his masculine scent was strong, stirring anticipation in her limbs.

She tried to shake away the feeling as she stepped inside. "Trey?" Her voice squeaked, so she cleared her throat and tried again. "Trey?" Still the volume of her voice wasn't very loud, so she stepped inside, nearly to the middle of the floor. Her heartbeat thundered in her ears, blocking out any other sounds.

What was she doing? This was wrong. She shouldn't be in his private chambers. But as she glanced around, she found her feet rooted in place and wouldn't move. His large bed was against the far wall close to the large fireplace. Several armoires stood around the spacious room along with a sofa and two cushioned chairs.

The room was different from what she'd expected. Perhaps it was due to his lifestyle, but it didn't look like a sultan's tent with silk and satin coverings. Instead, dark blue and brown colors were used in decorating. Against the other wall was a closed door. She didn't dare venture further to see where it led. Perhaps Trey wasn't here after all, but that didn't explain why lamps were lit. Nonetheless, she needed to get out. Now.

As she turned to leave, the floor in the adjoining room creaked. She jumped and swung around just in time to see Trey walk out as he fastened a towel around his waist. No other stitch of clothing covered his muscular body.

Her mouth turned dry as if cotton had taken up residence in her throat. Try as she might to divert her eyes, she gazed over his body in a slow inspection. Black, wet hair slicked back from his forehead. Wide shoulders and chest emphasized his muscular waist. Even with the small amount of light, she detected a sprinkle of hairs on his chest. His legs weren't as she'd imagined, either, as his calves practically bulged with strength.

He stopped suddenly, his eyes wide as he looked at her. Heat consumed her face, as well as her body, yet she still couldn't turn away. She opened her mouth to speak, but nothing came out.

His attention moved over her, and every inch of her burned with awareness. Within seconds, his smile widened.

"What a pleasant surprise." His voice dripped with sensual charm.

"I—I—" She cleared her throat. "I didn't know you were here."

One of his brows arched. "Indeed? Do you usually come into my room when I'm not occupying it?"

Embarrassment washed over her, and she could have died. Obviously, he enjoyed making her nervous. "What I meant was—" She swallowed the lump in her throat. "I was looking for you, but I doubted you were here."

"Ah." He nodded and folded his arms over his chest. "Good to know. So tell me, my sweet, how may I assist you?"

She licked her parched lips. "We need to talk." Her focus dipped to his towel, before she quickly lifted it back to his face. "If you don't mind, I would like you to change and meet me downstairs—"

"Why can we not talk here?"

She gasped. "Are you addled?"

Chuckling, he walked toward her, but turned and headed to the door first. "I believe you have asked me this question before." He shut the solid oak barrier. "And I refused to answer, for fear it would ruin my reputation."

Shivers started inside her, so she clasped her hands against her middle. Dear heavens! They were in his bedroom alone with the door closed, not to mention, he was wearing a towel! This was not a good thing.

Slowly, he walked toward her. Each step made her heart hammer faster. When he stopped, he took a lock of her hair with his finger and thumb, and rubbed.

"Judith? Why is your hair down? Are you aware how much I like it this way?"

She scolded herself for not thinking before she left her room. Now she regretted her most hasty decision. "I—I—" She swallowed hard. "I thought to retire for bed, but I really needed to talk to you first."

He stroked her cheek. "Which brought you looking for me in my room, I see. Whatever was on your mind must be extremely important for you to seek me out here."

"Please, forgive me for intruding upon your bath."

His manly scent of soap drifted all around her. The urge to lean into him and rub her face in the crook of his neck became overwhelming, but she shook the incredible, desire-stirring thoughts away. She must remain in control.

"You didn't intrude, my sweet. In fact, your presence has made my evening much better."

"Trey, would you please put on a robe? This is improper, and you know it."

He shrugged. "Nobody knows but us. I have dismissed my servants. We will not be disturbed."

Oh, dear... Why did he tell her that? Regardless, she needed to say what was on her mind and leave. Although telling her legs to move was a different story, entirely.

"It matters not. I would feel more comfortable if you put on a robe."

"As you wish." He picked up a robe lying on the foot of the bed and wrapped it loosely around himself, tying it at his waist, before coming to stand in front of her.

Using both hands, he cupped her face and stepped even closer. Automatically, she placed her palms on his chest to stop him. Her fingertips connected with the exposed skin and nearly seared her, sending a different kind of heat pumping in her body. His muscles were so hard, yet his skin so soft to the touch. She gasped and pulled her hands away as if he were made of hot coals. Touching him this way was detrimental to her health.

"What is it you want, Judith?"

Her mind fought an endless battle with her body. Yet giving in was not an option. Her heart would be hurt, and she couldn't bear it.

Chapter Twenty-Four

"TREY, STOP IT." She forced herself to take another step away from him. "I didn't come here for this."

"For what?"

"You really must get dressed. I cannot think with you like this. There's no way we can communicate while you are in this state of... of..." She swished her hand through the air.

He chuckled and moved closer. He grasped her hand and lifted it to his mouth before lightly kissing her fingertips. "Oh, I think differently, my sweet. I can think of a very enjoyable way to communicate while I'm in this state."

He placed her palm on his chest, and once again, it was like hot coals burning her flesh, except this time she couldn't pull away. His dark eyes entranced her, and heaven help her, she anticipated his next move.

"Judith, I don't mind if you touch me." His voice was deep, seductive. "In fact, I encourage it."

She licked her dry lips. "It's not proper," she whispered.

The corner of his mouth lifted in a lopsided grin. "Oh, but it is, my sweet. We shall say it's part of your learning. This is a very good way to communicate. It's intimate lesson number one; how to touch a man and make him melt."

Melt? He was certainly accomplishing that very thing with her. Yet he was going to teach her how to achieve making him melt. Although she should really protest, curiosity struck a chord in her, and she indeed wanted to be taught.

Staring at the exposed skin at the middle of his chest, she shook her head. Words had been lost in her head somewhere because she couldn't think of anything to say—or any kind of refusal.

"A man enjoys a woman's touch," he said deeply. Desire sparked in his eyes. "A man also enjoys a woman's curiosity. We... I don't want you to be shy with me."

Her heart tripped crazily. No longer was he discussing women in general. He talked right to her, telling her what he wanted. What he enjoyed. She enjoyed knowing this more than she should. What was happening to her? Self-control was within reach, yet she wanted to give it up for just a moment.

Then what?

His gaze dropped to her mouth. Kissing him would be very nice right now, but the way flames of desire licked through her body, she feared more would happen. She could not do this with a man who was not her husband—and more than likely would never be considered.

Trey made the first move, closing the space between them as he leaned forward, his mouth descending quickly. When his lips met hers, he brushed them in a gentle sweep over her mouth before moving down her cheek to her neck.

Warnings screamed in her mind, reminding her he didn't want a wife. He wanted what all rakes were after. And then he'd leave her to suffer the scandal and embarrassment as she searched for a worthy husband who would overlook her costly mistake. She couldn't let that happen.

"Trey, please stop." She pushed him away and walked backward toward the door, keeping her shaky hands clasped tightly against her stomach.

She stopped in front of the door and tried to regulate her breathing. Turning, she met his heated stare. "I didn't come here for this. I came to ask about Alex. I need to know if you have heard from your solicitor. I have given you ample time to try and locate my fiancé. If your solicitor has not found anything, then I shall look for Alex myself."

The pleasurable expression on Trey's face quickly disappeared as ragged breaths still shook his body. Silence stretched between them as he raked his fingers through his hair, then he took a deep breath and tightened the sash around his waist.

Folding his arms, he gave her a nod. "Very well. I suppose I can tell you what I have learned so far."

She lifted her chin and squared her shoulders, ready to hear what he had to say. "I would appreciate it."

"What my solicitor has discovered so far is not good at all."

Holding her breath, she waited.

"I fear your fiancé has not been very honest with you."

Slowly, she released the air from between her teeth as her heart knocked in a completely different rhythm this time.

"Apparently, Alexander Cutler is not a lieutenant in the Royal Navy."

She gasped. "What? How absurd. Of course he is."

"No, Judith. He has never been an officer. My solicitor checked this out thoroughly."

"But...but.... That cannot be."

"Tell me, Judith. Did you ever see him wearing a uniform?"

"Yes. It was the last time I had seen him before my parents died. Our meeting was very brief because he was leaving, but he was definitely wearing the uniform of a lieutenant."

Trey shook his head. "Then he must have stolen it, because there's no Alexander Cutler listed in the Royal Navy."

Anger shot through her and she fisted her hands by her side. "Alex did not steal anything, and he most assuredly did not lie to me."

"Then explain to me how my solicitor could not find him in the Navy? Does Mr. Cutler have a different name, perhaps?"

"No."

"So then why is he not listed?"

Confusion pounded in her head. None of this made sense. Why would Alex lie to her about being a lieutenant? He wouldn't. Didn't he know she could find out easily enough? "I don't know," she whispered.

Trey moved closer, standing in front of her. "Judith, I hesitated to tell you before I had more information." He laid his hand on her shoulder.

She slapped at his hand, knocking away his touch. "I think you have the wrong information. I don't know how, but I cannot believe he'd lie to me about that. We were planning on getting married."

Tears pricked her eyes, so she turned sharply and opened the door to leave. He grabbed her arm and swung her around to face him. Blinking, she hoped to get rid of the moisture before he noticed, but she failed miserably.

"Judith, my solicitor is still looking into this. We will find the truth, I promise."

"I appreciate all you have done, but something is not right." Her voice choked, so she cleared her throat.

He caressed her face then gently pulled her closer as his arms slid around her shoulders. With her palms against his chest, she tried to hold back, but he was stronger and her weak body fell against him.

Her cheek rested against his chest as she fought the tears still building. Although emotion tightened her bosom, she relaxed in his embrace as his hands stroked her back while soothing words whispered from his lips.

Curse him for doing this to her.

She should be thinking about Alex and why he hadn't come forth. At this point, she should be wondering if her dreams of being Mrs. Cutler were ever going to come true. Instead, all she could think about was how comfortable she felt in Trey's arms. Beneath her palm, his heartbeat thudded against her in a quick rhythm. She realized how quickly passion flared between them. She had to leave before her mind became weak.

Forcing herself to pull away was the hardest thing she'd ever had to do, but she stepped out of his embrace. He watched her with tenderness in his gaze, and she wanted to cry. She wouldn't. Not in front of him. "I must return to my room now. Good night, Trey."

She hurried out the door, not hearing what he'd muttered. It didn't matter anyway. Nothing he could say to her could stop the confusion swimming in her heart. Little by little, her life sifted away, and there wasn't anything she could do to stop it.

TREY LEANED AGAINST the white column of the porch as he gazed across the estate. Hawthorne had invited Judith to go riding this morning. And once again, they had ridden out of Trey's view. It was all he could do not to saddle his horse and follow.

Was Nic touching her right now? Wooing her with words of love?

Trey bunched his hands into fists, grinding his teeth. Why was Nic calling on Judith in the first place? Had his latest mistress become uneventful? That could be the only explanation. Besides, Nic didn't like women who spoke their minds as Judith did, so why was he even with her?

Trey had been on edge for two days since he'd caught Judith in his bedroom. Letting her leave his side that night was the hardest thing he'd ever done. Even while he watched her walk out the door, he wanted to pull her back into his arms and smother her with kisses until she agreed to stay.

He'd wanted her so much it hurt. Literally. The ache in his chest that night stayed quite a while. Her sweet smell of flowers had been in his room afterwards, and he'd lain awake all night in torture as he thought about her.

Plain and simple, the night had been pure agony. He'd wanted her, yet was relieved he hadn't compromised her. Judith needed a husband who would stay faithful to her as they had babies and lived happy, long lives.

He couldn't give her that, even if the idea tempted him. His father's blood ran deep, and inevitably, Trey would become tired of her and seek another companion, just as he'd done with all the women who'd been in his life thus far. Women had been nothing but objects, and when Tristan died, this idea was branded into Trey's mind deeper. He didn't ever want to love a woman so much he'd risk his life, as his brother had done.

Although in Tristan's situation, his mistress had lied to him. Lady Diana led Tristan to believe he was the only man for her. Unfortunately, her betrothed had different ideas. If only Trey had been quicker and more observant, he could have saved his brother that fateful night.

Since then, Trey realized how ruthless women could be. Judith may not be the deceitful person Lady Diana had been, but he wasn't willing to give her his heart. Neither did he want to break hers, which assuredly, he would. Ruining her life was out of the question, even for a taste of one night in heaven. And paradise it would be, indeed. Judith was more passionate than most of the women he'd been with, which made resisting her that much harder.

From up the drive, a single-horse buggy came. Immediately, Trey recognized his solicitor. Trey hurried down the steps of the porch and met the man just as the buggy stopped. "Good day, Mr. Lewis."

"It's a good day, indeed."

Trey smiled. "Does that mean you have more information?"

"I certainly do. Would you like to meet in your study?"

"Yes." Trey motioned toward the study. "Please, let's hurry with our meeting before Miss Faraday sees you. I don't wish to explain what you have discovered."

"Oh certainly, my lord. Especially right before her coming out ball. Isn't it tonight?"

"You are correct. She must have a lovely time at her ball and not worry about Mr. Cutler."

Trey led his solicitor into the study and closed the door. "Would you like a drink?"

"Thank you, but no. I promised my wife I would not indulge in spirits any earlier than one o'clock."

Trey chuckled and poured a small amount of brandy for himself. "Please, don't delay your findings, Mr. Lewis. I'm most anxious to hear what you have discovered."

The solicitor sank to the cushioned sofa and withdrew papers from his satchel. "Last we talked, I made mention about Mr. Cutler's income."

Trey nodded. "You said he was poor."

"That was what I had thought, but now I believe differently. That man has many secrets."

Excitement pounded in Trey's chest. Mr. Cutler was hiding more? The information would be well worth the wait, Trey was certain.

Chapter Twenty-Five

T REY WALKED TO his desk and sat on the chair. "What has Mr. Cutler been hiding now?"

"Three wealthy young widows have come forth with information about him. They have reported to be carrying on liaisons with the man. He used a different name each time, but their description of Mr. Cutler was the same. Apparently, he has a scar on his bottom lip. This was the feature they all brought up. When I talked to Mr. Cutler's relatives, the ones who were Miss Faraday's neighbors, they showed me a recent miniature of him, and indeed, we have the same man."

Trey crossed one leg over the other as he swirled his brandy in the snifter. "Who are these young widows, may I ask?"

Mr. Lewis shook his head. "I promised them I would leave their names out of my report."

"I understand." Trey motioned with his hand. "Please continue."

"Mr. Cutler had an affair with each, robbing them of most of their jewels before disappearing."

Trey sat up straight, his leg dropping to the floor. "He robbed them, you say?"

"Yes. They have each filed charges against Mr. Cutler, but the police have yet to find him."

"Good heavens, do you know what this means?" Panic

flowed through Trey as he rose and paced the floor. "When Mr. Cutler finds out how much Miss Faraday is worth, he will return for her." He bunched his hands into fists, thoughts clogging his mind with unanswered questions. "I will have to keep a closer watch over her so this man does not make contact."

"I agree, my lord."

Trey stopped and looked at his solicitor. "Do you think Mr. Cutler is dangerous?"

Mr. Lewis shrugged. "The widows didn't say. They said he's very crafty with his charm, and carries himself as a gentleman, which is why they fell for his deceit."

Shaking his head, Trey walked back to his desk and picked up his snifter, gulping down the rest. "We must not let that sway our minds. For all I know, he could be a murderer."

"Very true."

"Have you received any leads to where he's hiding?"

"Still nothing, my lord, but I shan't give up. After all, I did run across these three widows in my search. I'm quite certain I will find Mr. Cutler soon."

Trey took a deep breath and ran his fingers through his hair. "Miss Faraday thought she'd seen him the other day in town. Because I have never met him, I could not help her search."

Mr. Lewis shuffled through his papers and pulled out a miniature. "Here, my lord. This is yours to keep."

The picture stared back at Trey. He studied the man who might eventually cause harm to Judith. Rage grew inside him as he thought about Mr. Cutler laying one finger on her. If that ever happened, Trey would run him through with a sharp blade.

"Thank you, Mr. Lewis. Now I will recognize him if he ever comes to my door." *And I'll kill the thief on sight.*

The solicitor stood and gathered his papers, stuffing them back into his satchel. "I will keep you posted, my lord."

They walked out of the study and outside to the buggy. As the solicitor climbed in, Nic and Judith rode up the drive. Giving a nod to Mr. Lewis, Trey quickly dismissed him before Judith could ask any questions. Nic would know, and Trey only prayed his friend wouldn't tell her. News like this would be devastating, especially on the day of her special event.

Nic and Judith stopped their horses near Trey. He smiled wide at his mother's ward. Judith's cheeks were pink, and her eyes sparkled. The bonnet she wore hadn't held her ringlet hair together as wisps of locks fell across her forehead and by her ears. She was absolutely beautiful. He wished he didn't feel so protective, but she'd grown on him and wiggled her way into his heart.

Stopping his thoughts, he held his breath. *My heart?* Had he really allowed her to enter? Nonsense! After what had happened to Tristan, Trey vowed he wouldn't be another victim of love.

Once her horse stopped, he rushed to her side to help her dismount. Her gaze held his as he lifted her off, trying not to brush against her in the process, but her warmth still created havoc inside him. When her feet touched the ground, he released her and stepped away.

"How was your ride?" he asked with a smile.

"Perfect. I could not have asked for a better companion."

An invisible knife slid through his chest. Why did she have to say it that way? She knew how he felt about Nic taking her riding. Trey had told her of his jealousy the night of her dinner party. Perhaps this was her way of making him more envious.

"Splendid. I'm relieved you had such a good time."

She looked over her shoulder at Mr. Lewis' buggy riding away. "Who was that?"

He couldn't tell her. Perhaps after her ball, but not a moment sooner. "Just a business acquaintance." Trey glanced at Nic as his friend dismounted, challenging Nic with his eyes not to say anything. Hawthorne must have taken the hint, because he just smiled.

Trey took a deep breath and met Judith's stare. "Now, my dear, let's get you inside. Mother is worried about you."

"Why? I have ridden with Lord Hawthorne before."

Taking her hand, he squeezed as he hooked it over his arm. "Not on the morning of your ball. Mother says there are many items she still requires to go over with you. I promised her I would get you inside the moment you returned."

Judith swung her head in Nic's direction. "My lord, I want to thank you for a refreshing jaunt around the estate."

Dominic bowed. "The pleasure was all mine, Miss Faraday. I'm looking forward to seeing you tonight at your ball."

"As am I." She grinned.

Trey hurried them inside the house, not wanting to witness anymore flirty glances between the two. He'd never been a jealous man, but right now, he loathed his best friend and seriously thought about wringing the man's neck.

Before they reached the drawing room where his mother awaited, Trey slowed and took Judith's hand in his. He placed a kiss on her knuckles. "Until tonight, my sweet." Trey stepped back and turned.

"Wait."

Excitement leapt in his chest when he looked at her. "What is it?"

"I—I just wanted to tell you…"

He stepped closer and took her hands. "Yes?"

"Lord Hawthorne asked that I save the first dance for him. I told him yes. I hope you approve."

Jealousy squashed his excitement quickly, leaving a hollow ache in his chest. "Why, of course. I know Nic is just your friend." Although he said the words, he wished his heart believed it.

A soft smile graced her face. "Indeed, he is."

He patted her hands. "Fine. Then I shall see you tonight. You and Mother will have a splendid afternoon getting ready, I assure you. Before you know it, this night will be but a memory."

"Oh, I certainly hope so." She sighed. "I really didn't want your mother to go through so much trouble on my behalf, and really, I cannot wait until this night is over."

"Me, either." But for entirely different reasons.

"Thank you, Trey, for everything." She turned and walked into the drawing room.

Why did he feel as if she were saying good-bye, as if she were bringing a closure to their relationship? With a heavy heart, he walked away, knowing that tonight would be an ending, because without a doubt, men would be lined up at the door on the morrow, seeking her hand in marriage. Once Trey told her about Mr. Cutler's lies, she would assuredly find another man.

Sighing wearily, he nodded. As it should be.

Chapter Twenty-Six

JUDITH GAZED AT the full-length mirror at the unhappy woman staring back. Her parents would be pleased with everything the dowager had done. Judith imagined her mother and father looking down from heaven and smiling upon their daughter, pleased that she was finally entering into society.

Sorrow twisted Judith's heart. If only they could be here to share this night with her. But then, if they were, Judith wouldn't be having this evening. She wouldn't be living at the dowager's estate, and Judith certainly wouldn't be having improper feelings for her guardian's son. In fact, if her parents were alive, Judith might be married to Alex.

Another spasm shot through her heart. She couldn't possibly believe what Trey's solicitor had discovered. Alex *was* in the Royal Navy. Doubts filled her head and her heart leaned toward Trey's reasoning. If Alex were the honest man she'd believed him to be, he would have come for her. He would have met her at the woodsman's cottage and taken her as his wife. And he most certainly wouldn't have run from her when she called his name the other day in town.

Sighing, she ran her white-gloved hands down her gown, over the few ruffles and lace that created the ice-blue sensation she wore. The puffy shoulders and square neck bodice enhanced her slender figure and made her look more like a mature woman.

Her ringlet-styled hair wasn't as tight as she'd worn it, either. The dowager's hairdresser insisted that tonight Judith's hair should be alluring as it wove loosely into a bun and the relaxed ringlets swept across her partially bare shoulders, enticing the gentleman to her side.

Really, there was only one man Judith wanted to entice tonight—the very man she shouldn't. Yet, the excitement building inside her was because of him. She couldn't wait to see his eyes when she walked into the ballroom. Before, his gaze had always darkened with desire, and she hoped the same would happen tonight.

She should be put out with him for keeping secrets from her. This morning when she returned from riding, Trey and Dominic exchanged knowing glances. Immediately, she felt out of place, as if she'd entered into a secret conversation. It had to be that man who she'd seen leaving. Trey had said he was a business acquaintance, but she believed he was something more. Even the dowager had mentioned during their mid-meal that she'd seen Trey's solicitor leaving this morning. Obviously, Trey knew something, and he wasn't going to tell her. Tonight she'd get it out of Trey one way or another. If it was about Alex, she wanted to know now.

The chimes from her clock announced the hour. Time to make her grand entrance. Dominic promised he'd help to keep the money-hungry men away from her. What a dear man he was, and such a good friend. At first, she wondered about his interest in her, but now she knew he wasn't after a relationship. In fact, at times it seemed all he wanted to do was make Trey jealous, because the only times Lord Hawthorne fawned over her was when Trey was near. She grinned. She didn't mind helping the marquess with that task. It was quite enjoyable.

Slowly, she walked out of her bedroom and made her way down the grand staircase. The guests had already filled the hallway, spilling into the ballroom. She took a deep breath. *This is for you, Mother.*

As Judith descended, the room grew quiet and all eyes were on her. A steady rhythm beat in her chest as she tried to remain calm. She searched for Trey, hoping she'd find him immediately. No such luck. Isabelle Worthington waited at the end of the stairs by herself. The older woman's eyes shined with glistening tears as she watched Judith.

A movement caught her attention as a tall dark-head man hurried out of the ballroom. When Trey turned Judith's way, her heart leapt. He stopped and gaped wide. Beside him, Dominic whispered something to Trey that made him snap his mouth close and straighten, but his eyes remained fixed on her. Just as she'd hoped, they darkened with emotion the closer she came.

When she neared the bottom of the stairs, Trey moved silently through the crowd, meeting her at the last step. He took her gloved hand and kissed her fingers.

"You are absolutely breathtaking," he whispered for her ears only.

She curtsied. "Thank you, my lord."

He hooked her arm through his and escorted her into the ballroom beside his mother where they stopped and faced the crowd. Although Judith knew the dowager was here, she couldn't take her eyes off Trey long enough to see what the older woman was doing. Trey wore a black double-breasted over-jacket with tails, a white shirt and cravat, along with white trousers. A king couldn't have looked more dignified and regal at this moment.

The crowd gathered around them for an introduction. Judith smiled, nodded, and curtsied, but after ten minutes, all the names and faces became a blur. Trey stayed beside her, close enough that their arms touched. She liked that almost too much.

Finally, the dancing began. Just as Dominic promised, he swept her away into the ballroom. He was as tall as Trey, his shoulders were almost as wide. They were both very handsome men, but Trey outshined his friend in all aspects.

"Enjoying yourself?" the marquess asked.

She chuckled. "As much as I dare. Everything is still a blur to me. I just hope I don't disappoint Her Grace."

"I'm quite certain you will perform splendidly. After all, you were taught by the best." He winked.

"Who?" She bit back a laugh. "Lord Trey?"

"Who else can there be?" He chuckled.

"Oh, he didn't teach me, my lord, although don't let him know that. The knowledge would crush him, I fear." She leaned closer and lowered her voice. "You know what an ego that man has."

The marquess threw back his head and laughed, which lightened her heart. If all the men were like him, she wouldn't have to worry about her ability to communicate for the rest of the evening. Unfortunately, most men were like Trey, only wanting to steal a few kisses and take some liberties.

Before she knew it, she was in the arms of another man. For the life of her, she couldn't recall his name, but their conversation went well. At least the dance was more festive, and she barely had to touch him. As they moved around the room, she searched for Trey. He had definitely tried to hide himself tonight, because she couldn't see him anywhere. He hadn't danced with anyone, and from what she could see, he wasn't standing by the buffet table, either. Could he possibly be outside? Alone? Or worse—with another woman?

It didn't matter, she tried to convince herself. She suspected he had a mistress and had to put the poor woman on hold while he assisted his mother's ward. Still, it didn't stop Judith from searching for him every chance she got.

A man she hadn't seen since childhood occupied one of her dances. Her heart softened. Trevor Worthington, Duke of Kenbridge, had been a tease as a boy, but as he grew older, he treated her with kindness. He'd been the big brother she never had.

Although she wanted to squeal with delight and throw her arms around his neck, she didn't. They were no longer children. But his smile told her he hadn't forgotten their friendship.

"Good evening, Miss Faraday. What a pleasure it is to see you again."

Her grin stretched wider. "It's certainly a pleasure to see you, Your Grace."

The dance was slower, and Judith welcomed the rhythm. "I have not yet congratulated you on your recent marriage."

"I thank you."

"Did you bring your wife tonight? I would very much like to be introduced to her."

He shook his head. "She's laid up in bed. Doctor's orders."

"Then please pass on my regards to your wife. I hope she feels better soon."

Trevor looked too much like Trey, except the older brother didn't have the easy-going expression in his eyes. His gaze was too serious. Trevor seemed an inch taller, and maybe just a bit broader through the shoulders. But his dark hair and eyes were nearly the same. Thankfully, Trevor's personality was far different from his younger brother's. Trevor had always been London's greatest catch for a husband. Judith hoped his new wife appreciated him.

"So, Miss Faraday," Trevor said.

"Yes?"

"Has my brother treated you well during your stay?"

She studied Trevor's expression. His tight jaw and arched brows let her know his question was serious. Then again, he would know more than anyone what kind of man Trey portrayed.

Chapter Twenty-Seven

"HE HAS BEEN the perfect model of a gentleman," Judith lied, trying not to laugh at the same time. "I have to admit, the first few days of my stay were quite rocky, but we learned to get along."

Trevor chuckled. "I remember when my brother used to tease you as a child. It's good to know he overcame this habit."

"Well, it did take some time, but we eventually figured out a way to talk without any serious repercussions."

He laughed. For the remainder of the dance, his expression seemed more relaxed, which eased her mind. Apparently, Trevor worried about her innocence, too. He certainly had every right to think this way.

When Trevor left her side, another gentleman claimed her. By the eighth dance, she begged for a moment of rest. Her escort hurried to fetch a glass of champagne. She wasn't left alone for very long when several men gathered around to talk. They were charming, and quite handsome, but she dismissed them easily, knowing she was not choosing a husband tonight or any night, for that matter. It baffled her how many men sought her out due to her inheritance.

Men like that could not be trusted.

A flute of champagne was pressed into her hand, and she quickly took a long sip, moistening her parched throat. All around her people chatted about mundane things that made her want to scream. If she had to dance with every one for the rest of the evening just to get away from these people, then she would, the whole time praying the evening would end.

Now, where was the gentleman who was supposed to be her dance partner? Didn't he deliver her drink? But the man had conspicuously disappeared.

A warm hand cradled her elbow. Anger shot through her. Why, the nerve of that man who had touched her! Trying to hold her temper, she swung to scold the person responsible, and came face to face with Trey. He smiled, his blue eyes nearly melted her.

"Miss Faraday? May I have the honor of escorting you for the next dance?"

As the string quartet started the waltz, her heart skipped a beat. Finally, a moment she could enjoy. "Yes, of course, my lord."

He took her gloved hand in his as he led her to the middle of the floor, his gaze holding hers the whole time. Once she settled in his arms and their feet moved to the hum of the stringed instruments, she breathed a sigh of relief and smiled.

"By the sparkle in your eyes, I'm assuming you are enjoying yourself, my sweet."

I am now. "Actually, the sparkle in my eyes is probably due to the many glasses of champagne I have had tonight."

He laughed.

"But truthfully, I am enjoying myself. I have met some very fascinating people."

He arched a brow. "Have you taken a liking to any of them?"

"No. Am I supposed to?"

"I just wondered if anyone has caught your eye." He shrugged.

"My lord, I'm not looking for anyone to catch my eye." She tilted her head. "If you remember correctly, I'm still waiting for your solicitor to give us more information about Alex."

A flicker of panic crossed his expression before he lifted his chin, his body growing stiff. "Don't you believe what Mr. Lewis has discovered already?"

"That Alex is not in the Royal Navy?" She shook her head. "I want more proof before I condemn the man to hang, my lord. Until then, I shall continue to believe there's a simple explanation for all of this." She said the words, but deep inside it was harder to convince herself. Trey mustn't see her doubt. "However, my lord, I do believe you know more than you're telling."

His eyes widened. "Indeed? How pray, did you come to that conclusion?"

"Women's intuition."

He chuckled, and the deep timbre of his voice made her heart pitter-patter faster. Blast it, he always had this effect on her.

"Besides that," she continued, "I witnessed the exchange of knowing glances between you and Lord Hawthorne this morning after your business partner left."

Trey stumbled in his step but quickly corrected. She almost smiled with victory. He couldn't lie to her now.

"Knowing glances, my sweet? What are you referring to?"

"Oh, don't play coy with me. I believe your business partner was Mr. Lewis himself. Even your mother mentioned his name earlier this afternoon, and I know you talked to him." Her heart twisted in confusion and she frowned. "Please, Trey. Tell me what he said."

"Now, now, my lovely." He squeezed her hand. "I will not do anything to ruin your ball. My mother would have my head on a platter if I did anything of the sort."

Judith's chest grew heavy. "So you heard more bad news?"

"My dear," he said softly, "please stop this nonsense. We cannot have the most beautiful woman in the room frowning, now can we?"

She shrugged. "How should I know? Who, pray, is the most beautiful woman in the room? I shall promise not to make her frown."

Trey chuckled, his eyes twinkling again. "You know very well who I'm referring to." His fingers caressed her hand. "And I shall repeat what I told you earlier. You take my breath away. Indeed, I have never seen a more handsome woman than the one I'm dancing with now."

Judith wanted to smile from his compliment, really she did, but she wished he'd tell her the truth. Before another word was spoken, the music ended. Quickly, she stepped closer to him and whispered in his ear, "You *will* tell me what Mr. Lewis said. I shall pester you until you do."

When she pulled away, his smile stretched wide across his face. He lifted her hand to his mouth and kissed her knuckles. "I look forward to it, my sweet." He winked, hooked her arm over his arm and walked her back to the flock of men he'd rescued her from earlier.

She could have screamed. Trey would take back his words when she showed him her tactics of persistence. He knew something about Alex, and she'd not rest until he had told her every word. Yet, she knew how hardheaded Trey had been in the past. Teasing her was his greatest accomplishment. So how could she get him to confess? Perhaps she'd make a bargain with him of some sort. He'd told her many times before how much she tempted him.

She grinned. Yes, she'd tempt him the only way she knew how.

Giddiness was a perfect way to describe Judith tonight. Of course, the several glasses of champagne had much to do with her state of mind. With each glass of spirits, she flirted more, danced more, and laughed as if she didn't have a care in the world. Dancing seemed to go on all night, but she allowed man after man to take her out on the floor and swing her in their arms.

Dominic, her dear friend, saved her on a few occasions when a man or two had become overzealous, and she was thankful for the marquess' interruption. Dominic assured her she was acting normal and that the dowager was very pleased with tonight's events. He also kept assuring her that Trey couldn't keep his eyes off her.

It seemed strange Dominic would tell her such a thing, especially when he didn't know what intimacies had happened between her and Trey. Nonetheless, she smiled and accepted the praise. She also promised not to drink another glass of champagne for fear the room would spin more than it was already thus far tonight.

She had kept her word and occasionally captured Trey's attention, reminding him he had something to tell her. He laughed and handed her another glass of champagne, the rogue! The glimmer in his eye let her know he thought this a game.

A game, indeed. She would certainly show him how to play when she got him alone. And she would before the night was over.

When the last person left, she sighed with relief. Trey and his mother stood beside her as she bid their guests farewell and the butler closed the door. Judith turned to Trey and grinned, arching her brow, but before she muttered a word, the dowager took Judith in her arms and hugged her tight.

"Oh, my dear. This was the most magnificent night." Isabelle pulled away. "You made me so proud, as if you were my own daughter." She cupped Judith's face. "How can I thank you for allowing me to give you this? I know your parents are smiling down at us from heaven."

Judith nodded. "They certainly are. Thank you for your help, Your Grace." She turned to Trey. "And yours of course, my lord."

He bowed slightly. "The pleasure was all mine, my dear. Now, if you will excuse me, I must leave. I fear I still have some unfinished business to take care of in my study. Goodnight Mother, Judith."

Before she could stop him, he bolted down the hall as if his heels were on fire. Irritation boiled inside her and she fisted her hands. She'd get this resolved tonight whether he wanted it or not.

"Come, my dear," the dowager said as she tugged on Judith's

arm. "I shall take you to your room."

What else could Judith do but follow? Grudgingly, she walked beside her guardian until she opened the door to her bedroom and stepped inside. After the door closed behind her, she stomped to her vanity table and sat on the stool. Her maid had laid her nightgown on her bed, but she would not retire yet. Dealing with Trey was more important. Of course, she must wait a few minutes to make certain the dowager settled in her room, first.

While she waited, she pulled off her elbow-length gloves and removed her jewelry. She took out the ribbons weaved in her hair, pulled out the bun, then tugged at the ringlets. Using the brush, she finished straightening her hair. She remembered how Trey liked it down, and if she must tempt him tonight, she'd have to look the part. Getting him to confess what he knew was vital, and she'd do anything to get it.

Once her hair was the way she wanted, she left her room. With most of the lamps in the hallway extinguished, shadows followed her as she crept down the stairs to Trey's study. His door cracked open enough for a small amount of light to shine into the hallway.

Slowly, she pushed the door open. Trey sat at his desk, only a few lamps dimly illuminating the room as he stared at the papers in front of him, drumming his fingers on the oak. He had removed his over-jacket and waistcoat. Even his cravat was missing and his shirt hung open at the throat.

Indeed, he was a powerfully handsome man.

Taking a deep breath, she stepped inside.

Chapter Twenty-Eight

SILENCE FILLED THE room. Judith's heartbeat knocked against her ribs, and she feared Trey would hear. A pop from the fireplace jerked her attention to the low burning logs that had just broken. The heat made the room cozy, which in turn made her sleepy. Then again, that was probably the effect of the champagne.

"Please come in, my sweet. I have been waiting for you."

Trey's deep voice made her jump, and she placed her hand on her chest.

"Close the door, if you will."

Her hands shook as she did as he asked, wondering why she should be the one out of sorts tonight. She'd come for answers and wouldn't leave until he gave them. Then again, it was how she intended to get the answers that made her anxious.

She cleared her throat. "You've been waiting for me, my lord?"

Finally, he turned his head and stood. Even in the low lighting it was evident desire lit his eyes.

"But of course. After all, you did promise you were going to talk to me tonight. Did you not?"

"I did."

His bold gaze caressed every inch of her, inspecting her person as if she stood before him in her bedclothes. Her heartbeat thudded faster and her limbs quaked with nervousness. His nearness made her dizzy.

"Then pray, let's not wait another moment." Her voice shook, so she swallowed. "Please, tell me what more your solicitor has discovered about Alex."

Trey stepped closer, but she stood her ground, shoulders back, ready to do battle. He entwined a lock of hair in his fingers and brought it to his mouth, letting the waves caress his lips.

"You smell heavenly, Judith. Tell me," he said in a soft voice, "why did you brush out your hair?"

"I—I—" How could she admit she wanted to tempt him? "I had nothing better to do while I waited for your mother to retire."

He traced her face with the tips of his fingers. "Judith, do you know how lovely you looked tonight? I had no desire to take my eyes off you this evening, not even for a moment."

Warmth spread through her chest from his compliment. But enough of his flattery. She wanted answers. "Trey, please." She licked her dry lips. "Would you tell me what your solicitor has found?"

He frowned and stepped back to his desk. "I fear I'm reluctant to deliver bad tidings such as these."

She held her breath and clutched her hands against her middle. Did she really want to hear? Yes! She must know.

"What Mr. Lewis discovered about your fiancé is not good at all." He folded his arms and sat on the edge of his desk. "It appears Mr. Lewis was wrong about Mr. Cutler's finances."

Relief slowly seeped through her, but she dared not become too excited. She cocked a brow. "He was wrong?"

"Yes. Mr. Cutler is wealthier than we first expected."

Another bout of relief trickled out, but she held it in, just in case. Had the solicitor misjudged Alex? "I don't understand how this can be considered bad news."

"Apparently, your Mr. Cutler is quite a charmer, though. In the last year on three different occasions, with three different women, he has persuaded some young, wealthy widow to become his lover. Anyway, during these times, he proceeded to steal their jewels before he left without a trace. With each woman, he used a different name."

Shock vibrated through her body and her legs shook. She sat on the sofa, still clutching her hands to her body. It couldn't be true. Mr. Lewis had to be wrong. Alex wasn't the type of man who would have done that.

"How do they know it was Alex?"

"Each woman described your fiancé in the same fashion. They all said he had curly brown hair and a scar on his bottom lip." Trey lifted from the desk and sat beside her on the sofa. "Judith? Does Alex have a scar on his bottom lip?"

Her heart lodged in her throat and a deep ache filled her chest. She couldn't breathe, yet she feared if she did breathe she'd let out a sob. "Yes," she whispered.

"Apparently, he's hiding because the authorities are looking for him. All three of these women reported him as a thief."

Tears stung her eyes, and she blinked quickly to chase them away. Was this really the man she had intended to marry? The man she had met several months ago could have never acted this way. He'd been the perfect gentleman. Or was that just an act, too?

"Really, Trey. None of this makes sense. If he was only after me for my inheritance, why didn't he meet me at the woods-man's cottage?"

Trey stroked her arm. "Judith? Did he know about your in-heritance?"

An ache grew in her head, meeting the same pain as what was forming in her chest. "No." Her throat tightened with emotion, so she cleared her throat again.

"Oh, my sweet Judith." Trey cupped her face as he loomed near. "I didn't want to tell you. I cannot bear to see you hurting."

If he didn't stop pretending he cared, she was indeed going to cry. Releasing such emotion in front of him was out of the question. She must appear strong.

Pushing his hands away, she stood. "Thank you, my lord. Tell Mr. Lewis I'm grateful for this knowledge before I could exchange my vows with Mr. Cutler." She turned and walked to the door. "Now, if you will excuse me, I'm very tired and I must lie down. Goodnight, Trey."

Trey lifted himself from the sofa, but she hurried out of the room and rushed down the hallway before he could stop her. She didn't remember every step from there to her room, but once she was inside and the door closed, she ran to her bed. Tears streamed down her face as sobs choked her throat.

She'd been a fool for falling in love with a man she didn't know. Then again, had she really loved Alex or was it just the idea of marriage that she loved? She'd wanted to find a man to marry. All of her friends were married. So when she'd made Alexander Cutler's acquaintance and realized he found her interesting, she made it a goal to make him fall in love with her.

Slowly, she lifted from the bed and walked to her full-length mirror. She wiped the tears staining her cheeks and sighed. While growing up, she'd never been able to accomplish making the boys fall in love with her. Why did she think she could do it now?

She recalled all the times when she had fancied a boy, but they always found her friends more interesting. Judith could never keep her thoughts inside her head so she spoke her mind, which was her biggest downfall. Her friends giggled and batted their eyes and won over the boys every time.

Nothing had changed. Even tonight with her coming out ball, she could tell when the men found her interesting or not. Most of the time all she saw was their greedy nature, especially when they spoke of her inheritance. Indeed, money was their only interest. She had no desire for a man like that. The romantic side of her wanted to find a man who would love her for the woman she was, not what she could give them. She wanted a man who would treat her like a queen. The same way her father had treated her mother.

Would she ever find such a man?

A small knock rapped on the door. There was only one person who was awake at this hour, and in her confused and depressed state of mind, it was unwise to let him in.

Problem was, she truly didn't want to get rid of him.

"WHO IS IT?"

Trey stood in front of Judith's room, resting his palm on the door as if mentally reaching to her through the solid oak barrier. The crack in her voice said it all. Telling her about Mr. Cutler had broken her heart. Trey couldn't let her suffer alone. Whether or not she knew it, she needed him. Needed his comfort. Just as he needed hers.

"Judith, please let me in," he whispered, hoping everyone in the house had gone to bed by now.

From the other side, feet padded to the door and stopped. He waited for her to allow him entrance, but so far, that hadn't happened. He must convince her he was only here to comfort.

"Judith, my sweet. I cannot let you hate me like this."

"I don't hate you, Trey."

Her voice was too soft for him to believe her. "Please, let me in so I can explain."

The doorknob clicked and the door opened. She peered at him through the small gap and shook her head. "Go to bed, Trey. I don't wish to talk tonight."

His stomach clenched and his heart ached. "I fear I cannot leave. I must know you are all right."

Through the small amount of space the cracked door had to offer, he pleaded with his eyes as he kept hold of her puffy-eyed stare. Finally, she nodded and stepped away from the door. He pushed through then closed it.

Just like his study, not much light illuminated the room. Only a few candles cast shadows everywhere. He sucked in a quick breath. It would be nigh impossible to keep her at arm's length tonight.

She folded her arms and walked to the window. She pulled back the curtains only slightly, letting in a sliver of moonlight from outside.

"Judith, I want to apologize."

"Why? You were only trying to help," she said over her shoulder. "It's not your fault Mr. Cutler has deceived me and everyone else he comes in contact with." She lifted her fisted hand to her mouth as if she held back a cry.

His heart cracked with emotion. Seeing her distraught was more than he could bear. Taking soft steps, he moved closer until he stood behind her. Long chestnut hair cascaded over her shoulders and back in a seductive wave. Tenderly, he stroked the hair resting over her shoulder. "My heart is breaking for you, my sweet. Tell me what I can do to make your pain disappear."

Beneath his touch, her body quivered. Heat surged through him, stronger this time. She'd always responded well to him, and he smiled from the knowledge he still affected her.

"Trey," she whispered. "You really must leave. This is not proper."

She didn't need to tell him what his mind continually repeated every time they were together. Yet, right now, he couldn't abandon her.

He stepped closer, clutching both of her shoulders as he pressed his face into her hair. The scent of roses filled his head, making him dizzy with wanting. "You need not think in such a way. I'm here to share your pain. When you hurt, I hurt." He kissed her head. "It's because of me you are hurting, and I want to take it away. Please, allow me to comfort you, my love."

A deep sigh came from her as she leaned back against him. On impulse, he wrapped his arms around her shoulders, pulling her closer. She caressed his arms but didn't remove his hold.

He nuzzled her ear before moving his lips over her lobe. She shivered and clung to him.

"It tears me apart to see you cry, knowing I'm the one who caused you such agony," he whispered. "Did you really love him?"

She tilted her head back to rest on his shoulder and met his gaze. "I have been asking myself that very question tonight. I think I was in love with love and the idea of marriage, more than I was in love with Mr. Cutler. He was the first man to really give me attention."

"I cannot believe that. You are a very beautiful woman."

"Most men do not share your thoughts."

"They are blind fools then." He kissed the tip of her nose. "So you really didn't love Mr. Cutler?"

"Oh, I loved him, but probably not fully. Perhaps I was more infatuated than anything. Alex and I really never knew each other well." She shrugged. "Obviously, since he led a double life."

His heart leapt from her confession.

She licked her lips. "I would have been more crushed if we had never discovered his deceitfulness. Can you imagine how my life would have been ruined if I had married him?"

He dropped his gaze to her tempting mouth, wanting to sup her sweet nectar and lose himself in her passion. "I would have never let that happen."

A tender smile graced her mouth. "And pray, how would you have stopped it without knowing about his misdeeds?"

"You, my dear Judith, have lured me to your side these past few weeks, and I fear I cannot leave. I'm a greedy man, my love. I do not share."

She held her breath, her eyes growing wide. "What—"

"I would have never let him come near you." He lowered his mouth. "Not when I want you so badly."

Chapter Twenty-Nine

WHEN HIS LIPS met hers, she sighed deeply and answered his kiss. She turned in his embrace without breaking contact, and wrapped her arms around his neck. He crushed her body against his as his hands moved over her back in soft caresses.

She kissed him like a woman starved for passion, which indeed she was. He still couldn't believe no other man had kissed her in this manner. Not even Alex, the man she had dreamed of marrying. It surprised Trey that he had never quite felt the satisfaction with his other conquests as he had while holding Judith. Somehow she'd touched his heart, and he was reluctant to release this feeling.

Trey prayed she wouldn't stop him. She needed this pleasure as much as he did. He wanted to love her like no other man had.

But he wouldn't. He couldn't! He couldn't ruin her for other men—for her soon-to-be husband. Marriage didn't agree with Trey's plans like it did hers. He had to stop this now. In his mind, he repeated, *I will never make her a good husband.*

He broke the kiss and pressed his forehead against her, trying to get his breathing controlled. In a few moments, she looked up at him and smiled, cupping his face.

"You didn't have to stop, Trey."

"I know."

"Why did you then?"

He shook his head. "God knows I wanted to keep kissing you more than anything in the world, but I could not ruin you. You are too good of a person. You have a kind and loving heart. I could not do that to you."

Tears formed in her eyes, and when she smiled, her lips quivered. "Thank you."

He bent and placed a soft kiss on her mouth before pulling away. His chest grew tight with emotion. Not continuing what they'd both wanted had been the most unselfish thing he'd ever done, and he questioned his motives even though he knew. He wanted Judith more than any woman he'd ever known, but she would never be his.

Ever.

"Sleep well, my love." He kissed her one more time before turning and leaving her room. Each step made his heart heavier, and doubt trickled into his mind. Could he possibly love her and only her for the rest of his life? Could she possibly love him and want to be his wife forever and ever?

Shaking his head, he shoved the ludicrous notion away. The plain and simple truth was, he carried his father's passion for lust and desire. Trey could never be faithful to one woman. Eventually, Judith would bore him and he'd move on.

He couldn't do that to her. Indeed, he loved her, but he knew it wouldn't last.

As he stormed to his room, he cursed his father for ruining his life.

TREY LOVES ME!

Without a doubt, Judith knew this now. She smiled and climbed out of bed the next morning with a song in her heart. He had comforted her beyond her wildest dreams. He kissed like a man who couldn't get enough, and she answered with the same emotion. Never had a man made her feel so cherished, so beautiful. Only Trey.

Now she knew why she'd never had these feelings of desire for Alex. She was never in love with him. Trey had pulled her into his heart whether he wanted to or not. This was where she wanted to stay.

Forever.

She giggled as she slipped off her nightdress. Hard to believe she felt this way about him when the first day at the woodsman's cottage, she'd considered him the devil's spawn. Did he know he loved her or did he still deny his heart? Knowing how stubborn he was, he would deny it. She'd certainly try to help him overcome this problem and make him realize he loved her. Dominic's words came back to her, reminding her of what he thought Trey wanted in a woman.

She rang for her maid and dressed for the day. Trey wanted her, and she would be patient with him until he realized he loved her. She'd even prove they belonged together.

Within an hour, Judith had finished making herself presentable and hurried downstairs. Breakfast had long passed since everyone probably slept in, but she didn't mind. Her stomach didn't growl for food as much as her body yearned for Trey's affection.

As she neared the drawing room, the dowager's laugh rang through the silence. Trey's deep voice joined his mother's, making Judith's heart leap with excitement. It would be difficult, but she must act as if seeing Trey didn't set her body on fire. Neither Trey nor his mother was prepared for Judith to confess she'd found the man she wanted to marry. Another giggle reached her throat, but she quickly lifted her knuckles to her mouth in hopes of keeping the emotion contained. Soon they'd know of her decision, but now was not the time.

Taking a deep breath, she squared her shoulders and took another step closer to the drawing room. The dowager's voice vibrated through the air again, when the woman spoke about a list of men she had gathered. Judith slowed her feet and listened closer.

"Mother, I believe we have enough men on our list to start. This morning Bentley was overwhelmed with calling cards and invitations for Judith. She made quite an impression, and I'm certain a fine young gentleman will ask for her hand within a fortnight.

Isabelle Worthington laughed. "Oh, which one shall we choose?

"Mother, we will not choose any. This is Judith's decision."

"Are you certain? She's so young and innocent in all of this. I fear she will not know how to pick the right man."

"Mother," Trey's voice grumbled a little deeper. "You are underestimating our dear Judith. She has a good mind and she's very intelligent. Her wit is quicker and sharper than you think."

Judith smiled, her heart melting from his words. Although it hurt to think he and his mother were secretly devising ways to pick her future husband, Judith knew Trey would never allow any man to touch her. He'd told her that last night. She was his, and his kisses had branded her for life.

If she had to remind him of what happened, she would. One way or another, Trey and his mother would know Judith was not looking for a husband—unless the man was Trey.

Chapter Thirty

TAKING ANOTHER DEEP breath, Judith resumed her stance and strolled into the room. Right away, she gained the attention of Isabelle and Trey. Although Judith tried only to glance his way, hoping she wouldn't look at him like a woman in love, he jumped to his feet and smiled.

"Good afternoon, Judith," he said. "I trust you had a pleasant night's rest."

Heat moved up her neck toward her face, and she silently cursed the effect the double meaning had on her. "Thank you, Lord Trey. I did. I had an incredibly exhilarating night, which in turn helped me sleep as if I were floating on clouds."

He lifted a brow—and even the corner of his mouth turned up—as if letting her know he received the hidden meaning in her words.

"Well, my dear, I do say you look refreshed from your successful evening." The dowager smiled wide and held up a handful of cards. "Look at what we have received thus far. I know we will collect more as the day passes."

"Oh, how lovely." Judith moved to the sofa next to her guardian and sat.

"You have become a sensation, my dear." Isabelle beamed. "Now we must get you fitted for several more gowns."

"More?" Judith shook her head. "Don't I have enough already?"

Isabelle laughed. "Women never have enough, my dear."

"And when shall I plan for this excursion to Bond Street?"

The dowager nibbled on her bottom lip as she tapped her finger on her chin. During the few seconds of silence, Judith glanced at Trey. Casually, he sat in his chair with one leg crossed over the other, his dreamy gaze resting on her. A smile touched his mouth, making her heart flutter.

"How about we plan a trip to London in two days? Does that sound reasonable?" Isabelle finished.

Judith switched her focus back to her guardian. "Yes, it does. Will Lord Trey be joining us this time?"

Her comment brought him alert and he straightened in his chair, dropping his foot to the floor. "Me?"

"That sounds heavenly." The dowager clapped her hands. "Please consider coming with us, Trey. We shall have such a lovely time."

Panic crossed his expression, making his eyes wide and his smile disappear. Judith almost laughed. She hoped he agreed. Spending more time with him would help her convince him of his feelings for her.

"Um, well, I—I have business to attend."

"Trey, my dear," the dowager cut in. "I believe you can put off business for one day."

Judith leaned forward and touched his arm. When Trey's eyes met hers, his body seemed to relax from the stiff position he'd been in only moments ago. "Please," she said softly.

A slow smile stretched across his face. "How am I to resist two stubborn women?" He chuckled. "All right then. I shall come along."

Judith pulled away, pleased with his reaction. Perhaps it wouldn't be so difficult convincing him he was in love with her. She could only pray it happened quickly.

"I'm quite certain we will have many more calls from your young gentlemen friends, my dear. You will want to look your best." The dowager grinned.

"Of course," Judith said softly, not really wanting to impress anyone except Trey.

Isabelle patted her hands. "And if I were a betting person, I would say you will have at least a dozen marriage proposals within two weeks."

Judith's chest tightened. "So many? That soon?"

"Why of course."

"Whatever shall I do with so many proposals?" She sighed heavily and looked at Trey, who all of a sudden fidgeted in his chair.

The dowager chuckled. "Oh, dear Judith. You will have to make a choice which man you want to marry."

Frowning, she glanced at the duchess. "But what if none of them suit me?"

"No need to fret. Trey and I will be here to assist." Isabelle turned her head and looked at her son. "Is that not correct?"

"Yes, Mother. We will be here for support," he bit out his words.

Judith studied him closely. His irritation was obvious.

The dowager returned her attention to Judith. "It's not good to be too choosey, though. You will want to find the man who suits you the best, to be sure, but don't find fault with them just to pass them over. Do you understand?"

"I suppose."

Annoyance grew inside Judith. Why wasn't Trey arguing? Why was he siding with what his mother said? Judith knew he loved her, so why was he so eager to give her hand to the first available man? Beneath the folds of her dress, she fisted her hands. It didn't matter. She would not choose a husband unless it was Trey.

Bentley walked into the room and bowed. "Your Grace, Miss Faraday has a visitor."

Judith sucked in her breath and swung her gaze from the butler to Trey and the dowager. Hadn't Isabelle instructed

Bentley that Judith would be resting today?

"Who is it, Bentley?" Trey barked as he stood, arms crossed over his chest.

"My lord, it's Lord Hawthorne. He assured me Miss Faraday would want to see him."

The dowager motioned her hand. "Allow him in, Bentley. He can take tea with us."

Within a few minutes, Dominic made his appearance, his hat tucked under his arm and looking like he did whenever he took Judith riding. She grinned. Had he come to take her riding again? Whether he knew it or not, it was perfect timing. If she had to stay another moment in Trey's presence—especially with him set on finding her a husband—she'd be surely tempted to give him a good pounding whether it was lady-like or not. Dominic just may have saved the day.

Lord Hawthorne bowed. "Good day, Your Grace. I hope I'm not interrupting anything."

Isabelle smiled. "Of course not, my lord. You are always welcomed here." She motioned to the empty chair beside her. "Would you like to take tea with us?"

"Actually, Your Grace, I was in hopes that Miss Faraday would agree to ride with me. We have made it a habit of late to take a ride in the morning. Although it's afternoon, I would still enjoy a jaunt around the estate."

Judith's heart lightened. She couldn't wait to get out of this room.

Trey remained standing and folded his arms across his chest. "Hawthorne, don't you think Miss Faraday requires rest after her eventful evening that kept her up most of the night?"

Once again, Trey's double meaning caused heat to rise to Judith's cheeks. Where was her fan when she needed it?

"My Lord," she aimed her comment at Trey. "You need not fret. I feel well rested, thank you, and I would very much enjoy a ride with Lord Hawthorne."

She stood and walked toward Dominic. "If you will give me a

few minutes to change, I will meet you at the stables."

He nodded. "Of course."

She turned back to the dowager and Trey. "Please excuse me."

Isabelle nodded, but Trey's hard expression told Judith he wasn't pleased with her decision at all. She didn't wait for his answer, but turned and strolled out of the room. Besides, she couldn't let him know what was on her mind. She'd yell at him, to be sure. Maybe flirting with Lord Hawthorne would help Trey out just a bit. By the time she reached the end of the hall, her smile was so wide it hurt her cheeks.

Just as she rounded the corner to the stairs, someone called out her name behind her so softly she almost thought she'd imagined it. But hard-heeled shoes pounded on the floor, making her turn to see who came her way.

Trey walked up the hall, not looking as angry as he had a minute ago. She halted near the stairs, holding onto the railing. Her heartbeat quickened. Would she be able to hold her tongue? Or would her temper take over?

He didn't stop until he stood right in front of her, his hand covering hers on the railing. Her breathing accelerated and within moments, his desirable spicy scent surrounded her, making her want to cuddle in his arms.

"Do you want me, my lord?"

Trey's blue eyes darkened, just as they had last night. Her throat turned dry.

Chapter Thirty-One

"YOU KNOW I want you," Trey whispered before clearing his throat and straightening as he pulled his hand away. "Do you think it wise to go riding with Hawthorne today?" he said louder.

Judith shrugged. "I don't foresee a problem. Do you?"

His tongue darted out to swipe across his lips as his gaze dropped to her mouth. "Have you forgotten about last night so soon, my love?"

Her heart leapt. "I don't think that's something I shall ever forget," she whispered. "However, from what I have heard so far today, I believe *you* are the one who has forgotten about last night."

He arched a brow. "Are you jesting? I could not sleep at all because you were on my mind."

She wanted to sigh aloud from his comment. Instead, she lifted her chin, stubbornly. "Well, you definitely have a strange way of showing it."

"What do you mean?"

"If you enjoyed what happened last night so much, then why are you making a list of future husbands for me?"

He growled and ran his fingers through his hair. "You do not understand. It's the way things are done."

"Well, I certainly don't understand, nor do I approve." She

turned to continue up the stairs only stepping on the next higher, but he grabbed her wrist. His blue eyes pleaded with her, and her heart softened, if only slightly.

"If you don't approve, then why do you insist on going riding with Nic?"

"What?" She blinked, shocked of what he said. Did she detect a hint of jealousy? But of course. Trey had already admitted that he was envious of Dominic. "I enjoy riding with him because he's my friend. I love to ride, as well." She smiled and stroked the side of Trey's face. "Tell me the real reason you don't wish me to ride with the marquess." Her heartbeat quickened as she anticipated hearing his confession. He loved her—she knew he did, if only he would say the words.

"I—I—" His Adam's apple jumped. "I don't trust my friend around you, Judith. He's a rogue. Just like me."

She arched her eyebrow. "Just like you? I think not."

He took her hand off his cheek and kissed her palm. "You are correct. He's worse, which is why I cannot in good faith, allow you to continue going riding with him every morning."

"Trey, you should not fret. Lord Hawthorne has not made any improper advances toward me, nor will he ever. He respects you and your mother too much to do so." She squeezed his hand. "So please, have faith in me that nothing is going to happen."

Silence stretched between them, except for the occasional laughter down the hall from Lord Hawthorne and the dowager who were still in the drawing room. Trey's expression relaxed, but his mouth dropped into a frown.

"If you believe you are safe, then I will, as well."

She smiled. "Thank you, Trey."

She leaned in to kiss his cheek, but just before her lips touched the mark, he turned his face and his mouth met hers instead. A gasp of surprise left her throat, but she didn't pull away. The kiss was short, but so very sweet.

When Trey took a step back, he grinned, gave her a wink then walked back to the drawing room.

Excitement bubbled in her chest and she wanted to laugh out loud. True, he didn't confess he loved her, but she was one-step closer to convincing him.

Grinning like a fool, she lifted her gown to her ankles and bounded up, unlady-like, toward her room. Her heart swelled with happiness.

Much later as she rode across the estate with Dominic, thoughts of Trey still filled her mind. Once she and Dominic left the house, she hadn't said much as she tried to piece together her future. Riding had always helped her to think clearly, but so far it wasn't doing the trick.

"Judith, my dear, you have been abnormally quiet today. Are you out of sorts?"

Putting her thoughts away for now, she turned and looked at Dominic. "Please forgive me. I have much on my mind."

"Do you wish to share?"

She almost laughed aloud. Although she wished, she certainly didn't dare. "No."

He chuckled and brought his horse to a stop, so she followed his actions.

"You know, Judith, if I didn't know better, I would say you look quite smitten." He cocked his head. "Did something happen at last night's ball that I don't know about?"

Oh, did it ever. But once again, that was something she couldn't share. "You think I look smitten? Pray, what made you come to that conclusion?"

"The faraway look in your eyes. The soft smile on your lips, and especially the dreamy sighs I have heard repeatedly since we left the house."

Heat rushed to her cheeks, and she couldn't turn away quick enough. She realized when he noticed her blush because his grin widened and eyebrows rose.

"See. You are indeed, smitten."

She shook her head and urged her mare into a trot. "I shall never tell, my lord," she said over her shoulder.

He laughed and caught up to her, taking her reins and bringing her horse to a stop once again. His friendly gaze stayed on hers as he clasped her hand. "I believe I know who the man is."

Holding her breath, she didn't dare make a sound or a movement. He couldn't possibly know. If he did suspect, how could she keep it a secret?

"Do you think I'm blind, my dear? I notice the way you gaze at Trey. I have watched the way you act whenever he's near." He nodded. "You were in love with him before you knew the truth about Mr. Cutler. Am I correct?"

Oh, good heavens. Dominic did know her well. Then again, he was her friend, and friends should notice things like that. Relief swept over her. Finally, someone she could talk to about her feelings. "You are correct. It's Trey."

Dominic pulled back and chuckled. "Have you told him?"

"No. I have no desire to scare him."

"You believe it will?"

She arched a brow. "You are his friend, my lord. I think you know that answer as well as I."

He scratched his chin and nodded. "Correct. Telling him right now is not a good idea. We must wait until he's ready."

"We?" She leaned forward and touched his arm. "Are you saying you wish to assist me?"

"Why of course. I have known for several days that you are the right woman for my friend."

Tears of joy stung her eyes as excitement grew in her chest. "You don't know how pleased I am to hear that. I feared you would chase me away for trying to steal your friend."

"You are not doing that. Worthington and I will always be friends. You are the first woman I have approved of, and I have no desire to see him lose you."

She straightened and wiped away a stray tear. "Thank you. I worried I would not be able to do this alone."

Dominic winked. "My dear, I shall help you more than you anticipate, but you have to agree to work with me on this. I have a plan, and I believe it will work."

"What's your plan, my lord? I'm most eager to hear."

Dominic threw back his head and laughed. Enthusiasm bubbled inside her until she almost couldn't stand it. But she would be patient, because having Trey's love was the only thing that would make her happy and complete.

Chapter Thirty-Two

TREY PACED THE floor of the drawing room while his mother looked through Judith's prospective husbands checklist for the tenth time. She jotted down notes of what she knew about them. He passed the window and stopped to gaze across the meadow, watching for Judith and Hawthorne to return. They'd been gone a good hour.

Surprisingly, Judith looked more refreshed this afternoon when she entered the drawing room than he figured she should. Especially after last night. She didn't have dark circles under her eyes from lack of sleep. Instead, her eyes gleamed with luster when she'd first glanced his way.

Had he been the only one who'd lain in bed, tossing and turning, wondering why they could never be together?

Trey stopped by the window and looked out again. His life was torture, and knowing she was out with his best friend didn't help matters, either. Although Judith tried to assure him she was in good hands, Trey knew the way his friend worked. Hawthorne courted the women he wanted to make his mistress, making them think they had a chance to become the next Lady of the manor. Hawthorne didn't have a heart when it came to women. He used them for the same reasons Trey did.

Yet, somehow, he believed Judith didn't have those feelings for the marquess. Not when she looked at Trey with adoring eyes, and stroked him with a lover's touch like she had by the stairs earlier.

Groaning silently, he rested his forehead on the glass pane. He knew that look. It had been on Judith's face for a few days now. The same look most women gave him when they were infatuated. Judith didn't have a reason to love another man now. Could he have replaced Mr. Cutler in her heart already?

Although the idea caused excitement to stir in his chest, he tried to convince himself he didn't want her to think of him in such high regard. He didn't want her love, and to be sure, he didn't deserve it.

Or did he?

"Trey, dear?"

His mother's shrill voice jerked him out of his thoughts. "Yes, Mother."

"Do you think Lord Hawthorne would like to court Judith? He has been coming around quite often, but he has not made his intentions known."

Inwardly, Trey seethed. "I would not know, Mother."

"Well, I think Lord Hawthorne and Judith suit very well. I think he will make her a perfect husband. Do you not agree?"

He balled his hands into fists and shoved them into his pockets. Taking deep breaths, he tried to calm his ire. Why couldn't his mother see how wrong it would be to pair Judith with Nic?

"Mother," he began through clenched teeth, "I think it has slipped your mind that Lord Hawthorne is a titled rogue. Therefore, pairing him with Judith is out of the question. She does not need a man like that." He took another deep breath. "She requires a man who will stay faithful to her, who will love and cherish her forever."

He turned to look at his mother. Her frown deepened as she sank into the sofa, her shoulders drooping. He closed his eyes and cursed his inability to think before speaking. His mother had also deserved a better husband than the one she married. Unfortunately, there wasn't a thing his mother could have done about her marriage, short of divorcing, anyway.

"Mother, forgive me." He walked to her and touched her shoulders, giving them a gentle squeeze. "I didn't think—"

"No need to apologize, my dear," she said softly. "You are absolutely right. Judith is a very special young woman, and she deserves only the best." She patted his hand and looked up at him. "However, whether you have heard this or not, I have been told reformed rakes make the best husbands."

He grinned. "They do?"

"Mind you, I don't know this first hand, but I have friends who swear this is true."

He bent and kissed her cheek. "Then I'm quite certain Lord Hawthorne will make some lovely creature a wonderful husband. Unfortunately, it will not be our Judith."

She pulled back to look him in the eyes. "And pray, why not?"

He straightened. Once again, irritation flowed through him like water over jagged rocks. He didn't want his best friend touching and kissing the woman Trey could not get out of his mind.

"The subject is closed, Mother. Hawthorne will not be considered." He folded his arms and stalked across the room to the window again. "Dominic is my friend, and as my friend, he better have the decency to remain a gentleman in Judith's presence. I will not ever consider this match, so I expect you to drop the matter."

"Yes, dear."

His mother remained on the sofa as she looked at the list of prospective suitors. He'd like to toss the paper in the fire and never think of it again. The list turned his stomach in the worst way.

Letting out a deep sigh, he rubbed his forehead where a small throb started. How could he go through with this? How could he sit back and watch men court Judith and not stop it? There had to be a way to numb his heart. By allowing her to marry a man who would truly love her, Trey was saving her from a lifetime of heartache if she married him. Yet, convincing his heart it was the right thing was harder than he thought.

From down the hallway, jovial voices rang through the corridor. Trey hurried to the door, anxiously waiting for Judith and Nic to arrive. When Trey noticed their expressions, his gut twisted. Judith sashayed in the drawing room holding on to Nic's arm, both smiling wide as if they shared a delightful secret.

Balling his hands into fists, Trey shoved them behind his back before someone noticed. His mother beamed and motioned for them to come closer.

As they passed Trey, Judith's gaze met his briefly, her eyes twinkling with merriment. In haste, he studied her face, but thankfully, her lips weren't swollen from a lover's kiss as they'd been last night before he had left her room. That relieved him slightly.

"How was your ride, my dear?" his mother asked.

Judith's grin widened. "Absolutely wonderful."

"I must say, the weather has been very accommodating of late," the dowager replied.

Nic bent over Judith's hand and kissed her gloved fingers. "Thank you for such an enjoyable afternoon."

"The pleasure was all mine." Judith winked.

Nic straightened and nodded to Trey and then the dowager. "Now, if you will excuse me, I have business to attend."

Trey gnashed his teeth as his friend walked out the door, but what bothered him most was the dreamy-eyed stare on Judith's face as she watched Hawthorne leave.

"Judith dear, come sit by me," Trey's mother said. "We need to go through these invitations and see which ones to accept."

"Certainly, Your Grace."

The giddy expression on Judith's face was replaced and covered by a mask. The same mask he'd seen her wear whenever she was accommodating his mother. He knew it well since he'd worn it for many years. Pleasing his mother wasn't only necessary for her health, but his as well, especially if he wanted her to stop nagging at him for every little thing.

What was the real purpose of pleasing women? In his mother's circumstance, he did so because making her happy would pacify her curiosity and especially her harping. So, naturally, it was worth sugar-coating the truth just to see her smile.

What about Judith? What ways did he please her outside kissing her? Their conversations lately had been heated, and all he wanted to do was take her in his arms and keep her there. They'd gone on a few rides around the estate together, which he knew pleased her. But what else made her happy? He could tell she enjoyed playing him for a fool. He chuckled to himself. Oddly enough, it pleased him to make her laugh even when he was the target of humiliation.

Truth be told, he liked the way his heart raced whenever she was around. He enjoyed the way he could make her smile. And laugh. On occasions their conversations became heated, and yet little by little, he had come to enjoy talking with her no matter if it left him in a temper—or her.

Never before had he wanted to please a woman by just talking. Yet Judith was so very different. He wanted to do things that made her smile. Knowing firsthand how miserable life was when thinking about departed loved-ones, Trey wanted to make certain his Judith was smiling and laughing. He loved seeing her eyes light up with happiness…then darken with passion.

Was there more to their relationship? What were the things they had in common? True, they both loved roses. They both loved horses. But was there more?

Strange, but he didn't know this answer. Perhaps he should spend a few days getting to know her better. After all, he couldn't let his mother pick the right man for Judith, and how else could Trey pick the right man for her if he didn't know what Judith liked?

His stomach churned and bile rose to his throat. He couldn't even think about choosing her husband, but he was more qualified than his mother was. After all, he knew most of these gentlemen. He'd know if they would love his Judith the way she deserved.

Pain enclosed around his heart and squeezed. Hopefully, this ache in his chest would disappear very soon. He couldn't become emotional at a time like this.

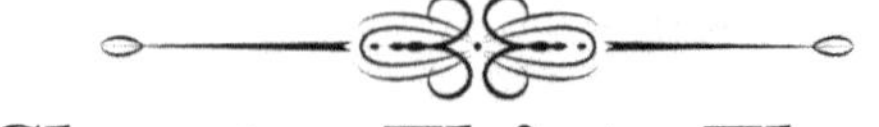

Chapter Thirty-Three

THE RIDE TO Bond Street didn't seem as long as when Judith had journeyed with the dowager the first time. Trey rode with them, which made her trip more enjoyable. With him in the vehicle, they had more topics to discuss. Trey's sense of humor showed quite often, which kept Judith thoroughly entertained. When they arrived at the dress shop, Trey excused himself to attend to business.

Disappointment washed through Judith. No longer would she be able to lose herself in his adorable blue eyes.

Before he walked away, he kissed her knuckles while his gaze held hers. Warmth spread through her body until he withdrew, bowed, and sauntered up the street. If Isabelle hadn't been standing beside her, Judith would have watched Trey until he disappeared. He was such a handsome man—inside and out.

Shaking herself out of dreamy thoughts, she turned and walked into the dress shop beside Isabelle. Her thoughts swam from the conversation she had had with Dominic yesterday. He admitted he knew she had feelings for Trey, and the marquess actually said he'd help her win Trey's heart. What a good friend he was.

For the next three hours, Judith was prodded, poked, and measured. She couldn't help but remember the last time she was here, and especially when she'd carelessly chased after Alex.

She frowned. Why had she been so gullible? And to think she would have waited for that man if the dowager hadn't rescued her by bringing Judith to the estate. Yet, it was Trey who had truly been her rescuer.

Finally, she and the dowager walked out of the dress shop. Right away, they met with other women who strolled along the walk. Isabelle stopped to talk to her friends, and Judith smiled politely, only nodding when the occasion called for some kind of recognition.

A few gentlemen strolled by, some she recognized from her ball. She gave them a nod. One stopped beside her and bowed.

"Good day, Miss Faraday. What a pleasure it is to see you again."

She scrambled to remember his name, but nothing came to mind. She curtsied and smiled politely.

Isabelle Worthington stepped beside him. "Good day, Mr. Pratt. How are you this fine afternoon?"

He bowed. "I'm having a pleasing day, Your Grace. And yourself?"

Isabelle grinned. "I'm taking my ward shopping."

The man's eyes beamed as his smile widened. "How lovely."

The dowager touched Judith's arm. "My dear, you remember Mr. Henry Pratt from your party. He's Viscount Newby's youngest son."

The name didn't ring any bells of familiarity, but she had no other choice but to act like it. "Of course I do."

"Mr. Pratt, I believe we received an invitation from your mother for a dinner social, did we not?"

His cheeks turned a dark red. "I hope so, Your Grace. I would very much enjoy getting to know Miss Faraday a little better. I fear her dance card was so full it was almost impossible to speak with her."

Judith chuckled. "What a whirlwind night that was. I look forward to talking with you during your mother's party."

He bowed again then walked away. When Judith's gaze fell

upon Isabelle and her friends, their wide smiles let her know they were up to no good. It was enough to make Judith scream.

"Mr. Henry Pratt would make a fine husband, Miss Faraday," the lady to her left said. "His father is an educated man and has taught him well."

"Indeed," another woman spoke. "His family holds strong to their religion. I heard Mr. Pratt intends to have his own Parish one day."

Judith kept her smile. She didn't know what to say. *Sorry, he's not like Trey, and I won't take anything less.* Of course not. That would be rude.

Isabelle told her friends goodbye, then turned and walked up the street with Judith by her side. The dowager continued telling her everything she knew about the Viscount's family. A year ago this would have interested Judith. Not now. Yet it seemed the older woman was insistent that Judith allow Mr. Pratt to court her to see if they would suit. She ground her teeth. This wasn't something she wished to do. However, she was still the dowager's ward and so must obey.

An idea jumped into Judith's head and she grinned. If Isabelle wanted Mr. Pratt to court Judith, she would, but she'd do it on her own terms. This particular courtship would not last longer than a day if she had her way.

Judith and the dowager entered a little shop at the end of the street, and after partaking of tea and crumpets, Isabelle moaned and placed her hand on her forehead.

"Oh, dear. I fear I've overdone myself today."

Judith touched the older woman's wrinkled, frail hand. "Do you wish to return home?"

"Trey said he would meet us here. I hope he comes quickly."

Glancing around the room, Judith didn't see him anywhere. "Do you wish me to find him now?"

"No, dear. I'm certain he will be here shortly."

Within seconds, the older woman's face turned white. Judith panicked. She pushed away from the table and ran to fetch someone who worked at the establishment. The man wearing an apron was the first person she grabbed.

"Sir, please help me. My guardian is very ill." She pointed to the direction of her table. "Do you have a back room where she can lie down?"

His eyes widened and he nodded. Judith rushed to the table with him by her side. He helped Isabelle up, and her legs wobbled as they took her to the back room. A small room with a cot was behind the kitchen, and thankfully, the room was warm and comfortable enough for the dowager.

Judith located a blanket and spread it over Isabelle.

"My dear, what are you doing?" the older woman asked with a cracked voice.

"Your Grace, you almost swooned out there."

"I did?"

"Yes, and you will lie right here until Trey comes for us."

The dowager nodded, her eyes drifting closed.

Judith stood inside the room, wringing her hands against her bosom. When was Trey coming? They needed to get Isabelle home, or to a doctor.

Soon, heavy breaths and soft snores came from the other woman. Judith left the room, closing the door behind her, and hurrying out into the dining area. Still, no Trey. She marched to the front door and peeked outside. The walkway was too busy for her to see anyone, so she stepped outside a little farther.

Coaches passed and she studied the crests painted on the doors to see if any belonged to the Worthington family. The wind picked up and teased the curls by her ears. Soon her arms grew cold, but she had to keep looking for him, so she rubbed her hands on her skin to keep herself warm.

Suddenly, the hairs on the back of her neck rose as the distinct feeling of being watched came over her. Fear inched its way up her spine, stilling her heartbeat. Slowly, she glanced around the area, searching for anyone with his or her gaze on her. Many people had looked her way, but they weren't the cause of the fright lodged in her throat. Her head warned her to hurry back inside and wait for Trey. Yet her stubbornness kept her outside in the cooling temperature.

Her name whispered through the wind and she swung around to see who was behind her. Once again, she didn't recognize anyone. So why did she hear her name being called?

The cool air turned chillier, and she rubbed her hands over her arms quicker. But the cold dread in her chest didn't disappear. In fact, it grew.

Looking from one person to the other, she searched every face that passed by, hoping to find the root of her worry. Heavy footsteps came up behind her and a strong hand clasped her shoulder.

Chapter Thirty-Four

JUDITH SQUEALED AND spun around, ready to defend herself with shaky fists. Trey stood before her, so close his spicy scent filled her senses, calming her.

He glanced from her balled hands up to her face before a grin broke out on his face. "My dear, this is a very awkward way to greet me, do you not agree?"

She sighed heavily and relaxed her arms. "Oh, Trey. I was so worried."

Immediately, he grasped her shoulders as his gaze narrowed. "Judith? Where's my mother?"

"She became ill and we took her to one of the back rooms. That is why I'm out here looking for you."

She grabbed his hand and led him through the eating establishment to the back room. When they reached their destination, Trey walked ahead and entered first. He knelt beside the bed and took his mother's frail hand in his strong one.

"Mother? Can you hear me?"

Her eyes fluttered open and she smiled weakly. "Trey. You are finally here."

"What's wrong?" He swiped his hand across her forehead. "You don't feel feverish."

She shivered. "Exactly opposite, I'm afraid. I'm very cold. I think we should return home now."

He shook his head. "Not with you feeling like this. I will take you to my townhouse, instead. It's only a few minutes away."

Isabelle's eyes widened and her gaze flew over Trey's shoulder and landed on Judith. "But…" She looked back at Trey. "We cannot go there. That's a bachelor's residence."

"Mother, I refuse to hear any arguments." He stood, but the older woman kept hold of his hand.

"What about your…mistress," she whispered.

Judith sucked in a quick breath. Trey glanced over his shoulder and looked directly at her. Guilt dulled his eyes before he turned back to his mother.

"We will not talk about such nonsense, Mother. I'm taking you there and that's final."

Judith's heart plummeted to the pit of her stomach, crumbling into a million pieces. He'd practically confessed. She sank against the wall as tears stung her eyes. The room became smaller and suffocating. Anger built inside her also, and that made her strong.

The man wearing the apron who worked here opened the door and walked in. "Is everything all right?" He directed his question to Trey.

Judith took the opportunity to leave since the door was open and Trey was slightly distracted. She pulled away from the wall and hurried out of the room. A tear slipped down her cheek before she realized she was crying. Angrily, she wiped the moisture away. She wasn't going to cry!

Within minutes, Trey walked out of the room with his mother on his arm. The older woman sagged weakly against her son as they made their way to the front door. Judith ran to her side, holding her other arm as she and Trey helped Isabelle outside and to the coach.

Once everyone sat inside the vehicle, Isabelle slumped against Trey and closed her eyes. Judith gasped and reached for the older woman. Trey shook his head and patted his mother's hands as he met Judith's gaze.

"Do not fret, my sweet," he said softly. "She's going to be all right."

Nodding, Judith sat back, clasped her hands in her lap and looked out the window. Hopefully, they'd make it to his townhouse or somewhere soon. She was out of sorts, and she didn't enjoy this confused feeling.

"Judith?"

Her heart beat faster. Now was not the time to talk to Trey. "Yes," she answered without looking at him.

"What happened this afternoon? What wore Mother out?"

She shrugged and focused on her fingers. "I have not a clue. She was fine, I thought, until after we partook of tea and crumpets. Then she felt ill and nearly lost consciousness a couple of times." Judith breathed slower, hoping to calm her anger. "I'm relieved you arrived when you did. I didn't know what to do."

Silence lasted only a few minutes before Trey cleared his throat. "Judith, look at me."

Taking a deep breath for courage, she lifted her gaze. His frown tugged at her heart, and she scolded herself for caring.

"I know why you are upset." His voice was low, probably for his mother's sake. "Mother was mistaken. I don't have a mistress."

Confusion filled her head even more, especially when her heart leapt with excitement. Why was she so willing to believe? Was it because all rogues had mistresses? Or was it because she'd once trusted Alex and was greatly deceived?

She pulled her shoulders back and lifted her chin. "How very decent of you, my lord. I'm quite certain your confession will ease your mother's worries."

The corner of his mouth lifted. "And what of yours?"

She shrugged. "I don't have them any longer."

"You are not a very good liar, Judith."

She arched an eyebrow. "Neither are you."

"Are you saying you don't believe me?"

"I'm saying I will believe whatever I may, but I cannot take anyone's word any longer. I have been burned by doing that, or have you forgotten?"

He shook his head. "I have not. But why don't you believe me?"

Oh, how she wanted to, so much her chest ached. "If you please, I would rather not talk about this now." She turned her gaze to the window again.

The clip-clop of the horses' hooves and the rattle of the coach filled the silence. Just as the vehicle came to a stop, Trey touched Judith's knee, and she looked at him.

"We will finish this conversation today. I assure you."

She gulped. Was that something she wanted? Although she desperately needed to hear the truth, she knew how Trey's charming conversations progressed with her ending in his arms while he kissed her passionately. And heaven help her if she wasn't looking forward to it.

TREY SPLASHED WATER on his face, hoping to relieve the tension of the trying day he'd had. The physician had checked his mother, telling Trey she just needed rest and would be back to herself in a few days. Now that one worry was out of the way, he needed to reassure Judith he had not kept a mistress since before she came to stay with his mother.

Before leaving his bedroom to find Judith, he removed his cravat and waistcoat, feeling more relaxed without them. A grin tugged at his mouth when he remembered the time he talked to Judith wearing a towel. Now that had been very enjoyable.

He hurried downstairs to the drawing room, hoping that's where Judith waited for him. When he entered, he immediately noticed her sitting behind the harpsichord, lightly stroking the keys as if she wanted to play.

He stopped inside the room, softly closing the door so she

wouldn't hear. Leaning against the barrier, he folded his arms and grinned. "Please play something for me."

She jumped and spun around, her eyes wide and mouth agape. "What?"

He motioned to the instrument. "Play for me, and don't tell me you don't know how. I'm quite certain this is another thing your parents taught you while you were young."

"Although I do know how to play, my heart is not in it tonight. Forgive me."

She moved away from the instrument and walked past him to the sofa. Her flowery scent moved with her, reminding him how much he loved that smell.

Trey walked around the couch and sat next to her. He turned and brought his arm across the back of the furniture, facing her. Still, she hesitated in meeting his eyes. His heart clenched. How could he prove to her he didn't have a mistress?

He exhaled deeply. "Now, about that misunderstanding."

She arched her eyebrow. "What misunderstanding?"

"About my mistress."

Judith's shoulders squared and she lifted her chin a notch. A trait he had always admired in Judith—her stubbornness.

"My lord, I thought you told me you didn't have one."

"I don't. Not now."

"But you did at one time?"

He nodded. "I'm not going to lie to you." He moved his hand and caressed the lock of hair near her ear. "I had a mistress, but our relationship ended about a week before I received my mother's letter informing me about her new ward."

The tightness around Judith's lips softened, as did the gleam in her emerald eyes. She was enchanting. Irresistible. And to think he had to resist her.

"Truly?" Her voice was soft.

"Yes. If you want me to prove it to you, I can. I will have my secretary tell you the very day I sent the missive to dissolve our relationship."

Her whole body relaxed and she shook her head. "That will not be necessary. I believe you."

He scooted closer and placed his hand over hers resting in her lap. Using his other hand, he slid it across her shoulders to pull her closer. Thankfully, she didn't resist.

"Now, I want to know why you care if I have a mistress or not?"

Her tongue slipped out and moistened her lips as the blush in her cheeks darkened. "Well, you see—" Her throat jumped as if she swallowed hard. "I have come to have deep feelings for you, Trey."

He stroked her cheek. "As a friend?"

Her chuckle sounded uneasy. "Well, of course. We are friends, are we not?"

"I certainly hope so." He drew his thumb along her jaw line, heading toward her sensual mouth. "However, due to what happened the night of your ball, I feel we have become more than friends."

Her skin turned hot under his touch. He wanted to laugh, but refrained.

"Yes," she whispered. "I feel we have become more than mere friends."

Excitement drummed inside his chest and he cursed the effect she had on him. Although he wanted to hear the words from her mouth, he knew nothing could come of it. Perhaps this was the time he needed to tell her so she didn't fall completely in love with him.

He couldn't bring the words forth. They wouldn't form on his tongue. Instead, the need to kiss her, hold and touch her overrode everything.

Chapter Thirty-Five

S HE TOOK HIS hand from her jaw and brought it to her mouth, placing a sweet kiss on his palm. "Trey, I want to be more than just your friend."

Groaning, he cupped her face and brought his mouth to hers. He kissed her gently at first, then raw hunger took over and he wrapped his arms around her and crushed her against his body. Her deep sighs thrilled him, and he wanted nothing more than to bring back the passion they'd shared in her bedroom not long ago. Her hands slid over his chest, wandering. His muscles clenched wherever she touched.

"Oh, my love. You know how much I want you," he muttered.

"Trey," she sighed. She cupped his face and brought his attention to her eyes. "Trey, I have no desire to be your next mistress."

Pain exploded in his chest, suffocating him. Her confession wasn't a surprise. He'd suspected she was in love with him.

"I know you don't."

"Then why…" She took a deep breath. "Why are you still trying to find me a husband?"

Cursing under his breath, he pulled away and leaned his head back against the sofa, closing his eyes. This wasn't what he'd wanted to discuss. Yet, he needed to bring his past out in the open no matter how hard it was.

"Oh, Judith. You don't understand."

"Help me understand," she pleaded, grasping his hand.

After inhaling deeply for a couple of minutes, he finally opened his eyes and looked at her. She wore her heart on her sleeves, because the love illuminating from her eyes nearly shredded his heart to pieces. Why did love have to hurt so much? This was exactly what his father had warned him about falling in love.

"I'm incapable of love, my sweet Judith." There. He finally confessed. So why didn't it make the pain in his chest disappear?

"How do you know?"

Her question made him want to laugh. She was so innocent. "Believe me, Judith, I do know. I have the same blood as my father. I'm following in his footsteps. But I will do one thing he never did."

"What is that?"

"I will not break a woman's heart and ruin her life by marrying. My mother had a miserable marriage. Were you aware of that?"

She nodded as her eyes moistened with tears. "Lord Hawthorne told me about it the other day."

"I grew up watching the way my father treated my mother. I could never do that to my wife. So in order to keep that from happening, I will not marry. Ever."

She leaned toward him and stroked his face. "Your father didn't love your mother. That's why he was able to treat her so unkindly."

"I know."

"So are you saying you will never fall in love?"

He wanted to take her in his arms and let her show him all about falling in love. But he didn't dare. He knew too many men that had given their heart to a woman only to have it ripped out of their chests later. His brother, Tristan, was a prime example that men shouldn't give away their souls like trinkets.

He took her hands from his face and kissed her fingertips. "I cannot…I will not allow myself to fall in love."

She pulled away. Tears brimmed in her eyes. Emotion clogged his throat and he wanted to weep. What a fool he was for letting himself become this attached to his mother's ward.

"Trey, I don't believe that. Deep inside of you there's a loving heart. I have seen it." She placed her fist on her bosom. "I have felt it."

"You are the one with the loving heart." He kissed her lips, gently, then pulled back. "This is why you will remain innocent until my mother and I find the right man to marry you."

Anger creased her forehead and the lines around her mouth. Tears slid down her cheeks as she shook her head. Letting out a groan, she turned and marched out of the room.

His heart crumbled. He hadn't wanted to hurt her. The truth needed to come out. Maybe now she wouldn't tempt him and the feelings between them could end.

"JUDITH, YOU DON'T need me there," Isabelle said and adjusted the blankets over her legs. "Trey is capable of escorting you to Lady Newby's dinner party."

Judith frowned, mainly for the dowager's sake. It wasn't a good idea to have Isabelle know of the plans swimming in Judith's head for tonight's party. For certain, the older woman would have heart palpitations.

"I'll miss you," Judith said, trying not to grin. "Will you be all right without us here to take care of you?"

The dowager chuckled and flipped her hand through the air. "Now that I'm home and in my own bed, I will be just fine, I assure you."

"Then if you will excuse me, I need to hurry to my room and get ready for tonight."

"Have a pleasant time, my dear. I will enjoy myself by reading a book." She patted the hardbound lying next to her on the bed.

As Judith exited the room, her smile grew. From what she'd heard about Mr. Pratt from Isabelle's friends, the man's family was in hopes of him becoming a man of God and having his own Parish. That told her Mr. Pratt was very conservative. He wouldn't want a wife who thrived on wearing the most expensive gowns, not to mention the most gaudy.

Taking her time with her toilette, Judith made certain her appearance tonight would tease Trey in more ways than one. She would flirt outrageously, which was definitely something Henry Pratt wouldn't want in a future wife, and she hoped Trey's jealous streak would make itself known.

Trey would love the gown she chose for tonight's entertainment since it showed more of her womanly attributes than her others. The dressmaker, Mrs. André, assured the dowager this was the latest fashion in France. Instead of a square neck, the bodice dipped dangerously low between the breasts, displaying an ample amount of bosom. The white mull was encased in silver tinsel embroidery. An elegant gown even a princess would wear. Judith's maid styled her hair the way she did at her coming out ball. Ringlets fell around her head loosely, but the back was curled into a relaxed bun.

From down the hallway, the grandfather clock bonged nine times. Judith grinned. Time to go. Before leaving her room, she wrapped her long cloak around her, not showing a hint of what lay beneath. The unveiling would come later.

She was put out with Trey last night, only because she wanted his love desperately. She realized he wasn't ready to admit he loved her, so she must have more patience. Dominic had mentioned making Trey jealous would do the trick. She would start the marquess' plan tonight.

Trey met her at the front door. He looked regal in his deep green over-jacket, waistcoat and black breeches. His cravat was perfectly knotted against his throat, and Judith realized she preferred his neck bare so she could touch his skin.

He helped her outside to the coach, took her hand and assisted her inside. Once he was sitting across from her, he rapped on the wall to inform the driver to start their journey to Viscount Newby's estate. Even in the semi-darkened vehicle, Trey's warm gaze rested on her as a smile touched his sculptured mouth.

Trey cleared his throat. "Mother tells me Mr. Pratt is interested in courting you."

"That's what I hear," she said softly.

"Has Mother told you about him?" Trey asked.

"Yes, she has, along with a few of her friends. While on Bond Street yesterday, we came across him in front of a shop. Your mother's friends were playing matchmaker, but not very subtly. They told me how he will have his own Parish someday."

Trey nodded. "Henry Pratt will make God proud, to be sure. He comes from a respectable family. Any lady would consider herself fortunate to be his wife."

"Even me?" She cocked her head, keeping her stare on him.

He shrugged. "I don't see why not. You, my dear Judith, will please most men, I'm quite certain."

"Except you, correct?"

His smile disappeared and he folded his arms, moving his stare to outside the window. "Judith, I would rather not discuss this again. You know my feelings."

"Indeed, I do, just as you know mine."

The remainder of the ride was filled with silence, except for the clip-clop of the horses' hooves and the wheels crunching on the graveled roads. Occasionally, Trey cleared his throat or shifted in his seat, but he didn't say another word.

When the coach stopped and their footman opened the door, Trey climbed down first, turned and reached his hand out to assist her. Gently, she slid her fingers against his palm. She held his gaze until she stood beside him. Her heart wrenched with frustration. Would he ever love her and give her a chance to make him happy? Or would his past secrets keep him from the one woman who could love him forever?

He tucked her hand around his elbow as he escorted her inside. The butler stood ready to take their wraps. Trey handed his garment to the older servant, before turning to assist Judith once again.

Holding back her grin, she tightened her mouth as Trey removed her cloak. He must have not noticed her gown at first because he handed her cloak to the butler without acting as if he was stunned by her appearance. But once he turned to her and held out his elbow for her to take, his gaze moved over her in a leisurely sweep. His eyes widened and his mouth hung open.

This was exactly the response she wanted.

Judith held herself from grinning too wide. Victory filled her, and she hoped it would remain throughout the evening.

Trey hitched his breath. "What the devil are you wearing?" he muttered before his gaze bounced up and met her eyes. "Why are you dressed like that?"

It was a good thing he kept his voice lowered for their ears only.

She gave him a shrug of innocence. "What do you mean, my lord?"

His eyes narrowed. "Do not play coy with me, my dear. You know what I mean." Once again, his gaze moved over her body. "Why are you wearing that gown? It's so…so…"

"Provocative? Seductive?"

"Yes."

She grinned and lifted her chin. "I want to look my best, Trey darling. How else am I going to land a husband?"

Leaving him behind, she walked ahead and into the room filled with dinner guests. Immediately, she spotted Mr. Pratt, so she sashayed toward him. It was hard not to notice the gasps and stares from the others as she passed. Her appearance shocked the older women in the group, and made most of the men stare with open mouths, pretty much the way Trey had when he first noticed her.

When Henry Pratt finally looked her way, his eyes widened and his face flamed a brilliant red. Judith stopped right in front of him and curtsied low. When she finally stood straight and met his eyes, they were diverted elsewhere as he stiffened his body.

"Good evening, my lord."

He nodded and glanced very briefly at her. "Miss Faraday."

"I must pass on the dowager duchess' apologies for not coming tonight. Yesterday afternoon she became quite ill and she has not fully recovered."

Although she watched his every move, he tried not to look her way at all, and when he did, his gaze dropped to her bosom.

"Oh, I understand." He quickly looked away again. "I pray she has a speedy recovery."

From the corner of the room, an older woman with silver hair rushed to Henry Pratt's side. Judith didn't need to be told this was the over-protective mother. But before Judith could say anything, someone's warm hand brushed against her arm. She knew who it was. Her body had become familiar with Trey's touch by now.

"Mr. Pratt. Lady Newby." Trey bowed. "It's a pleasure to see you again."

When the older woman looked upon Trey, her smile reached her eyes, making them sparkle. But when the viscountess moved her attention to Judith, loathing darkened the depths of her brown eyes.

"Lady Newby," Trey began, "I don't think I have introduced you to my mother's ward, Miss Judith Faraday."

"No," the older woman snipped. "You have not."

Judith curtsied, as was customary, but didn't dip as low this time. Obviously impressing Henry's mother wasn't necessary. "It's a privilege to meet you, Lady Newby."

"Likewise, I'm sure." The lady's face remained solemn.

"Lady Newby, Mr. Pratt, if you will excuse us, I must have a word with my mother's ward."

"Very well." The viscountess lifted her chin, her gaze still shooting daggers at Judith.

Wrapping his hand around her elbow, he urged Judith to follow, which she did. They passed other couples she recognized, and she smiled and nodded in greeting. Trey didn't appear put out, but the tight grip he had on her elbow proved otherwise. He pulled her to the corner of the room and stopped, facing her and blocking her from the other guests. She didn't mind. She'd rather have his attention than anyone else's.

"I'm certain you know you have insulted the hostess tonight." His voice was low.

She nodded. "A blind man would have been able to see the heated sparks of anger coming from the viscountess' eyes."

"And yet you continue to smile?" He arched a brow. "Pray, Miss Faraday, does this not worry you?"

"Not at all, my lord. Everyone has a right to their own opinion."

He blew out a deep breath and pinched the bridge of his nose. "Yet now I'm the one who has to repair the damage."

"Damage?" She studied his worried expression. "What damage?"

His gaze moved across her bodice again, this time, his eyes darkened with desire. Her heartbeat quickened, and her palms grew moist. She wished they were alone. Because they weren't, she anticipated his next move. Would he indeed do something scandalous?

"You are not dressed properly, my sweet," he muttered. "You were told how this family lives, and so you should have dressed accordingly." He finally lifted his eyes to hers. "Your gown is most daring."

"I know." She smiled. "I was in the mood to wear it tonight."

"Why? Because my mother is not here?"

She chuckled. "Perhaps."

He shook his head. "I don't know how to repair this."

"Should we leave?"

"Not yet. That will make it worse. We must remain a little

while longer, but then not overstay our welcome. I also want you by my side. I saw the look of lust on some of the men here, and I don't feel like making any threats tonight or calling anyone out. Is that understood?"

Warmth spread through her and she wanted to sigh aloud. "Ah, Trey," she whispered. "Always my rescuer."

He growled. "And stop looking at me that way."

"What way is that?"

"That you are enamored with me. You don't want tongues wagging, do you?"

Her grin widened. "I shall never tell, my lord." She pushed passed him and proceeded to visit with the other guests, ignoring his instructions. He couldn't call any man out tonight, but she would definitely start gossipmongers in action.

As the night wore on, she accomplished her goal. The more Trey's forehead creased and his eyebrows drew together, the more she flirted. Dinner went well. She was seated by Henry Pratt, which she gathered was done before they knew what gown she wore, but Judith made the best of an awkward situation.

While chatting, laughing, and batting her eyes at Mr. Pratt, Trey sat down across the table from her and glared at her the entire time. She'd hear plenty when they returned home, and she couldn't wait for their heated debate.

Chapter Thirty-Six

TREY'S HANDS ACHED from bunching them into fists, not to mention how his jaw hurt from grinding his teeth. When the proper time came, Trey made excuses to both Henry and the viscountess, which they accepted happily.

The little actress he couldn't keep ogling tonight walked beside him to the coach and he helped her inside without shaking some sense into her. No, he'd do that in private. It wasn't good to have a scandal with his mother's health declining.

Once the vehicle started on its way, Trey sat back and folded his arms while he stared at Judith. Her attention was on her fingers as they rested entwined on her lap. A grin touched her beautiful face, and he wanted to scold her about her behavior tonight. Then after he was done, he wanted to hold and kiss her.

For sure, he'd become one confused man since she had entered his life.

He adjusted himself on the seat. "So, Miss Faraday, do you have anything to say for yourself?"

Her gaze bounced up and met his, her smile growing wider. "No."

Inwardly, he growled. "Was your performance on purpose? You know what kind of man Henry Pratt was, and yet you still insisted on wearing a provocative gown."

"Yes."

He rolled his eyes. "Would you answer both parts of my question?"

She tapped her finger on her chin. "There were two parts? The first half was clearly a question, but the second sounded more like an observation. It was your opinion, so why should I be expected to answer that?"

Taking a deep, calming breath, he rubbed his forehead. "Judith, you are being very obstinate, you know."

"Yes, I do."

"So tell me why. Knowing about Henry Pratt, why did you still wear that gown?"

Her eyes drooped half-mast as she plucked the tie of her cape, opening it to reveal the lovely gown again. She shrugged the garment off her shoulders.

"Do you not like it, my lord?" Her voice was lower than before. "I wore it because I thought you might approve."

Desire leapt inside him again, and he balled his hands into fists, keeping himself from reaching for her and taking her in his arms. "My opinion is not in question here. The way you acted tonight made me wonder if you were purposely trying to cause a scandal."

The corner of her mouth lifted. "Indeed?"

He leaned forward, grasping his knees. "I think I know what you are trying to do, and it will not work."

"And what is that, my lord?"

"You are trying to trap me into marriage. I recall telling you before that women have tried many times, but they have not succeeded. I will not play these games, Judith."

Sighing heavily, she relaxed against the seat. "Honestly, Trey. Do you really believe I wanted to court Henry Pratt? Do you really think we suit? You know me well, so tell me honestly. Would I have been happy married to him?"

He studied her solemn expression, and the way she gazed deeply into his eyes. Why did she have to ask that question? Why did she fight him so? Yet it was in her nature to go against his opinion. She enjoyed debating issues with him. And God help him, he loved it. That was one of the things he admired most about her, her willingness to use her brain instead of her body.

He chuckled. "No."

"You didn't answer all parts of my question." She arched a brow.

He grinned wider. "No, no, and no. There. Is that better?"

She kept silent for a few moments as her gaze wandered over him. With each second that passed, her smile softened.

"No, that's not better," she said, then lifted off her seat and moved to his, sitting right beside him. "Now this is much better."

He groaned and closed his eyes, resting his head back against the wall of the coach. It was dangerous for both of them to be this close. He couldn't fight her. He didn't want to. But he must.

"Trey," she whispered as she stroked his chin, turning it to look her way. "I wore this gown for you and only you."

"What am I going to do with you?" Opening his eyes, he shook his head.

Her smile widened as she cuddled beside him. "Do you really want me to answer that?"

"No." He cupped her face. "I already know your answer."

"Tell me why you continue to find me a potential husband when you know I will fight you every step of the way?"

"You are a stubborn woman, Miss Faraday." He ran the pad of his thumb along her bottom lip. "You are also refusing to see the truth of the matter."

She leaned into him, her mouth hovering below his. "Trey, I know you want me. Why can you not see I want you just as much?"

Groaning, he brushed his lips against hers. His heart hammered against his chest, threatening to break his ribs. Did he care? Not at this particular moment.

Judith cupped his face as she met his soft kisses, but the more she pressed against him, the more hunger invaded his senses, and being gentle drifted further and further out of his mind. With a loud moan, he wrapped her in his arms and crushed her against him as he deepened the kiss.

She pulled away, looking into his eyes. Emotion etched itself all over her expression, and although she didn't say the words, he knew she was in love with him. His heart leapt, yet his mind tried to crush it. He couldn't have her saying those words to him. He didn't know how he'd react.

As she opened her mouth to speak, he shook his head, not wanting her to say the words for fear he'd break her heart when he didn't repeat them back.

"Trey, I—"

"Shh…" He said, then kissed her lips again. "Don't say it."

"Why?"

"Because I don't wish to hurt you anymore."

"Then don't."

"Can't you see? I have no other choice. It's the kind of man I am."

Scowling, she pulled away from him and crossed her arms over her chest. "I refuse to believe that rubbish."

With a deep sigh, he relaxed and pushed his fingers through his hair. "Oh, Judith. Why can't you believe me?"

"Obviously, I know you better than you think I do. The man I know is kind, understanding, and forgiving."

"Then I have put on an excellent performance."

"No, I don't believe it. Trey, you act yourself when you are around me. You can never hurt me."

"Never say never. Neither of us knows the future. How can you say I will not hurt you? I'm too much like my father. Someday I will be unfaithful. I go through women quickly. I get restless easily, so I move on."

She tilted her head, frowning. "Have you ever been in love with any of these women?"

"Of course not. Don't be ridiculous."

"Have you ever considered this is the reason you move on to your next conquest so quickly?"

He shrugged. "Perhaps. But I refuse to let any woman have my heart." Maybe if he said it enough times, he'd believe it. The burning sensation in his chest whispered she might be correct in her guess.

"Why, Trey?" She stroked his face, then his neck. "Love is not something to run from. It's what makes two people complete."

The ache in his chest continued to expand to where it was impossible to breathe. Confusion swam in his head and looking into Judith's understanding eyes was making it worse. She didn't know what he knew about love, and he hesitated to tell her. Yet he must. There was no other way she'd know what pain stayed in his heart from the past.

He shook his head and pulled away from her tender touch. "No, Judith. You cannot understand what agony I have suffered. I know very well what love is capable of doing to people."

"How, when you have admitted you have never been in love?"

"I have seen what it's done to those around me."

"Do you mean your parents?"

"Yes, them. And others."

"But Trey, were your parents truly in love?"

He frowned. "No."

"Then—"

"But Tristan was."

Her eyes widened and a gasp escaped her throat. "Tristan? All of this is about your brother?"

"Yes."

"Why?"

Sighing, he rubbed his eyes. He couldn't talk about it. The only person he opened up with was Hawthorne. Even Trey's mother didn't know the truth. He couldn't open up the grave of guilt eating at his heart.

A soft hand touched his and removed it from his face. Caring eyes stared back at him as she lowered his hand to her lap, still clutching it.

"Please tell me."

Her heart-felt plea knocked down one of the walls of ice protecting him. Agony squeezed his chest. He'd tell her. Maybe then her ridiculous idea of wanting him for her husband would disappear. Once she knew the truth, she'd certainly find another man to please.

Chapter Thirty-Seven

T O JUDITH'S DISAPPOINTMENT, the coach stopped before Trey could speak another word. She pulled the cloak together and readied herself. Once the footman opened the door, Trey climbed out first then assisted her.

She held his stare as she stepped onto the ground, and although he let go of her hand, she wouldn't let him get away. Quickly, she slipped her hand around his elbow and followed him inside the house.

The halls were quiet and dimly lit. Had the servants retired for the evening? She sincerely hoped so. She wanted more time alone with Trey, especially since he acted as if he had something very important to tell her. It must be imperative if it was keeping him from loving her.

He stopped just before they reached the stairs, and turned to face her. "Would you like to change into something more comfortable?"

"What I would like is to sit somewhere with you so you can finish telling me about Tristan."

When he smiled, it didn't touch his eyes. Sadness still lingered in their depths.

"I have no desire to talk here and have servants overhear, or heaven forbid my mother interrupt us."

"How about a walk outside?"

Nodding, he took her by the hand and led them outside into the moonlight. Only a few lanterns lit the side of the house, and the farther away they walked, the more shadows thickened around them. Soon, their only light became the moon.

He kept her hand in his while his other hand stroked her arm. She didn't say anything, hoping he would speak first. When his steps slowed, she grew hopeful.

Stopping, he looked up into the night sky. She admired the shape of his handsome face and stubborn jaw, then shifted her eyes to his irresistible neck that made her want to nibble to her complete satisfaction.

After taking a deep breath, he looked at her. "What do you remember about Tristan?"

Memories flooded her mind, and she couldn't stop the smile stretching her mouth. "He was an enjoyable person. He laughed a lot. He also teased, although it was not anything like your teasing."

He chuckled.

"And I remember he made friends easily," she added. "He was the person to talk with because he would listen and understand."

Trey nodded. "He was a man with a huge heart, and his caring heart was the very thing that killed him in the end."

She shook her head as confusion filled her. "I don't understand."

He turned and led them toward a stone bench. They sat together, but shadows from the nearby tree made it hard to see his face.

"Two years ago," Trey began, "Tristan fell in love. He fell hard. She was the daughter of a baron, and her father wanted to find the best match for her. Tristan would do anything for that woman. He wanted to marry her, but her parents would not allow the match because Tristan was the second son, and other lords—with higher titles—were vying for her attention, too. Lady Diana led my brother to believe he had a chance, making him hope her parents would eventually give in and allow her to marry him. One night, he went to her house to talk her into eloping with him, but instead he found her in the stables with another man."

Judith gasped and covered her mouth. "Were they…you know…"

Trey shrugged. "Tristan would not tell me, but he hinted that Lady Diana was there against her will. So upset at Lord Hollingsworth, Tristan challenged him to a duel." Trey shook his head. "Now that I think back on it, I realize Lady Diana didn't do anything to stop it. If she had pleaded with my brother, he would not have gone through with it. Makes me wonder if she indeed wanted him to duel the other man."

He sighed heavily. "Anyway, Tristan asked me to be his second and I agreed. My brother was an excellent swordsman, but the man he had challenged was deceitful. Deep in my heart, I knew I had to be there to protect my brother."

Her heart ached hearing Trey's agony. The pain he had suffered was evident in the lines on his face and his tight frown. She wanted to caress him, to kiss him and make him feel better, but instead, she let him talk.

Leaning his elbows on his knees, he rested his forehead in his hands. "I was right. Lord Hollingsworth could not be trusted. As Tristan and I stood on the field waiting for the others to arrive, Tristan was shot. Hollingsworth hid in the trees and shot my brother."

"Oh, Trey. No!" She stroked his stiff shoulder.

"Tristan didn't die immediately. I wrestled Hollingsworth to the ground, ready to kill the man myself. Tristan fought with Hollingsworth's second, but due to his weakened state, the other man was stronger. Before I knew it, they were near the edge of the cliff. I broke away from Hollingsworth and ran to assist my brother, but—"

His voice choked, which made emotion clog her throat. Tears stung her eyes, but she continued to caress Trey's shoulder.

"He fell over the cliff before I could stop it from happening. I was almost there, but I was not fast enough." His voice broke and he covered his face with his hands. "My brother died because I could not save him."

Tears streamed down her face and she wrapped her arms around Trey, trying to turn him toward her body. He resisted at first, but he soon let her comfort him. She hushed him and stroked his hair, placing kisses on his forehead. Her heart broke for his sorrow, and helplessness settled around her.

"Trey, you cannot blame yourself."

He shook his head, still covering his face. "You don't understand. I should have stopped him from dueling." He pulled away enough to look at her. "But I encouraged my brother to fight Hollingsworth for touching the woman Tristan loved. I wanted to believe in love back then. I wanted to believe Lady Diana and Tristan's love would overcome all. Because I believed in such nonsense, my brother was killed."

"No, Trey. Don't say that. You cannot think this way. Tristan made his own decisions. He could have refused to duel, but he didn't."

Trey pushed away from her, stood, and ran his fingers through his hair. "For several days I searched for his body in the water. I could not find him." He pounded his fist against the nearest tree. "It was then when I realized he had died for love. The same artificial love my parents were married for, yet my father continued to insult my mother and cheat on her. The same faux love that tore my mother apart and made her cry when my father stayed out late, preferring his mistresses over her."

"Trey, no—"

"Which is the very reason I quit believing in it. I refuse to give my heart to any woman and suffer the agony." He spun around and faced her. "Judith, please don't force the issue. You know my mind now. This emotion called love is not worth the pain."

More tears streamed down her face, but she wondered if he could even see them in the darkness. He'd hardened his heart, and she didn't know how to break through. Her chest ached with agony, and helplessness flooded through her.

"You know the worst part?"

She shook her head.

"Lady Diana married Lord Hollingsworth two weeks later. Apparently, she had been betrothed to him for months, yet she still led Tristan to believe she loved him."

"I'm…sorry."

He held out his hand. "Come. It's late and I need to return you to your room."

Nodding, she stood and slipped her hand into his. As they walked back to the house in silence, her mind whirled with all the information, trying to find the right words to say. Sadly, there was nothing she could come up with.

Perhaps there was no way to break through his hardened heart. Maybe they were not meant to be together. The tightness in her chest kept her from sobbing aloud, but she was on the verge. He probably wouldn't care anyway.

When they reached the hallway, she pushed away from him and ran to her bedroom, knowing he wouldn't follow this time.

"MY DEAR, MISS Faraday. Your beauty has outshone the sun today."

Judith forced a smile, hoping she didn't appear like she wanted to roll her eyes and gag with distaste. The insipid fop who had called on her today was terrible with his words.

"You are much too kind, Lord James. I fear I don't deserve such a compliment." And truly, she didn't. She'd heard Lord James was after a woman who he could put on display—the kind he'd be proud to have on his arm as they walked through the park. A woman to make other men jealous. He would have definitely approved of the gown she wore for Henry Pratt's dinner social. But instead, she chose to wear drab brown, and pull her hair back so tight in a bun that her eyes nearly popped out of her head. She even draped a shawl over her shoulders, to keep any hint of skin from showing.

"Oh, but you are the um—" His gaze swept over her as panic laced his eyes and tightened his lips. "You are extremely lovely." He pulled his shoulders back and grinned. "Would you care for a walk outside today?"

"Are you insane?" She laid on the theatrics and gasped, placing a hand on her chest. "The wind is blowing. It's much too chilly to walk outside. I might catch my death out there."

"Nonsense. The weather is perfect."

Judith bundled her shawl tighter. "Not for me. I fear I get cold easily. Perhaps another time…or another season."

"But—it will not get warmer than this since it's mid-summer."

Thankfully, Lord James left not long after that. She really shouldn't have pushed him away, but she didn't have any interest in him. Or any man.

Save for one.

The two weeks since Trey had confessed his feelings to her had passed in a blur. Every day Judith had a different suitor, and every day the men left with their shoulders sagging, pretty much like Lord James had done. None could make her heart pitter-patter.

Not like Trey had been able to accomplish.

Dominic has been out of town, and she missed their morning rides. She also missed talking to him. He'd be the only one to understand. Apparently, his plan to make Trey jealous enough to admit his love hadn't worked. Now her hopes were crushed and she lingered in a foggy world without any dreams for her future.

Although Trey still resided in the dowager's house, he was rarely around during the day. It hurt to think he didn't want to see her, but she understood. She knew he was falling in love with her, and since this was something he didn't want, it would be easier not to see each other constantly.

Did Isabelle know what was happening between Judith and Trey? At quiet times, Judith caught the older woman looking at her with a pained expression. Whenever Judith asked if something was wrong, the dowager smiled and shook her head. If only Judith could tell her guardian what was going on, but she didn't dare. The dowager was unable to do anything about it, anyway.

Isabelle had been busy lately planning her own birthday ball. Judith offered to help, but the older woman refused. Although Judith wasn't in any kind of mood to celebrate, at least it would keep her mind busy and her thoughts off of Trey. But Isabelle took over and didn't allow Judith to do anything.

Sighing heavily, Judith rested the sewing sampler in her lap and looked out the window. Perhaps she should stop trying to thwart the dowager's plans of finding her a husband and let her guardian pick a man. Now Judith's life seemed dull and pointless. If she allowed herself to get to know some of these men, maybe she'd fall in love again. It would definitely take a stalwart man to make Trey disappear from her heart.

Boot steps echoed on the floor out in the hallway, and she swung her gaze toward the door. It wouldn't be Trey. He usually didn't return home until late, but her heartbeat still picked up rhythm in anticipation of seeing him.

Chapter Thirty-Eight

INSTEAD, DOMINIC WALKED into the room. Disappointment washed over Judith, yet she was pleased to see her dear friend, nonetheless.

Instead of wearing his riding clothes, he looked as if he'd just come from a social gathering of the aristocrats. His long tailed velvet blue over-jacket matched well with the topaz stitches on his satin vest. Deep velvet trousers complimented his attire.

"The dowager told me you were in here. I hope you don't mind a visitor."

She set her sampler aside and stood, reaching her hands out to his. "I would love a visitor, especially you."

He chuckled and walked toward her. When he grasped her hands, he pulled her close for an embrace. Surprised, she sucked in a quick breath, but the warmth from his body blended into hers and comforted her. He'd never been this close to her, yet right now was when she needed him the most.

Burying her face against his chest, tears filled her eyes and emotion clogged her throat. Oh, she needed this comfort. Needed it badly.

Dominic withdrew and looked down at her with wide eyes. "What's this? Tears? Did you miss me that much?"

She laughed softly. "I have missed you, but only because I have needed a friend."

He ran the pad of his thumb across her cheek, catching a tear. "Shall we sit? I fear this might take a while."

"It will." She smiled and took his hand, pulling him to the couch. Once they were both sitting side by side, she took a deep breath. "Much has happened during your absence."

His gaze wandered over her as confusion creased his forehead. "I had gathered as much. You look as if you are already married to Mr. Pratt." He shook his head. "Those colors on you practically make you look ill."

She nodded. "I have been discouraging suitors, and this is the way to accomplish it. I tried to do as you had suggested a while ago by trying to make Trey jealous. Instead, I made him upset. He knows I'm in love with him."

"You told him?"

"I didn't say the words, but I didn't have to. He knows."

"And?"

"As you probably expected, he tried to dissuade me. On the ride home from Viscountess Newby's dinner party, Trey brought up the subject of his brother and how Tristan had given his heart to a woman, which was the reason he died. I convinced him to tell me about what really happened and why he feels this way."

Dominic's eyes widened. "And he did?"

"Yes."

He clasped her hands. "This is wonderful. He trusts you enough to confide in you. Don't you see? He's never done this before."

"No, Dominic. It does not matter."

"How could it not matter? Trey opened up to you and told you things he has never told his mother. Does that not show you how much he loves you?"

A sob rose to her throat and she swallowed it down. "It didn't work that way. He may trust me, but he's not going to give me his heart. He told me that." She shook her head. "I don't know how to convince him otherwise. I have no desire to give up, but I don't want to love him if he cannot love me in return."

"Oh, my dear Judith." He cupped her face. "I promise your love will win him. Don't give up. Eventually he will see how loving you is the best thing in the world."

Biting her bottom lip, she took deep breaths, trying not to cry again. "Why don't I feel the same? You didn't see him that night. You didn't see the agony in his eyes and especially in his voice."

He nodded. "I talked to him days after Tristan died, and yes, I did see the guilt and the pain he went through. He built a wall around his heart, and it's going to take a very special woman to break it down, but it's not going to happen quickly."

"I'm not strong. I cannot love him if he will not return my affection." She sniffed. "I fear I'm not that woman he needs to melt his heart."

"That's not true. I know you are. I have known Trey for many years, and you are the first woman he's ever acted this way with. The other women who have come into his life leave quickly. He didn't care for them. He has never cared for them. He's never been jealous of other men, either." He winked. "Trey is a jealous man when it comes to you. I saw the envy on his face while he watched you dance with others at your coming out ball. I stood beside him as he admired you descending the stairs that evening. The man was speechless. He couldn't stop staring like a wide-mouth bass."

She smiled, although her heart wrenched with emotion. How she wanted Dominic's words to be true. "So how do I tear down the wall he has around his heart if he will not let me near?"

Chuckling he stroked her ear. "I thought I had that worked out, but apparently, it was not doing what I'd hoped. Perhaps I shall have to think more on this."

She rested her hand on his chest. "Do you know where he is now? He's gone most of the day and does not return until late."

"He's been at his office in Town. I have visited him a few times there just this week, in fact."

"He's not..." She swallowed hard. "He's not with his mistress, is he?"

"Oh, my dear Judith." Dominic rubbed her cheek. "You have no need to fear. No other woman's company can compare to yours. Trey cannot get you out of his system, therefore, any other woman will not do."

Once again, tears welled in her eyes. This time, she couldn't stop them from falling in buckets down her cheeks. "How I wish that were true."

"Shh…" He pulled her against his chest.

Squeezing her eyes, she held in the sobs, but the tears continued to stream.

"Please, Judith, don't cry." He kissed the top of her head.

"I'm sorry." She looked into his caring eyes. "Thank you for being here. I have kept this bottled up inside me for two weeks. I'm so pleased you are with me now."

He gave her a soft smile. "I'm your friend, am I not?"

"Yes."

"Then I will always be here."

He kissed her forehead again, but this time his lips lingered a little longer on her skin. When he pulled away and looked at her again, the color of his eyes was darker. She hitched a breath. Oh no. He couldn't possibly be considering what she thought.

Dominic's gaze dropped to her mouth, his smile relaxing. Her heartbeat quickened. He wouldn't try to kiss her. Not here. Not at a time like this when he just said he was her friend.

Or would he?

He stroked his thumb across her mouth, making her lips part. Lowering his head, he moved closer. She stiffened and her mind turned blank until he pressed his mouth to hers in a soft kiss. Tenderly, he brushed his lips across hers while his hands bracketed her face. He pecked lightly as if encouraging her to participate.

What could he possibly be thinking? He'd just told her how she shouldn't give up on Trey; that she was the woman who would break through to his heart. Dominic loved Trey, so why was he taking liberties with her?

"Excuse me for interrupting." Trey's voice boomed from the doorway.

Judith jumped. She pushed away from Dominic and clutched her throat, focusing on Trey. Strength sapped from her limbs. Even the words in her mind wouldn't form on her tongue. All she could do was stare, and wish she could hide in a hole.

Chapter Thirty-Nine

I NWARDLY, JUDITH DIED. Why did Trey have to choose this time to come home early, especially when he hadn't done so in two weeks?

Casually, Dominic stood and adjusted his waistcoat. "Trey. What a surprise to see you this fine afternoon."

Her heartbeat thudded in a crazy rhythm as she watched Trey. Anger lines creased his forehead and around his mouth, and his beautiful blue eyes were dulled with pain. Slowly, her heart broke, piece by agonizing piece.

Trey lifted his chin. "I'm quite certain it is a surprise, Hawthorne." His gaze briefly touched Judith before he glared at Dominic. "Tell me, what are your intentions toward my mother's ward?"

Straightening, Dominic clasped his hands behind his back. "Purely honorable, if you must know."

"Of course I must know. You were caught kissing her, you jackanapes."

She stepped forward and reached out to Trey. "It's not what you think—"

"Judith, my dear," Dominic interrupted. "Let me take care of this."

Oh, no! This wasn't good at all. Trey would never forgive her. She had to make him understand she didn't encourage

Dominic's kiss. For some reason, she doubted Trey would believe her. Emptiness consumed her chest and she couldn't breathe.

"Hawthorne," Trey barked. "All I want to know is if you are going to make your intentions known. You had mentioned a while back how you wished to court her, and I clearly discouraged your request. Now I see you have gone against my word." He folded his arms across his chest. "What are your plans with Miss Faraday? Are you going to lead her to believe she will be the next Lady Hawthorne like you do to most women?"

Dominic glared. "That was uncalled for. You know Judith is different from those other women."

She wrung her hands against her middle. Dominic wanted to make Trey jealous in hopes he would realize his love for her. Should they continue with the ruse? If Trey's reactions were not as Dominic had planned, would the man she loved be lost to her forever?

"Trey, I request permission to speak with you in private," Dominic said.

Trey's jaw hardened, his mouth pinched in a frown. His accusing gaze switched to Judith and her world slowly slipped away. He wore his feelings on his shoulders, and it was obvious his soul was aching as much as hers. All she wanted to do was run to him and hold him, kiss him and let him know everything was all right.

"Judith? Do you wish to say anything at this time?" Trey asked.

Oh, what a loaded question. What could she say that he would believe, anyway? She shifted her shoulders back and lifted her chin. "I will speak with you in private too, my lord. However, I shall wait until you have spoken with Dominic."

Trey nodded, then looked at his friend. "Meet me in my study in ten minutes. Don't be late." He spun around and marched out of the room.

Groaning, she sank to the couch and covered her face with her shaky hands. What had they done?

"Judith, my dear." Dominic sat next to her, removing her hands from her face. "Don't fret. All will be made right, I promise."

"Are you insane?" She blinked with wide eyes. "He caught you kissing me. I can only imagine what he's thinking." She scowled. "Which reminds me, I would also like you to explain that kiss. Not more than five seconds before, you were convincing me how I was the right woman for Trey."

Dominic grinned. "It was a pleasant kiss, I must admit, but I heard Trey coming up the hall. I knew he would see me kissing you."

She gasped. "Why?"

"Why do you think? We must make him jealous. How else is he going to realize his true feelings for you?"

She wiped the moisture from her eyes. "But, did you see the way he looked at me? I fear he will never forgive me now. How can he love me when he thinks I have feelings for you?"

"Now, now, Judith." He patted her hands. "You must trust me. I know Trey better than you. When I talk to him, I will make him see how much he cares for you."

She sniffed. "Dominic, I pray you know what you are doing. I don't think I can live with the knowledge that Trey loathes me."

He leaned forward and kissed her forehead. "Please don't fret. Trust me."

TREY PACED HIS study as he poured the full snifter of brandy down his throat. Pain spewed through his veins as quickly as the alcohol burned down to his belly. The heavy cloak of confusion and betrayal hung thick around him and he couldn't think straight.

How could Nic do this to him? Worse, how could Judith? She knew how he felt about love and the circumstances that made him harden his heart.

Obviously, he shouldn't have changed his opinion of women. He should have treated Judith just as he'd done the others. At one time he thought she was different, but she wasn't. She flew to any man who opened their arms and showed a little affection. He should have realized how flighty she was. First with Mr. Cutler, then with Trey, and now Nic.

Agony wrenched Trey's heart again and he doubled over. He couldn't react this way. He was stronger than this, and…he was *not* in love with Judith.

Taking a deep breath, he straightened and gulped down another swallow of brandy. He needed a level head when talking to Nic, and especially Judith. Trey couldn't become weak now.

A knock on the door brought him out of his thoughts and he looked toward the sound. Hawthorne stood holding his hat in his arm, looking like he was coming to call. The imbecile! Why was he acting so superior when Trey could crush him with one step of his boot?

"Come in, Hawthorne and close the door," he snapped.

Nic did as instructed then moved to the brown leather chair and sat. The steady gaze of his friend remained on Trey until he walked to his desk and planted his butt in the chair.

"So, Hawthorne, what are your intentions?"

"Miss Faraday is my friend."

Trey rolled his eyes and snorted. "When have you ever kissed your friend? In fact, the whole time I have known you, I have never met a woman friend who was not your mistress."

"There is a first time for everything."

Trey arched his brow. "Come now, Hawthorne. Be truthful with me."

"I am. Judith is my friend. I was kissing her because…well, because…"

"Go on." Trey leaned back in his chair and folded his arms. His friend wasn't going to get out of this one very easily without lying.

Nic huffed and rose to his feet. "The reason I kissed her was because I knew you were coming up the hall."

Trey blinked and shook his head, not believing what he'd heard. "You did it because you wanted to be caught?"

"Yes."

Chuckling, he gulped down the remaining brandy in the glass before standing. "Tell me, why would you do something like that?"

"To see your reaction."

"Hawthorne, you are not making any sense."

"Forgive me, my dear friend." Nic walked closer until he stood right in front of Trey. "I wanted to see how you would react when watching another man kiss the woman you love."

They stood eye to eye in silence. Trey glared at Nic. This was not a game of words. His friend was serious.

Trey pushed past Nic and stormed toward the liquor tray. "You don't know what you are talking about. I don't love her. I love nobody."

"No, you love Judith. I can tell."

Anger filled Trey as he poured a good amount of brandy in his glass. "Hawthorne, I'm beginning to think you have gone insane. You, out of all people, know how I feel about that." He turned and faced him. "Why would you think such a thing?"

A grin stretched across Nic's mouth as he came closer. "Because I have watched the two of you together. I see the passion on your face, I hear the emotion in your voice, and I see the tender way you touch her. You care deeply for a woman you claim not to love, my dear friend."

Trey tightened his grip around his snifter as he took another long swallow, his glare never leaving Nic.

"It's all right to admit you care about her," Nic continued. "Lightning will not spear from the sky and strike you dead if you admit your true feelings." He shrugged. "It's easy to see why you fell in love. I have been riding with her for a while now. I know the woman she is, and I can only hope to find my true love as you have."

Trey's heartbeat pounded against his ribs, while the strange emotion that consumed him since meeting Judith filled his chest. "I cannot love her, Nic," he said softly. "I have no desire to suffer as Tristan suffered."

"You won't."

"I most certainly will," he shouted as he threw his drink in the empty hearth, watching it shatter. "I have seen firsthand what love does to a man. And I have seen it tear apart my mother for loving a man who could not return her feelings, and every night she cried herself to sleep and the pain nearly killed her."

Trey leaned against the wall and dragged his fingers through his hair. When would the alcohol start to work? He needed the magic to dull the pain in his head and in his heart immediately. Emotion grew in his chest, making it harder and harder to breathe.

"You forget one thing, my good man."

Trey glanced over his shoulder at Nic. "And what is that?"

"Judith is not your mother. Nor is she Lady Diana."

"I know this. What difference does it make?"

"Your father was never in love with your mother. Lady Diana was never in love with Tristan." Nic grinned. "Judith is very much in love with you, and you feel the same for her, but you are too stubborn to admit it."

Growling, Trey pushed the heels of his hands against his eyes, willing the confusion inside him to disappear. "I don't want to love her," he muttered.

"Do you not wish to be happy? Judith would make you very happy. Trust her. Trust in her love. She will not disappoint you."

Trey sighed and lowered his hands. His head throbbed, and he wanted it to go away. He wanted Nic to leave, too. His friend's words were very confusing and he didn't want to think about this right now.

"How do you know I will not get hurt?"

Nic shrugged. "Name one man you know who has not been hurt a time or two in his life. It's something we all must experience, my dear friend. Because to experience this helps us to love stronger and deeper."

Chuckling, Trey rolled his eyes. "When did you become so educated on the subject? You are a rakehell just as me."

"Very true. But I'm a romantic at heart. I do want the right woman to come along and sweep me into another world and make me fall in love with her and only her."

Trey shook his head. "Who are you and what have you done with my friend?"

Nic laughed, walked to him and clapped his hand on Trey's shoulder. "I'm here. I will always be here, and I will always be your friend. Even if it means kissing the woman you love to make you jealous enough to admit your true feelings."

Trey chuckled and pushed Nic away. "Get out of here you awful person, and don't come back."

"Do you wish me to send Judith in here?"

Trey froze, yet his heart accelerated. Could he talk to her now? No, he needed more time to think about what Nic told him. Needed more time to debate whether he should take his friend's advice or continue to live his life as he's done so far.

He needed to choose whether he could be miserable without Judith or blissfully happy as her husband.

"No. Tell her I don't want to see her yet. I have much to think about." He rubbed his head. "Plus I have drunk more than I should and I don't think I will be responsible for my actions around her."

Nic nodded. "As you wish. But I beg of you, don't take too long in deciding. Judith is a woman, and women are impatient when it comes to men."

"This I know very well." Trey smiled, and for the first time in a long time, it felt good and didn't make him feel guilty.

Chapter Forty

J UDITH COULDN'T CONCENTRATE on anything. Dominic had informed her of his conversation with Trey, and she cried again. What an emotional sap she'd been lately, but she couldn't help it. She loved Trey deeply.

So far he hadn't talked with her about his feelings, and it had been nearly five days since he had walked in on Nic kissing her. The dowager had finally allowed Judith to help with her birthday party, which kept Judith busy. But she still couldn't wait to talk to him. Unfortunately, she had to give him more time.

Her heart lifted whenever he looked at her. Anger wasn't embedded on his face. Instead, he smiled, and it actually reached his eyes, making them sparkle. The heavy burden of worry still rested on her chest, but every time he looked her way with a pleasant expression, it lightened her heart.

For the birthday party, Judith dressed in one of her new gowns, white muslin embroidered in white glass beads with an ivory silk square collar. Short puffy sleeves were also trimmed in ivory silk and silk cording. She wore white gloves that reached above her elbows. Her hair piled on top of her head in a knot, but she left wisps of ringlets to hang on her neck and ears.

Judith really had to put on a performance tonight. Lately, she'd been pushing suitors away, which she was certain had upset many people. Isabelle hadn't said anything to her about this behavior, but Judith knew it didn't make the dowager look like a respectable guardian.

Once Judith was ready, she hurried downstairs, eager to see Trey. They hadn't spoken for almost three weeks, and she feared his mood would be sour like it had been before.

He stood by his mother at the doorway of the ballroom, and when he saw her, his eyes widened along with his smile. Her heart leapt, hoping he'd missed her as much as she had him.

More handsome than she'd seen him before, he wore a charcoal overcoat with a high collar. His dark blue vest had gold stitches embroidered in the material. Charcoal gray breeches fit his legs to perfection, and reminded her once again what a muscular man he was underneath.

Trey stepped away from his mother and toward Judith. He took her white-gloved hand, lifted it to his mouth and placed a kiss on her knuckles. "You are breathtaking tonight."

Heat flooded her cheeks and she curtsied. "May I give the same compliment to you, my lord?"

His grin widened, and the dimple in his cheek flashed at her. "You certainly may."

"Oh, Judith," the dowager exclaimed as she hurried to her side. "You look ravishing. Thank you for being here to help me greet my guests. I'm very grateful for you and Trey. I wish Trevor could be here as well, but he just sent a note. He'd be detained for an hour but will arrive soon afterward." The dowager took a deep breath. "I just want everything perfect."

"And it shall be, Mother."

It was hard for Judith to pull her gaze away from Trey, but she did smile at the dowager. "Trey is correct. So far everything has turned out wonderfully. Happy Birthday, Your Grace."

Isabelle patted Judith's cheek. "Thank you, my dear."

As she stood beside Isabelle and Trey, Judith wished they'd stop making small talk. Of course, airing their feelings in front of the dowager wasn't a good idea, either, but Judith wanted to know if Trey had thought about them—about her love and what she had to offer. Would he give her love a chance and trust her to make him happy?

Throughout the evening, Trey kept his gaze on her, just as she watched him. It didn't matter if she danced with someone else, or if he stood with a group of people, she always knew where he was every minute. Sometimes she could read his expression, and it gave her encouragement. On a few occasions confusion crossed his gaze, making her heart sink. If only she could get him alone and talk to him.

After their dance was over, her partner escorted her back to the dowager, but before reaching the older woman, Trey stepped away from his group and stopped her.

"May I have this dance?"

She smiled wide. "Yes," she sighed.

The tune was slower than the country-dances the stringed quartet had played thus far, which Judith was grateful for. The first few moments, she was lost just staring into his warm eyes. He didn't smile, nor did he frown, but the intense focus in his eyes made her heart hammer faster.

Finally, the corners of his mouth lifted in a grin. "You really do look radiant tonight. I cannot keep my eyes off you."

She wanted to moan aloud. "I know the feeling. I keep watching you to see if you catch the eye of another woman."

He chuckled. "It would be hard when I'm looking at you, and only you."

"Trey, about the other day—"

"Shh…" He squeezed her hand. "There's no need to bring it up. You have given me much to think about, and only I can come to a decision."

She nodded. "I understand."

"But please, don't fret. I want you to enjoy yourself tonight."

"I will." She glanced briefly across the crowd. "This is a wonderful party, and I'm certain your mother is elated to have such endearing guests."

"Yes. She thrives on being in the limelight."

A commotion from the corner of the room started, and gained Judith's attention, especially when the dowager strode across the room toward her servants wearing a scowl. Judith stopped, hoping to see what caused the voices to grow. Trey must have noticed, because he turned in the same direction.

"What's going on?" she asked.

"I don't know. It almost looks like an uninvited guest is causing trouble. Come. Let's put a stop to it."

Taking her by the hand, he led her off the dance floor. The closer they came to the crowd, the more her heartbeat quickened. People looked at her with accusing glares, and when she passed, they whispered behind their hands.

Suddenly, a loud voice rang through the room, quieting even the musicians. The familiar voice struck her and her heart sank.

Alex!

Judith stood frozen as she stared at the man from her past who was dressed in the uniform of a lieutenant of the Royal Navy. Two of Isabelle's servants held him back, and he struggled against them. When Alex saw her, he pointed his head in her direction.

"There she is," he said loudly.

"Oh, no, it's Alex." Her voice was low, but Trey heard it and looked at her.

Trey's quick breath was noticeable, and he marched up to Alex. "What is the meaning of this?"

"I'm here to rescue the woman I love."

"And whom might that be, may I ask?"

"Miss Judith Faraday, my fiancée."

Whispers in the room grew louder and Judith's head began to swim. No. This couldn't be happening. Fear kept her in place, staring at the man she didn't know any longer. Why was he dressed as a sailor when Trey's solicitor discovered he wasn't in the navy?

"I highly doubt that sir," Trey snapped. "She's my brother's ward, under my mother's care. I think I would know if she had been engaged."

Alex yanked his arms away from the servants, dug his hand inside the double-breasted red coat and pulled out a scrolled paper. "Here is the legal document that betrothed us before her parents died."

Gasps rang through the room. Judith's was the loudest. She swayed, and a strong arm clutched hers, holding her up. She glanced beside her to see Dominic being her support. His scowl was aimed at Alex, looking as if he was ready to stand beside his friend and kill the intruder.

Trey grabbed the paper from Alex and opened it, his eyes swiftly reading over each word. By the time it reached the bottom, his mouth turned down into a frown. He looked at Judith and shook his head.

"It's signed by a clergyman."

Finally, anger snapped her out of her daze, and she pulled away from Dominic. "That's ridiculous." She hurried to stand beside Trey, reading every word on the document.

"Did you sign this with him?" Trey asked softly.

Slowly, the pieces of her mended heart broke again. She did sign it. They were alone that day, making a promise to each other. It was before her parents died. But… No, this wasn't right.

She moved her glare to Alex. "This is not legal, and you know it. There was no clergyman witnessing our signatures that day."

Alex tilted his head and smiled. "Oh, my darling, Judith. You cannot deny this. We were betrothed in front of witnesses."

"My parents did not even know about you."

A loud moan came from behind as the dowager swooned. Dominic rushed to her side and helped her into a chair while another woman fanned Isabelle's face. The dowager opened her eyes and met Judith's gaze.

This wasn't good for the older woman's health. Why did Alex pick this day to come? She turned her attention back to Alex. "Will you leave? You are not wanted here."

He shook his head. "I'm not leaving without my fiancée."

"I'm not that person."

"The document proves otherwise."

Panic consumed Judith, making her breathing quicken. She looked from the dowager to Dominic, then to Trey, silently pleading with them for help. How could she get out of this? Answers weren't coming to her at all, and she feared what would happen if she left with Alex.

"I—I—" She swallowed hard and looked at Trey again. Confusion clouded his blue eyes as his gaze switched between her and the betrothal document.

"Alex," she begged, "you don't understand. I cannot leave with you."

"What's not to understand? You are mine. Not theirs. We belong together."

Tears swam in her eyes and she turned to Trey one more time for help. But there was no help available. Nothing could be done. The false document said it all. If she didn't leave with Alex now, her name would be ruined, along with the dowager's. Judith couldn't do that to her guardian. Not after everything the woman had done for her.

Nodding, she ducked her head and took a step toward Alex, but suddenly, a firm hand grasped her arm, stopping her. She swung her gaze to Trey.

"No," he said loudly. "I cannot allow her to leave with you, Mr. Cutler."

"Why not?" Alex snapped.

"Because she has broken the betrothal."

Alex's eyes widened. "And how, may I ask, did she do that?"

"She…" Trey's deep stare penetrated her, his jaw hardened as his lips thinned into a line. He lifted his chin and met Alex's stare. "Miss Faraday and I were alone together quite a few times since she's been here. I'm a rogue, Mr. Cutler. Need I say more?"

Judith lost her breath. Yet her heart pounded with excitement. Why did he say that? He hinted to everyone that they'd been intimate. Did he know he'd have to marry her now? And worse, would he blame her for trying to trap him?

Another loud groan came from the dowager as she covered her face with her hands. Gasps ricocheted off the walls and whispers filled the room and grew louder by the second.

Alex's eyes widened and his mouth dropped open. "Is this true? Were you intimate with him?"

She nodded, trying not to smile and let everyone know how pleased she was that Trey saved her. "Yes."

Trey ripped the betrothal document in three pieces and shoved them at Alex's chest. "Now take this and get off my mother's property before I call in the guards and have you arrested."

Alex glared at Trey, then turned his fiery eyes on her. "Mark my words, this is not over." With that, he turned and marched out of the house.

Standing still, she dared not glance around the room. All eyes were on her and Trey. Heated accusation glares nearly pierced through her.

Cautiously, she looked at Trey. His attention was aimed at the floor as he swiped his fingers through his hair. Several earth-shattering moments passed before he lifted his gaze to hers. She couldn't read his expression. His eyes were wide, and his mouth still pinched in irritation. He looked as helpless as she felt.

He turned quickly and walked to his mother. Judith couldn't hear what was being said, but it was obvious by the older woman's swollen moist eyes and red nose, she wasn't taking the news very well.

Groaning, Judith rubbed her forehead. All of this because of her foolish mistakes. What would happen to her life now? How could she make up for everything she'd done? She glanced at Trey who wouldn't meet her eyes. Did he think she trapped him? That had to be the reason for his actions.

The walls closed in on her, making it difficult for her to breathe. She pushed through the crowd—who parted quickly— and hurried out of the ballroom just for fresh air. Once she reached the stairs, she headed for her room as fast as her feet would take her.

Tears flooded her eyes and streamed down her cheeks before she reached her room. As she ran inside and closed the door behind her, a sob caught in her throat. Her knees buckled beneath her, and she sank to the floor and cried.

Chapter Forty-One

JUDITH REMAINED IN her bed curled on her side as she stared at the wall. The day had passed slowly, and she'd slept most of it. Meals had been brought to her. She ignored the food. How could she eat when her world had crumbled down around her?

Nobody came to her room to see to her welfare. That was fine. She knew she'd severed ties with the Worthington family whether she had wanted to or not. Strange to think how she'd wanted to get away from them when she first arrived, and now she didn't want to leave.

One of the upstairs maids bustled into her room to tidy up, but Judith didn't want to talk. Thankfully, the woman didn't either. She wouldn't even glance at Judith.

Had she really been shunned from the family? Any moment Trey would come to her room and instruct her to pack her things and go far away, never to return.

Tears filled her eyes. As much as the idea frightened her, she doubted Trey would do that. After all, he was the one who made the confession. If he didn't do the right thing and marry her now, his reputation would be ruined, also. Then again, he was a rogue, so maybe it wouldn't hurt him at all. He had told her several times that he would not be trapped into marriage. That's exactly what happened.

A knock came upon the door, but she refrained from moving.

The maid turned and looked at Judith. "Miss, do you want visitors?"

"No." Judith flipped her hand. "Send them away, please."

"As you wish."

By the second knock, the maid opened the door.

"I'd like to speak with Miss Faraday."

Judith gasped and turned in bed, bringing the covers with her as she stared at the towering man at the door. It was the duke, Trey's older brother, Trevor.

"Your Grace, she's indisposed," the maid curtsied and replied.

His hard stare met Judith's from across the room. "Get up now and put on your wrapper. I will not wait to discuss this with you."

Nodding, Judith jumped out of bed, pushed her feet into slippers and yanked on her wrapper. Trevor walked to the couch on the other side of the room where he sat. On shaky legs, she moved to the other chair across from his and sank down on the cushion.

"It's nice to see you again, Your Grace," she said in a small voice. "When did you arrive?"

He arched a brow. "I arrived just shortly after the entertainment last night."

Heat flooded her face and she swallowed hard. "I see. I'm sorry I missed your arrival."

"I'm sorry I missed the main event."

Trevor kept his narrowed stare on her in silence for a few awkward moments. His eyes were a dark blue...a frightening blue. She'd never seen him so cross before. Although he had the Worthington's handsome looks, his scowl could frighten young children, she was sure.

Judith fidgeted in her chair and wrung her hands against her middle. Would he yell at her? Demand she leave posthaste? If so, she wished he'd do it soon. Worrying about the unknown was killing her.

He let out a deep sigh, sat back and folded his arms over his chest. "So tell me, Miss Faraday, how has my brother been treating you?"

She stared at him with wide eyes. Was he being humorous? That wasn't a trait she thought he had. He'd always been so serious. "I do not understand your question."

"Fine, I shall put it bluntly. Was my brother telling the truth when he announced to my mother's guests that he'd been intimate with you?"

She dropped her gaze to her lap and ran her finger along the seam of her wrapper. "Yes, he was telling the truth."

"That scoundrel. The last time I talked with him, he promised me you were safe under his care. He said you would remain innocent."

"Oh, he hasn't done anything to compromise my virtue," she said quickly as she snapped her head up to look his way. After the words were out, she silently cursed herself for blurting that out.

Trevor grinned, reminding her a lot of the way Trey smiled. Even the dimple on his chin flashed at her—something she hadn't seen since they were children.

"He has not compromised your virtue?" Trevor tapped his finger on his chin. "What an interesting change of events."

Her face flamed, but she kept her eyes on him anyway.

"It makes me wonder why Trey led everyone to believe he had? Especially to a room full of gossipmongers."

She shrugged. "I pray it was because he knew I didn't want to leave with Mr. Cutler. Alex lied about the betrothal agreement, but I had no way to prove it at the moment. I was sinking fast, and I didn't know how to get out. I silently pleaded with Trey to help me, and I prayed he could see it in my eyes."

Trevor nodded. "So my gallant brother came to your rescue?"

"Yes. That's the way I look at it. However, I seriously think Trey is not thinking the way I am."

"What do you suppose he's thinking?"

"I fear he thinks I have trapped him in some way."

"But you were not the one who confessed the secret."

"I know, but I desperately wanted him to help me last night."

He shook his head. "That does not mean Trey is going to think you have trapped him."

"I don't know, Your Grace. I know how he feels about love and marriage."

Trevor tilted his head, his eyes widening. "He's shared with you his feelings on the subject?"

"Yes."

"So the two of you have grown rather close, both physically and emotionally?"

"Yes. He knows I'm in love with him."

"Does he now." His grin stretched across his face. "So I'm assuming you do not mind marrying him after all."

"I do want to marry him, Your Grace, but I don't want him to think I trapped him."

"I see." He nodded.

She leaned forward. "Do you think he will marry me?"

Trevor chuckled. "Oh, he will do the right thing by you. I can promise that."

"Are you saying you will force him?"

He held up his hands and shrugged. "You put me in an awkward position, Miss Faraday. If my brother does not do it first, I must force him to do the right thing."

Her heart flipped with excitement, yet she worried Trey would eventually blame her. If he hadn't done so already.

"Did you come here to tell me to leave?" she asked.

"No. I wanted to know how you felt about my brother, and especially how he feels about you." Trevor stood, walked to her and patted her shoulder. "Keep up the good work." He winked. "You are the best thing that has ever happened to my brother."

Tears gathered in her eyes and she smiled. "What does your mother think? Does she hate me for ruining her birthday party?"

"I shall let my mother talk to you herself. Do not fret, though. She's a very understanding woman."

"All right."

As Trevor walked out the door, her heart lifted slightly. Trevor would see that she married Trey. But would he hate her if that happened? She must talk to him, and to his mother, of course. Thankfully, Trevor was on her side.

Judith jumped up and hurried to get dressed, suddenly having the energy to make it through the evening. Not bothering to style her hair, she brushed it away from her face and tied a ribbon around the bulk that lay against her neck. She didn't plan on having company, and hopefully nobody would mind her hair hanging down her back.

She hurried out of her room and down the stairs. As she expected, the house was abnormally quiet. When one of Isabelle's servants walked by, she stopped them. "Can you tell me where the dowager is right now?"

The maid curtsied. "She's in her room and does not wish to be disturbed."

Judith frowned. "I suppose I shall talk with her later."

"Yes, Miss." The maid bobbed again then turned and left.

Sighing deeply, Judith walked down the hall to Trey's study, but it was empty. Should she allow him more time to think of his hasty decision? If she gave him more time, would he feel as if she was trapping him? *Oh heavens.* Why couldn't she think about anything without worrying?

She wandered through the house, but soon stepped outside. The weather was lovely for riding. Too bad she wasn't dressed for it. Walking was good, too, as long as she did it before the sun set on the horizon.

As she strolled through the dowager's flower garden, she smiled in remembrance of the time she and Trey had walked through here on her first day. Things had been so different back then. Now she was glad he'd talked her into staying and allowing his mother to sponsor her into society.

From the corner of her eyes, there was a movement at the gazebo. Curious, she stepped closer until the man sitting inside came to her view. Her heart leapt. *Trey!*

She must have caught his attention too, because his head snapped up and his gaze met hers. They stared at each other for a few seconds before he motioned for her to come nearer. Each step closer, her heart beat harder. He wasn't smiling, yet he didn't have that hard look on his face, either.

When she entered the rotund center, he scooted over on the bench and patted the empty space next to him. Her body shook, either with excitement or fear, she couldn't decide, but she did as instructed.

This evening he wore only a loose shirt and black breeches, appearing more casual than she thought he should. Had he been in his bedroom all day, as well?

Silence filled the space between them, and she knew if he didn't say anything, her heartbeat would soon echo in the night. His eyes were toward the opening of the gazebo, but she remained staring at him, praying he didn't hate her.

He cleared his throat. "So, that was Mr. Cutler."

Her heart knocked crazily against her ribs. "Yes," she said in a small voice.

"Somehow I pictured him differently. My solicitor showed me Cutler's picture, but he does not look anything like it."

"His hair is longer than I remember, and he's sporting a mustache whereas he had not before."

"I'm curious to know where he obtained that uniform since my solicitor discovered he was never in the navy."

She shrugged. "I cannot fathom. Just one of his disguises, I suppose."

Trey finally looked at her. Still, his expression was unreadable.

"I don't know why I did not think to have him arrested last night. If you remember correctly, my solicitor also discovered Mr. Cutler had stolen jewelry from three young widows."

"Yes, I recall that now." She licked her dry lips. "I suppose you didn't think to have him arrested because it was such a shock to see him at your mother's party, and making false accusations."

"True." He pushed his fingers through his hair, leaned back on the bench and looked at the ceiling. "But I sent out a letter this morning to my solicitor, informing him of Mr. Cutler's actions. Hopefully, the police will be able to find Mr. Cutler before he does more damage."

"Yes, I pray they will, too."

Judith swallowed hard, still keeping her eyes on him. Would he say anything about his confession or would she be the one to bring it up? The suspense nearly killed her. How could he act so calm at a time like this?

Sighing heavily, he met her stare again. "So, I suppose we should plan a wedding now, shouldn't we?"

Worry shook her body as tears stung her eyes. Still, she didn't know if he was mad or if the idea of marrying her was agreeable to him. "I suppose." Her voice cracked, so she cleared her throat.

"Usually when situations like this happen, a speedy marriage accompanies it. Do you understand?"

"Yes. We should be married within the week."

"Indeed. Such a torturous task. Don't you agree?"

Her vision blurred and her heart broke. No excitement showed in his eyes, and pain laced his throat. No hint of his teasing grin was there, either. Obviously he didn't want to marry her. He'd even called it torture. Her worst nightmare had come true. He blamed her. As much as she loved him, she couldn't marry him when he didn't return her love. She wouldn't be like his parents, and she'd save him from the same fate.

She had to leave. Not just here, right now, but leave the manor. She couldn't bring shame to the Worthington family. Hopefully, the Dowager would understand.

Standing, Judith swiped the tears from her eyes and faced Trey. "We should be married quickly, but we won't. I cannot let it happen this way, Trey. I will be gone first thing in the morning and you will never have to worry about me again."

Judith darted out of the gazebo, not wanting to face Trey. Lifting her dress above her ankles, she quickened her steps and ran. He called her name, but she ignored him and focused on the side doors. *Almost there.*

Her tears blurred her vision, but she didn't wipe them in her pursuit to get inside the house and separate herself from Trey. Her legs shook, but she pushed herself forward. She couldn't become weak now.

The doorknob was within reach. She stretched her hand and held her breath. But a large hand grasped her arm, stopping her flight.

"Judith!"

Trey's voice came out forceful. Demanding. She looked over her shoulder at him, and realized his voice didn't portray the worry on his face.

"Good heavens, woman. Have you gone insane?"

She shook her head and tried to pull her arm away, but he held it tightly.

"What possessed you to say what you did back there?" he asked.

Taking a deep breath for courage, she straightened her shoulders, ready for battle. "I will not let this happen, Trey. I'll not marry a man who thinks of marriage as torture." She swallowed the knot in her throat. "And I'll not let what happened to your parents happen to us."

Trey's eyes widened. Within seconds, the look of surprise left his face and he grinned. "Oh, my sweet Judith."

He pulled her against his chest. She wanted to fight him, to pound her fists into his solid muscular frame and sob until she relinquished all her tears, but his caring voice stopped her. The emotion illuminating from his blue eyes eased her fears.

"Forgive me for using the wrong word, my love. I don't think of marriage to you as being torturous. The reason I said it that way was because I was being humorous."

"Humorous?" Her voice shook slightly and she looked up at him. "You showed no expression of humor, Trey."

He stroked her cheek as he stared deep into her eyes. "Forgive me again. The shock of what's happened is still very real. I cannot believe I said what I did last night."

"Do you wish to take your words back? Tell me your feelings now. Don't hide them any longer." She gripped his shirt, praying he'd say what she wanted to hear.

"No. I don't wish to take my words back." He kissed her forehead and rested his mouth against her hair. "Judith, I could not let Mr. Cutler take you, even if it meant causing scandal."

"I didn't want to leave with him."

"I know."

"But I worried you would think…" She swallowed the knot in her throat again.

"What?" He pulled back and looked down at her.

"I didn't want you to think I was forcing you, or trapping you." Her eyes watered again.

"Why would I think that? I know you are not trapping me. I said what I did of my own free will." He stroked her bottom lip with his thumb. "I said what I did because I didn't want you to leave me."

Her chest tightened with happiness, making it harder to breathe. She couldn't jump to conclusions. "I will not leave you, Trey," she whispered. "I—I love you."

Groaning, his mouth swept down and captured hers as his arms circled around her. She held onto him as she answered his passionate kisses with urgency. He pushed her against the door.

She sighed and met his urgent kisses. Immeasurable pleasure swept through her. He loved her and wanted to marry her!

Breaking the kiss, she leaned her head against his as she took in deep breaths. "Trey?"

"Yes, my darling."

She smiled. "I will make you very happy. Please believe that."

"I know you will." He winked. "And I will do my best to make you a good husband."

She nodded. "I shall make sure of that, my beautiful lord."

Chapter Forty-Two

THE NEXT MORNING, Judith walked down the hallway with a straight back and chin held high, trying to give the appearance of having strength. She couldn't go another minute without talking to the dowager. Although, her nerves jumped inside her stomach and she wrung her hands, showing her weakness.

She didn't want to disappoint Isabelle. In the last little while, the older woman had replaced her mother, if only in small measurements. Judith loved the dowager more than she realized she would when she first arrived.

Would Isabelle be distraught, wasting away in her bed, stressing over the scandal Judith and Trey had caused? If so, could she ever make things right with the older woman?

Judith reached Isabelle's bedroom door and knocked. Her hands shook so she quickly clasped them together and held them tight against her breast. From the other side of the door, footsteps padded on the floor in hurried steps.

Finally a voice rang through the room, telling Judith to enter. When she walked inside, the curtains were closed and only a few candlesticks were lit. The dowager lay in bed, the covers pulled up and tucked underneath her arms as they rested on the blankets. Ringlets of hair spilled from underneath her frilly nightcap.

"Your Grace, I hope you forgive my intrusion, but I must

speak with you. I cannot wait a moment longer."

Isabelle glanced across to the room to her maid who was sitting in one of the cushioned chairs reading a book. "Mary? Will you leave us, please?"

"Yes, Your Grace." The servant bobbed and hurried out of the room.

Isabelle lifted her hand and motioned. "Come closer, child so I can see you better."

On shaky legs, Judith did as instructed until she stood next to the dowager's bed. Taking a deep breath, she prayed for strength to say the right words. She also prayed Isabelle would forgive her and Trey.

She swallowed the lump in her throat before saying anything. "I wanted to talk to you about what happened during your birthday party. I'm extremely saddened by the turn of events. I honestly didn't think Mr. Cutler would come."

"Tell me about this man. Is he really your fiancé?"

Judith shrugged. "Yes, and no. Before my parents died, I started seeing him in secret. I knew they would not approve because he was not of noble birth. Although we discussed marriage, there was no legal document signed. The one he showed you the other night was false, I assure you."

The dowager nodded. "Why did you not tell me about him when you first arrived?"

"I made an agreement with Trey. He said he would hire a solicitor to look for Mr. Cutler if I would allow you to prepare me for my coming out ball. Trey knew I was very displeased with coming to your estate. I felt I was too old for a guardian, and I certainly didn't want to have a ball."

"Why?"

"A month before my mother died, she had started to prepare one for me. The memories weighed heavily on my heart and I could not bear to let someone else take my mother's place." Tears pricked Judith's eyes and the lump in her throat returned. Still, she fought for control over her emotions.

"I see," the dowager said. "And how do you feel now? Do you feel you need a guardian?"

"Not really, Your Grace. I'm very grateful for everything you and Trey have done to help me in my time of need. I feel I have made friends with you over the past few weeks, and I shall never forget your generosity and kindness."

"Did Trey ever find information about your Mr. Cutler?"

"Yes." Judith cleared her throat. "He found out some very upsetting news, in fact. The night of my ball, after the guests were gone, Trey told me what his solicitor discovered. Apparently, Mr. Cutler had deceived a lot of people. He was not the man I thought he was."

"Is that when Trey seduced you?"

The dowager's voice held a sharp edge, yet the woman's eyes almost twinkled. Judith scrunched her forehead. For some reason, Isabelle appeared almost delighted to think Trey had seduced his mother's ward.

"Yes and no. Trey had turned on his charm way before my ball."

Isabelle's eyebrows lifted. "Indeed?"

"Yes. I know he was fighting his attraction for me, just as I fought it. Yet it was inevitable. Whenever we were alone, sparks flew between us, either in verbal swordplay or physically."

The dowager rubbed her chin, still not taking her eyes off Judith. "I should have suspected something was amiss. Trey usually never stays around the estate more than a few days."

Judith sat on the edge of the bed and clasped the older woman's hand. "Please believe me when I say this was not meant to happen. When I first arrived, I disliked Trey's very presence. He felt the same about me, too."

"Are you in love with my son now?"

Peace settled in Judith's chest, making her smile. "I'm completely in love with him. I think I fell in love before my coming out ball."

Suddenly, the dowager's face relaxed and she grinned. "I

noticed the changes in Trey the longer he was with you. I wanted him to love you, Judith. I have been praying for that since you two were young and he used to tease you."

Judith gasped. "What? You have wanted this for that long?"

"Yes." She shrugged. "I have secrets, too. Please do not be angry with me, but this was one of the reasons I brought you to my estate after your parents died. I knew you were old enough and independent enough to take care of yourself. I also knew you did not need instructions on how to give a dinner party, or to dance. Your father left you a large inheritance, but I wanted you here to tempt my son. I wanted him to fall in love with you."

Shock vibrated through Judith's body, along with the bubble of laughter that sprang from her throat. "I cannot believe this."

"Please don't blame an old woman for playing matchmaker."

"Oh, Isabelle." Judith wrapped her arms around the older woman and hugged her tight. The dowager returned her hug and kissed Judith's cheek.

"I have always wanted a daughter, you know. Because your mother was my best friend, I wanted you as my daughter, too. Now my wish has come true."

Judith laughed again and pulled away. "Does Trey know about this?"

"No, although I believe he suspects I'm hiding something."

"Then I have you to thank for my happiness right now." Judith smiled.

"No, you have Trey. I feared he would not come up to scratch. He has had a hard life, and his father was not a decent example. I worried Trey would grow up to be like him."

"That's one of the reasons he fought the attraction the way he did. He didn't want to become like his father."

The dowager shook her head. "He's not. Trey has a heart. My husband did not."

Judith squeezed Isabelle's hands again. "Thank you for telling me. I do love your son, and I want to make him a good wife."

"You will. I have no doubt. Now, let me up so we can plan a

wedding."

Laughing, Judith stood and helped the older woman out of bed. Falling from her lap spilled a deck of cards to the floor.

Judith lifted an eyebrow. "What's this?"

The dowager shrugged. "I had to keep myself entertained while pretending to be out of sorts. I'm so relieved you decided to come talk to me. I fear I would have bored myself to death waiting for you and Trey to make the first move."

"Indeed, you are full of surprises, Your Grace." Judith shook her head. "Trey is exactly like you. He does not have to worry about being like his father, because Trey's sneakiness comes from you."

They laughed together and hugged. Judith's stress eased considerably. Now she had a wedding to plan, and her heart beat with renewed life.

Chapter Forty-Three

WEARILY, JUDITH WALKED out of the drawing room where she and Isabelle had been discussing the wedding plans for most of the afternoon. Although spending time with the dowager was pleasant and the plans were exciting, the stress of the past few days had Judith feeling very exhausted. All she wanted to do was crawl into bed and sleep.

Dominic had arrived earlier this afternoon and met with Trey. She wanted to break away from Isabelle just to greet her friend, but she didn't dare. The last time she and Dominic were together, things hadn't turned out very well.

Or had they? Was it due to Dominic's kiss that Trey changed his mind about marriage? Or was it Alex who had forced Trey to admit his true feelings? Either way, she was happy with the final result.

She turned down the hallway and headed toward the study. Trey's heated voice echoed in the corridor, overriding her soft slippers clicking on the marbled floor. What had made him angry? Hopefully, not Dominic.

As she reached the door, which was cracked open slightly, she slowed her steps. She couldn't see through the space into the room, but both Trey and Dominic's voice rose in volume.

"I will not do it," Trey shouted. "That poor woman has been through enough already. I'm not going to distress her unnecessarily."

"If she does not hear it from you first, she will be put out," Hawthorne answered.

Trey growled. "Don't you think I know this?"

"When will Mr. Lewis be in touch with you? When will he know for certain?"

"I don't know."

Judith's heart sank. Were they talking about her? About Alex? They'd have to be since they mentioned Mr. Lewis' name. So what was it that Trey didn't want to tell her?

She shouldn't eavesdrop but couldn't help it. The need to know overrode anything she'd been taught about manners. As she leaned toward the door, she bumped it with her shoulder and it squeaked open.

Cursing under her breath, she quickly straightened. Trey stood by the window, facing the door, and Dominic who'd been sitting on the leather sofa, jumped to his feet. Neither man appeared pleased to see her.

She smiled her best and walked in. "Good evening gentlemen. I hope I didn't disrupt anything important."

Dominic jerked his attention to Trey and scowled but said nothing.

Trey walked toward her, his grin stretching. His smile wasn't real because there was no light in his eyes, which confirmed to Judith the conversation she'd overheard was indeed about her.

"My dear Judith." Trey took her hands and kissed her on the cheek. "How was your day with Mother?"

"Very enlightening." She chuckled. "We accomplished a lot."

"Splendid." He lifted her hands to his mouth and kissed her knuckles.

"Trey? Forgive me for asking, but were you and Dominic just talking about me? Or more importantly, about Mr. Cutler?"

Trey's body stiffened and his eyes widened. Behind him, Dominic hitched a breath, the sound spilling through the room.

"Now, my dear," Trey said as he pulled her into his arms.

"You needn't worry your lovely head about what is going on."

"Is it about Alex getting arrested? Did your solicitor find him and arrest him?"

"Shhh…" Trey placed his finger on her lips. "It's like I told you, there's no need to worry."

Arching her eyebrow, she cocked her head. "Trey, you are purposely putting me off. I want you to tell me."

Dominic cleared his throat and moved past them toward the door. "If you will both excuse me, I shall leave now."

"Hawthorne, don't go far," Trey said, still holding Judith's gaze. "We still have things to discuss."

"As you wish." As Dominic left he mumbled something she couldn't quite understand, and closed the door behind him.

Trey's arms tightened around her, bringing her closer to his body. "Alone at last."

"Please stop, Trey. I want to know what is going on. I heard your raised voice from down the hall. I know something is upsetting you."

He kissed her nose, then her cheek, and moved to her lips, but she pulled away before he could do anymore. She knew Trey well. He was trying to distract her. She wouldn't let him win this time. "I mean it, Trey. I want answers."

He sighed heavily. "Yes, the conversation Hawthorne and I were having was about Mr. Cutler."

"Did Mr. Lewis find him?"

"No."

She frowned. "So what's happening?"

"Mr. Lewis has discovered other things about Mr. Cutler which he will investigate. Until my solicitor has solid facts, there's nothing we can do."

"What did Mr. Lewis learn?"

Trey shook his head as he caressed her cheek. "It's very upsetting information and I don't dare tell you only because we don't know if it's the truth yet."

She scowled. "Trey. You cannot tell me this and leave me

hanging."

"You wanted to know, my sweet, so I told you."

"But you did not tell me everything."

He pulled away from her, turned and ran his fingers through his hair as he paced the floor. "Judith, I just cannot. It's killing me inside, but it will be worse if the information I give you is false."

Anger built inside of her, making her want to scream. She understood his reasoning, but it upset her when he didn't want to be truthful with her. "Please, just tell me," she pleaded.

He stopped in front of her and cupped her face. His blue eyes were dulled with worry as he shook his head. "This is the time you need to trust me. Trust that I know what I'm doing."

Trust him? Of course she trusted him. Didn't she? Then why was her chest aching with doubts? She didn't know what possible information Mr. Lewis could have gathered on Alex, but why did Trey not love her enough to be honest?

Trust runs two ways, and he wasn't proving he trusted her.

Tears stung her eyes. "I trust you," she whispered.

He took her in his arms again and kissed her neck before burying his face against her skin. Tingles ran through her, but the pain and doubt in her heart stopped desire from entering her body.

"Believe me, my sweet. In due time I will tell you. It's just too soon to do so now."

A tear slipped free and ran down her cheek. She quickly wiped it away before Trey noticed.

He lifted his head and kissed her mouth again, but she broke the contact and pulled away. "I'm tired. I'm going to lie down while you finish your meeting with Dominic."

"All right. I will come wake you when we are done."

She nodded, turned and walked out of the room, hurrying down the hallway toward the side door. As she stepped outside, tears streamed down her cheeks. Marriage would be difficult between them at first, especially since they both needed to learn how to trust each other.

Trey had always thought he was right. She thought she was the one who had all the answers. They'd definitely have a lot of compromising to do. It hurt to think he wouldn't tell her about Alex.

In the horizon, the sun began its descent, turning the sky a maroon tint. Billowy clouds hung thick, threatening a rainstorm in the near future, and the cool wind had picked up since earlier today, guaranteeing the storm would be coming soon.

She walked past the flower gardens and into the gazebo. This was the perfect spot to sit, relax and think. Especially now.

Tilting back her head, she closed her eyes and breathed deeply. Were her emotions on her sleeves due to her exhausted state? Perhaps. Of course her pending marriage took a lot out of her, also. If only they could marry quickly and get it over with. But the dowager wanted it to be a grand occasion.

Judith chuckled. Had Isabelle forgotten about the scandal created at her party two nights ago? Then again, it didn't matter. The older woman had always wanted Judith and Trey to marry, so why not make it a big event?

Bushes rustled behind the gazebo. It couldn't be the wind, because the sound was too forceful. Had a small animal been caught in the branches?

Investigating, she hurried out and cautiously walked toward the bushes, crouching the closer she came. She strained to hear any sounds of distress from a kitten, but only the howling of the wind pierced the air.

As she stood, the rustling came again, but from another direction. When she turned to look, the blur of a person dressed in dark clothes came toward her, holding up a blanket. Before she had time to scream, the covering was tossed over her as a rope tied it to her body. Her arms were imprisoned against her sides.

"Let me go this instant!"

The suddenness of it all caught her off guard and she stumbled. She braced herself to hit the ground, but sturdy arms wrapped around her, keeping her from going down.

"Who are you?" she cried out. "What do you want with me?"

She was dragged into the bushes and struggled with her kidnapper. When he didn't answer, she screamed. The person stopped, stood her upright and shook her hard, which jerked her head back and forth violently.

"Listen, my dear. I swear to you right now if you scream once more I will kill Lord Trey personally, and anyone else who comes to your rescue. Do you understand?"

She inhaled sharply. "Oh, no! Alex?"

"Yes, my dear. Did you miss me?"

Darkness surrounded her because of the covering. The heavy scent of horse stung her nose and made her gag. Her heart beat in a fierce rhythm. This couldn't be happening. "Alex, if you let me go, I promise to have Trey's solicitor stop investigating you. You will be free to do whatever you wish."

A deep chuckle rattled through his chest. His head pressed against hers, and the strong scent of alcohol wafted through the material of the blanket.

"I told you once that you would be my wife. Do not doubt me again. Your lover's life is at stake. If you want him to live, you will follow my instructions."

"Please, Alex. Let me go. I don't love you," she sobbed.

He yanked her, making her stumble into him as he led them away from the estate. "You will change your feelings eventually. I have faith you will find the love we once shared."

She didn't know how long they walked, but her feet hurt and her body ached from his abuse. But she didn't dare scream again. Alex was able to forge the betrothal agreement, so what else could he be capable of? She shuddered to think. Would he indeed kill Trey?

Finally, he stopped and lifted her onto a hard surface. She rolled on uneven boards. Broken pieces pierced her skin and she whimpered. Nearby, a horse snorted. It felt as if she'd been put in a wagon.

"Alex? What are you doing with me?"

"I'm taking you to our love nest."

"Release me at once, Alex. I mean it." It was hard to be firm with him when her voice shook.

He laughed. "I will remove the horse's blanket as soon as we arrive at the inn."

"What inn? Where are you taking me?"

"We are on our way to be married, my dear. We will stop at an inn to rest the night. By this time tomorrow, we'll be at Gretna Green where we'll be married.

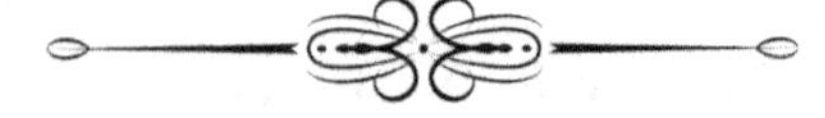

Chapter Forty-Four

T REY AND NIC'S business lasted longer than anticipated. He told Nic to spend the night and they would continue their dealings in the morning. As Trey climbed the stairs to his bedroom, his heart wrenched with worry. It had hurt to see the pain of doubt fill Judith's eyes, but he didn't dare tell her the truth. Not yet. How could he tell her about the newest findings of good ole Alexander Cutler? Trey couldn't.

Not when Alex was being investigated for murdering Judith's parents.

Agony twisted Trey's stomach. Her parents' death was still too recent. Judith continued to mourn for them. Opening old wounds would be painful, and Trey couldn't allow her to suffer in such a way. Not until they knew for certain if Alex had done the crime.

Trey stopped at her bedroom door and knocked softly. When no answer came from the other side, he grinned. She must be asleep. He'd wake her up in a very enjoyable way.

He opened the door and walked inside, but came to a quick halt. The bed was empty. Could she be waiting for him in his bedroom? He didn't know why, but anticipation had him rushing down the hall and into his room. He stopped again when his bed lay empty, too.

Had his mother occupied more of Judith's evening? He

doubted it, especially because she was so exhausted when he talked to her earlier.

He left his room and practically ran down the stairs to the drawing room. Empty. He hurried to the dining room. Empty.

Growling, he dragged his fingers through his hair. Where was she?

"My lord?"

He jumped and turned toward one of his mother's servants. The older man wore the black and white uniform, holding out a folded piece of paper.

"My lord, I was instructed to give this to you."

Trey took the paper. "Who instructed you to hand this to me?"

"A man who came to the door earlier this evening."

"Did he leave his name?"

"No, my lord. Just this."

Trey nodded. "Thank you." He turned and walked into the drawing room as he opened the letter and stopped near a light to read.

"Dear Trey. I have realized how wrong I was about everything. I'm still in love with Alex and I want to marry him. Please know I never wanted to hurt you, but I must follow my heart. Sincerely, Judith."

Trey's breathing stopped as he sank to the nearest chair. An invisible knife ripped through his chest, leaving him hollow inside. He stared at the letter, not believing what he'd read. She couldn't have gone back to that man.

Numbness spread through Trey's mind and body like icy fingers. None of this made sense. They'd been so happy last night and this morning. She'd told him she loved him. So why did she now change her mind? Was it because he didn't tell her about Alex?

Angered, he crunched the paper in his hand, making a fist. Something wasn't right. She loved him! Why would any woman go back to the man who'd lied to her?

In a flash, the memory of Tristan and Lady Diana crossed his mind. Was Judith like Lady Diana? Had Trey been right about women this whole time and had a moment's weakness around Judith?

He groaned as he dropped his face in his hands. It hurt to breathe. Hurt to think. Hurt to feel.

The shuffling of feet echoed from down the hallway. Voices raised and grew closer. He didn't care. All he wanted to do was curl up and die. He wanted to get away from the pain this so-called love had brought him. The very pain his father had warned him about.

"Trey?"

Nic's panicked voice brought Trey out of his thoughts and he jerked his head up. Nic and two servants entered the drawing room. The upstairs maid wrung her hands just under her breast as she stood in back of Nic.

"Trey, something has happened to Judith," Nic said.

Trey shrugged. "I know. She returned to Alexander Cutler."

Nic narrowed his stare. "What are you mumbling about? She didn't go back to Mr. Cutler. She does not love him."

Trey brought forth the crinkled paper. "Then why did she write this note for me?"

Nic yanked it from his hands and skimmed over the words. "This is not her writing."

Jumping to his feet, Trey stood in front of his friend. "How do you know? You don't know her handwriting."

"Do you?" Nic rebutted.

"No. But why else…" Trey shook his head. "Why don't you think she wrote this?"

Nic motioned the upstairs maid to come forward. When she stood in front of Trey, she curtsied.

"My lord, not too long ago I saw Miss Faraday outside by the gazebo. I looked away for a moment, and when I looked back, she had a blanket wrapped around her and was being dragged by a man wearing dark clothes."

A different emotion washed over Trey and he straightened. "Someone was forcing her to leave?"

"Yes, my lord."

He almost cried with relief. How foolish he'd been to jump to conclusions about her. Why hadn't he put his trust in her love as he should have? She did love him, and he must believe it.

When he thought of her being forced from the estate, anger surged through him again. He looked at Nic. "Mr. Cutler has taken her."

Hawthorne nodded. "That's who I thought it might be, as well."

Trey shook the paper in his hand. "This was probably written by the man himself." He glanced at the writing again, realizing it didn't appear feminine at all. Judith's handwriting would have been precise. Perfect. Just like her.

He glanced back at the maid. "Did you see where he was taking her?"

"No, my lord. By the time I found somebody to tell, they had left the estate."

Trey held his pounding head in his hands as he paced the floor. Where would that man have taken her?

"Trey?"

He stopped and faced Nic. "What?"

"Mr. Cutler knew about Judith's inheritance. I have no doubt."

Trey nodded as he squeezed his eyes closed. "I believe you are right."

"Being the calculated, underhanded man Mr. Cutler is, there's only one place he would have taken her."

Trey snapped his attention to Nic as they both said the same thing.

"Gretna Green."

Chapter Forty-Five

A FEW TIMES during the ride, Judith had fallen asleep. Alex had taken off the horse's blanket and they moved to a different vehicle. Now the coach they rode in was covered as a driver took them toward the inn.

She'd cried all of her tears. Exhaustion wouldn't let her shed anymore. Weary, she could hardly hold herself upright, and slumped against the corner of the conveyance as it jerked her body to and fro.

Alex talked to her, but she didn't listen. She couldn't. Not when her heart ached to have Trey come to her rescue and all she wanted to hear was his voice. That wouldn't happen. Alex told her about the letter he'd written for Trey to read after they'd left. He would believe she was out of his life for good. He hadn't wanted to believe in love. Now he would close his heart to love once more.

She had no other choice but to marry Alex. If she didn't, he'd kill Trey. She loved Trey too much to have him die for her. It was Tristan and Lady Diana's story all over again.

The coach slowed, which made Alex peek out the window. Night was upon them, and she doubted he could see anything, but when he sat back in the seat and smiled wide, she knew he had. They must be at the inn.

Releasing a defeated sigh, she closed her eyes. Could she

convince Alex that marrying her was wrong? She didn't love him, and she'd repeatedly told him. So why was he continuing this?

My inheritance.

He must know about the money.

The conveyance stopped and the driver opened the door. Alex jumped down, turned and offered his hand. Ignoring his help, she pushed his hand aside and climbed out by herself.

The inn was small. Not at all what she'd expected, but there was a large barn out back to keep the horses. From where she stood, it didn't appear to be full since there weren't any carriages waiting nearby. Just her misfortune. She may not find anyone to help her get away.

He grabbed her hand and hooked it around his elbow. Holding himself straight, he strolled toward the building. She rolled her eyes. He'd always wanted to be a gentleman. Too bad he'd never achieve that goal.

He ushered them inside and paid for their lodging. Bile rose in her throat. They were going to share a room. If he tried to touch her, she'd fight him every second.

While Alex talked with the man at the desk, she blocked out what they said and scanned the room, searching for a way out. If given the chance, she'd run. Where would she go? She was in the middle of nowhere. And at night. No, she couldn't escape now. Morning would be the best time.

Morning may be too late.

Worn out tables and rickety chairs filled the nearly empty area. A few people loitered in the dining area, not paying attention to anything but their mug of ale in front of them.

In the corner, a lone man slumped against the wall. His gaze rested on her. A long dirty brown beard hung from his face, the same color of his long, matted hair. His ragged clothes looked as if they could stand on their own. Shivers of disgust crawled over her skin. By his unkempt appearance, she assumed he was not somebody she could trust. He, too, had a mug sitting in front of him on the table.

When Alex started walking, she pulled her attention away from the man in the corner and followed beside Alex. Perhaps it was a good idea to stay close to him no matter how much she loathed his presence.

Alex found a table for them. Her weak legs didn't want to move, so she plopped on the chair. It also didn't matter how sticky the table was, because she rested her elbows on the top so she could hold up her head with her hands.

"When will the room be ready?" Her voice was low, mainly because she didn't have much strength to speak.

He glared at her. "Did you not hear anything while I talked to the owner of the inn?"

"No."

"He said our room would not be ready for another hour."

She groaned and covered her face with her hands. "I will probably fall asleep way before then. Wake me when they are ready."

He leaned across and grasped her arm. Pain shot up from her wrist and she cried out.

"You are not going to fall asleep. We are supposed to appear like a couple in love, and you are going to act like the proper fiancée."

She glared back. "If you wanted a responsive woman, you should have kidnapped someone else."

"Lower your voice," he snapped, tightening his grip.

"You are hurting me."

"Act accordingly, and I won't have to."

When he released her, she rubbed the bruise forming on her arm. Across the room, she noticed a movement. The man in the corner had straightened in his chair. His eyes stayed on her, but appeared more alert. A strange sensation swept over her. His features looked hard, his eyes narrowed and lips thinned as he gazed her way. Her heart beat wildly. She hoped she wouldn't have to fight off two men tonight.

She glanced back at Alex. He drummed his fingers on the

table as he lustfully eyed one of the barmaids who walked past.

Judith groaned. "Alex, can you answer some questions for me now?"

His head swung back toward her and he smiled. "Anything, my dear."

"Why did you lie to me?"

"Pardon?"

"While we were secretly courting, you told me you were in the Royal Navy. That was a lie, was it not?"

He shrugged. "I suppose it was a little white lie."

"Little?" She arched a brow. "I would not call your lie little. Did you know the navy can press charges against you for wrongly impersonating an officer?"

He flipped his hand through the air. "That's rubbish."

"And what about your other crimes?"

"I don't have any others."

She shook her head. "You think you are invincible? How pathetic."

Once again, he reached across the table and gripped her wrist. This time she didn't cry out, but the pain still shot up her arm.

"What other crimes are you referring to?" His voice deepened with a warning.

"Alex, when you steal from people, you are going to get punished."

"I have not stolen anything."

"Indeed? Then what about the three widows you had a torrid affair with this last year?"

He released her hand and pulled away, his eyes widened. "How do you know about them?"

"Lord Trey had his solicitor investigate you. Apparently, you stole money from these women. They, too, are going to press charges."

He sneered. "As I have mentioned before, I have not stolen anything."

"Then why do they say differently?"

"They are probably heartbroken because I left them to find another woman."

Although not a humorous moment, she chuckled, not believing the words coming from his mouth. "Oh, Alex. I'm quite certain they were not heartbroken. Each widow said after you had left, they noticed their expensive jewels and money missing." She shrugged. "Very coincidental, don't you think?"

He leaned forward on the table and glared. "They all lied then. The reason I moved on was because they couldn't please me. They gave me their jewels. I didn't steal anything."

"How strange you never used your real name." She tapped her finger on her chin. "Can you tell me why? If you had no intentions of stealing their money, why would you not use your real name?"

His angry glare nearly burned through her, but she held her back straight and met the challenge in his eyes. A few minutes passed in silence, but by the nerve jumping in his neck, she knew he was desperately trying to think of another lie.

Finally, he sat back and smiled. His whole body relaxed as he folded his arms across his chest. "My dear, innocent Judith. You don't know men at all. The reason I did not use my real name was because I had no desire for a relationship with them."

"Plausible story, Alex, but I don't believe you. Since I found out about you, I know all you want is money."

"And pray, how did you come to this conclusion?"

"Simple, really. You know I don't love you, yet you are determined to marry me. Why? Because you know how much money my parents left me when they died."

He cocked his head. "How would I know that?"

"I don't know, but sneaky, conniving rats like yourself always find a way."

"How do you know I don't really love you?"

She rolled her eyes. "Because not too long ago when I was on Bond Street shopping, I saw you. I called out your name. You turned and looked at me, but you never responded. Instead, you ran the other way and ignored me. If you really loved me, you would have come when I called. If you had really loved me, you would have met me at the woodsman's cottage that first day." She shook her head. "But you are just a pathetic little man who is no better than a common criminal. You use people to get what you want. I'm so fortunate Lord Trey came into my life when he did, or I would be married to you by now."

A scowl marred his face mere seconds before he lashed out at her, his fingers digging into her shoulder. "You little hussy. How dare you say those things about me!"

"They are true."

"I don't use people for money, but I do know about revenge. I know when I'm tired of being the man stepped on all the time. The snobbish nobility have always looked down at me as if I was dung on their shoes. I'm not. I have feelings, too."

"Only when it suits you."

"You sound just like your parents. Do you know that?"

She blinked with wide eyes. "What are you talking about? You have never spoken to my parents."

"On the contrary." He let go of her and sat back in his chair. "You didn't know this, but they knew about us."

She gasped. "How could they?"

"I don't know, but they approached me one day and offered me money to stop seeing you. I discovered at that time how wealthy your parents really were."

Her throat tightened with emotion and moisture filled her eyes. Her parents hadn't said a thing. Obviously, they knew Alex was all about money. They loved her enough to pay the freeloader off and get him out of her life.

"Why had they not said anything to me?" she whispered, more to herself than to him as she looked down at her hands.

"Probably because it was the day before they died."

She snapped her attention to him. "How do you know when they died? I didn't send you a letter until a week afterward."

A mischief grin crossed his face and he shrugged. "I know these things."

Chapter Forty-Six

PIECES BEGAN FITTING together in her mind. He knew they were wealthy. He knew when they died. When her parents' carriage accident was investigated, the police told her it was a terrible mishap, but in the back of her mind, she doubted.

"Oh, no…" she said slowly. "You killed them, didn't you?"

His eyes widened and his smile stretched. "Forgive me, Judith, but I never gave you credit for having a brain. You proved me wrong just now."

Jumping out of her chair, she screamed and lunged for him. The table knocked over, and when she landed on him, his chair collapsed, bringing them both to the floor. She clawed at his face and beat on his chest. Anything to punish him. Tears clogged her vision, but she continued to bring upon him as much pain as she could.

He finally grabbed hold of her hands and rolled them until he loomed over her. He lifted his fist and it swooped down, connecting to her jaw. Pain exploded in her face and her head jerked back and hit the hard wooden floor.

Sounds all around her faded in and out as she struggled to keep from sinking into an unconscious state. The more she tried to focus on the murderer in front of her, the more pain filled her skull.

Closing her eyes, she rested her head against the ground and breathed deeply, fighting to keep from going into the black abyss. Other voices swarmed around her, none that sounded familiar. Her head spun, and waves of nausea assailed her stomach. If she didn't move, she would be fine. The deeper she breathed, the quicker her stomach eased.

A strong pair of hands lifted her up. Dirt and sweat wafted around her, making her want to gag again.

"Miss? Are you all right?"

The small amount of alcohol on the man's breath wasn't a lot, but mixed with the other smells surrounding him, caused her to turn away.

"I will be in a moment."

She sat on the floor, still keeping her eyes closed until the dizziness settled. His hands continued to hold her shoulders.

Slowly, she opened her eyes. The man from the corner of the room sat in front of her. His dull blue eyes staring deep at her face as if studying her.

She shook away his touch. "Thank you, but I'm feeling better now."

As she tenderly touched her throbbing jaw, she glanced around for Alex. He lay on the ground, unconscious. She looked back at the man next to her. "What happened?"

"I gave him a good pounding. I could not allow him to harm you that way."

Not many strangers were so kind. She smiled, then winced when her cut lip bled. "I thank you again, sir."

She struggled to stand, and the man helped her up. When she swayed, he grabbed her shoulders again to steady her. Glancing down at Alex, her heartbeat quickened. Was he out cold? Now was the time to escape. But, where would she go to hide?

"Miss?" the stranger asked.

She looked back at him. "Yes."

"You look very familiar."

Underneath all the dirt, there was probably a man she'd like to meet. Obviously he had a giving heart even though his straggly hair and beard, and ragged clothes kept her from looking deeper. Unfortunately, his stench was enough to make a pig swoon. Yet, there was something familiar in his blue eyes. If only his hair was shorter and clean, maybe she'd know him.

"I don't know, sir. I'm Miss Faraday. What's your name?"

He frowned and dropped his hands. "That, I do not know."

"Pardon? How could you not know your name?"

He shrugged. "That slips my mind, also. I had a head injury a while back and I cannot remember anything."

She sucked in her breath. Amazing. She'd heard of things like this happening, but she'd never met anyone with this problem.

On the floor, Alex groaned and stirred. She jumped away from him, closer to the stranger.

"Is he your husband?" the man asked.

"No. He has kidnapped me and intends to take me to Gretna Green to get married." She turned toward him and clutched his filthy shirt. "Please help me. He killed my parents." Her voice broke and tears gathered in her eyes again.

The stranger's face hardened. His blue eyes darkened as he glanced back at Alex. The man grumbled before bending and slamming his fist into Alex's face again, knocking him out.

The stranger took her hand. "Come. I will get you out of here." He pulled her outside and toward the barn.

"Where will we go? There's nowhere to run. Alex will find me."

"I will think of something. Give me a moment."

He rushed them into the barn and toward the back. His gaze flew over every wall. "There has to be some kind of tool I can use as a weapon against him."

She shook her head. "I don't think it will do much good. He has a pistol."

The man stopped and faced her. He clamped his hands on her shoulders and looked deep into her eyes.

"I will not let him harm you, Judith."

Gasping, she took a step back, breaking the contact. "Pardon me, sir. How do you know my name? I didn't tell you my Christian name."

He stood frozen for a few moments as he looked at her. Confusion creased his forehead and narrowed his gaze. "I don't know, but I know you are Judith Faraday."

"Do you know my parents?"

He gazed in the distance for another few seconds before meeting her eyes again. "Is your father Viscount Manderville?"

She sucked in a quick breath and covered her mouth. Tears fell from her eyes quicker than before. "Yes. You do know him. How?"

The man shook his head. "I cannot recall." He scratched his head. "But when I see you in my mind, you are a young girl."

"I—I wish I recognized you, but I cannot say I do."

Through the stillness of the night, Alex's voice shouted, calling her name.

"Oh, no!" She clutched the stranger's hands. "He's coming."

"He won't get you. I promise."

He led them further back in the barn. Alex's voice grew nearer toward the front. He'd be in sight at any moment.

"Look, there is a back door." He pointed and hurried them toward it.

It took a couple of hard pushes, but the stranger finally opened the door. He grabbed her hand and led her out, then closed the barrier behind them. Down the road, two horsemen rode fast toward the inn. In the moonlight, the figure of the lead rider looked familiar. It wasn't until he was almost to the inn when recognition struck.

"Trey!"

She yanked away from the stranger's grasp and ran toward the man she loved. He'd heard her because he stopped the horse and jumped down.

"Trey," she screamed and ran with outstretched arms.

He ran toward her, and when they met, he held her tight in his embrace and swung her around once.

"Oh, Trey. I never thought I would see you again," she sobbed, pulling herself closer to his body.

"Shhh… I'm here now, my love." He kissed her forehead. "Where's Alex?"

"He was in the barn." She looked over her shoulder in that direction. She didn't see him, but the stranger stood back a ways, studying Trey through hooded eyes.

From around the corner, Alex stumbled away from the barn, holding a pistol. Trey moved Judith behind him, blocking her from Alex's aim.

"Let her go, Lord Trey. She's not yours."

"Yes she is, and I will not let her go."

Alex waved the pistol as he walked closer. Judith noticed Dominic slowly sliding off his horse, trying not to be seen. Taking careful steps, he crept through the shadows toward Alex. She prayed Dominic reached him before he shot Trey.

Alex shook his head. "I cannot let you take her. I have gone through a lot in order to make her mine."

"Yes, I know. You killed her parents."

She gasped and clutched the back of Trey's cloak. How did he know? Unless… Was that what he and Dominic talked about this afternoon?

Throwing back his head, Alex laughed. "Exactly, so you know why I cannot leave without her."

Finally, Alex stopped and aimed the weapon. No longer was his hand shaky. "Give her to me now, or I will kill you, Trey Worthington."

"Then shoot, you coward, because I will not give her up."

She sobbed and buried her head against his back. Why did he say that? Dominic wasn't close enough to Alex to stop him yet.

"As you wish, *my lord*." Alex narrowed his gaze on Trey.

"No!" The voice of the stranger shouted in the stillness.

Judith jerked her head up just in time to see him run toward Trey. The pistol fired. Smoke filled the air, and Trey's body went limp. She screamed.

Chapter Forty-Seven

THE FORCE OF the strange man slamming into Trey's body caused him to lose his breath. He sagged against Judith who stood behind him. But the bullet didn't hit him. Instead, the man who'd saved Trey's life fell to the ground at his feet, clutching his shoulder. Trey glanced up in time to see Nic's pistol fire and Alex crumble to the dirt in a motionless heap.

Hawthorne looked his way. "Are you all right?"

Trey nodded. "The bullet hit this man, instead."

Judith sobbed and wrapped her arms around Trey. He pulled her to his chest and she clung to his shirt. Burying his face in her hair, he held her tight. "I'm all right," he whispered.

Nic ran closer to kneel beside the stranger who'd taken the bullet. "I think he's still alive."

Trey pulled away from Judith and crouched beside the unconscious man, rolling him from his side to his back. Blood coated the stranger's shoulder and down his arm.

"We have to stop the bleeding," Nic said.

Judith stepped beside Trey and lifted her gown, showing her petticoats. "Use this."

Trey took the bottom hem and ripped a long strip while Nic removed the man's filthy coat.

"Who is he?" he asked Judith.

"I don't know, but he knows me somehow."

Trey looked up at her. "He does?"

"Yes, but only when I was a young girl. He does not know his name. He says he has a head injury and does not remember anything."

Not much light shone on them from the half moon, and Trey couldn't see the man's face very well. With all the hair covering his features, it was hard to detect anything. Trey concentrated on bandaging the man's arm, hoping it would stop the flow of blood.

As Nic finished removing the man's shirt, the stranger's arm fell across his chest.

"Look!" Nic shook his head and pointed to a ring on the man's finger. "Trey, isn't that—"

Gasping, Trey ignored his bandaging and lifted the stranger's hand.

"What is it?" Judith asked.

"He's wearing my ring."

"How can it be your ring?"

Trey shook his head. "It's a ring with my family's crest." He peered closer at the unconscious man. Moving the long hair out of his face, Trey studied him until familiarity sneaked upon him.

Good heavens! It couldn't be.

Emotion lodged in his throat as he gently rolled the man to his side so Trey could look at his back. When the old bullet wound just under his shoulder blade caught Trey's eye, he gasped. "It's Tristan."

Judith fell to her knees and hiccupped a sob as she covered her mouth.

Nic's eyes grew misty and he shook his head. "How is that possible?"

Trey rolled the man back toward him and swiped the hair away from his face again, studying him closer. Tears built in Trey's eyes, but it was his heart that told him this was really his brother. "Tristan!" Trey's voice cracked as he gently shook his brother. "Open your eyes and look at me."

With tender prodding, Tristan finally blinked. When he met

Trey's stare, he smiled. "Trey," he rasped.

Trey's chest tightened and tears leaked down his cheeks. He gathered his brother in his arms and hugged him. "I cannot believe you are alive."

Tristan sniffed. "I remember now. Thank God, I remember!"

Trey pulled away and cupped his brother's face. "Where have you been?"

"I don't know. I have drifted from one place to another. Nothing was in my memory. Not even my name." He looked to Judith. "Until I saw her. Somehow I knew her."

Crying, she leaned forward and hugged him.

"When she yelled your name," Tristan told Trey, "another memory hit me. I knew you were my brother."

Laughing with happiness, Trey wiped his moist eyes. "I...we all thought you were dead."

Tristan looked on the other side of him at Nic and smiled. "Hawthorne, old man. How are you?"

Nic chuckled and gave him a bear hug.

Trey couldn't believe the waves of emotion he'd experienced in one day, but the happiness flowing through him was worth every ache and sorrow he'd suffered. "Let's get you home and cleaned up, Tristan. You look awful."

Everyone laughed.

Judith scooted next to Trey and he wrapped his arm around her, pulling her closer. He winked and kissed her on the mouth.

"Tristan," Trey said as he looked back at his brother. "I want to introduce you to my fiancée."

His brother's weak hand lifted toward Judith and she grasped it with both of her hands. He kissed her knuckles and smiled. "It's a pleasure to meet you. Again."

As Trey helped his brother stand, his attention moved to the motionless body still on the road. "Nic? Did you kill him?"

"Yes."

"Splendid. If you hadn't, I would have."

Trey's heart sang with joy. Never did he think he'd feel this elated, especially after he thought Tristan had died, and again today when he thought the love of his life had left him. His chest still tightened, but there was a cleansing emotion spreading through him.

Smiling, he looked up at the darkened sky. If his father was gazing down from heaven—or up from hell—Trey hoped he knew how happy the prospect of marriage and family made him. He'd never follow in his father's footsteps again.

TREY SMILED AT his beautiful Judith asleep curled up beside him on the couch. Her chestnut hair fanned across his arm and her white billowy nightdress made her appear virginal. Desire crept into his body, and he couldn't wait until they were married.

The past few days had been dreadfully exhausting for Judith, and he feared she wouldn't be able to keep alert any longer. Although she tried her hardest to have a strong spirit, she still needed protecting and loving. He would be the lucky chap to give it to her for the rest of their lives. Their wedding was only days away, but he needed to be with her now. Never again did he want to be separated from the woman he loved.

Quietly, he tucked a blanket around her as he cuddled her closer to his side. The household had retired, and he knew he could be with her like this all night and nobody would notice.

Tristan's joyous homecoming took a lot out of the family. Mother's first reaction to seeing her son back from the dead caused her to swoon, and rightly so for such a frail woman. After she gained consciousness, she kept Tristan's hand in hers and wouldn't let it go, holding him as if she didn't want the dream to end.

Grinning, Trey stroked Judith's arm, staring at her lovely face. He knew how his mother felt. He didn't want his dream to end, either. It had taken him many years to become this happy, and he still worried something would snatch it away.

He cupped Judith's face and rubbed this thumb across her bottom lip. Slowly, her mouth stretched into a grin. She blinked her eyes open and looked at him as he loomed over her.

"Is it morning?"

He chuckled. "No, my love."

"Am I still on the couch?"

"Yes."

"Why are you here?"

"Because I want to be with you always."

"Hmm…" She turned toward him and snuggled her face against his chest. "This is nice."

"Nice is good." He kissed her lips. "But I have plans to make it better."

"Better than nice?"

"So much better."

"You do have ways of accomplishing that, don't you?"

"Indeed, my lady." He kissed her mouth. "In fact, I have decided where we are going to live after we are married."

Her forehead crinkled and her eyes narrowed. "Where?"

"During the Season, we can live in my townhouse—unless you want me to sell it and get another one. But during the off months, I thought we could live in *your* house…where you grew up."

She gasped, her eyes widening and sparkling with excitement. "You really want to live there?"

"I do if you do."

"Oh, yes." She threw her arms around him for a tight hug.

When her body relaxed, she left her head resting on his shoulder and looked up, her hand stroking his face. "We should retire to our room, don't you think?"

He lifted his head enough to gaze into her sultry green eyes. "No, I want to stay right here. I will never leave you. Ever. I must be with the woman I love more than life itself."

She gasped, her eyes widening. "Trey? You just told me you

loved me."

"Indeed I did. Was there any doubt?"

Tears gathered in her eyes. "I knew you did, but you have never said it before."

"I shall say it every day for the rest of our lives, because I mean it, Judith. I love you completely."

She threw her arms around his neck and pulled him down for another kiss. No longer did she act like a tired woman, but instead one that was eager to be kissed good and hard. He wouldn't disappoint her. Ever again.

The End

About the Author

Marie Higgins is an award-winning, best-selling author of clean romance novels that melt your heart and have you falling in love over and over again. Since 2010, she's published over 100 heartwarming, on-the-edge-of-your-seat romances. She's broadened her readership by writing mystery/suspense, humor, time-travel, and paranormal, along with her love for historical romances. Her readers have dubbed her "Queen of Tease" because of her twists and unexpected endings.

Website – www.authormariehiggins.com
Facebook – facebook.com/marie.higgins.7543
TikTok – tiktok.com/@author.mariehiggins
Instagram – instagram.com/author.mariehiggins
Bookbub – bookbub.com/authors/marie-higgins
Twitter – @mariehigginsxox